OTHER WORKS BY MICHAEL TOBIAS

Literary

World War III: Population and Biology at the End of the Millennium;
A Vision of Nature—Traces of the Original World;
Rage & Reason; Environmental Meditation;
Life Force: The World of Jainism; Fatal Exposure;
Voice of the Planet; Mountain People (ed.);
After Eden: History, Ecology & Conscience;
Deep Ecology (ed.); Deva; The Mountain Spirit (ed.);
Believe (with William Shatner); Harry & Arthur;
The Autobiography of a Boy; Tsa; Dhaulagirideon

Films & Television Series

A Parliament of Souls (13 part); A Day in the Life of Ireland;
Voice of the Planet (10 part); The Making of Voice of the Planet;
Black Tide; Ahimsa-Nonviolence; Antarctica—The Last Continent;
Cloudwalker; Kazantzakis; Ozone Crisis; Animal Rights; The Gift;
Space Futures; Sand and Lightning; Science Notes (32 part);
The Power Game (4 parts); The Sixth Annual Genesis Awards;
The Fifth Annual Genesis Awards

A Naked Man

by
Michael Tobias

JAIN PUBLISHING COMPANY
Fremont, California

COVER PHOTO: Courtesy of Nancy Webber

Library of Congress Cataloging-in-Publication Data

Tobias, Michael.
    A naked man / by Michael Tobias.
       p.   cm.
    ISBN 0-87573-027-2 (pbk.)
    1. Men—United States—Religious life—Fiction. I. Title.
PS3570.028N35   1993
813'.54—dc20   93-49547
                                                      CIP

Dedication

I dedicate this novel to my wife, and best friend, Jane Gray Morrison Tobias.

To my dear comrade, Robert Radin . . .

And to all Jains throughout the world, and throughout time . . .

Contents

Acknowledgements

I owe special gratitude to Mukesh Jain, the inspired publisher of Jain Publishing Company for his belief in this work.

Special thanks goes to Dr. Mukund Lath, English translator of the *Kalpasutra, Eighth Chapter of the Dasasrutaskandha of Bhadrabahu*; to the Editor & Hindi Translator, Mahopadhyaya Vinaya Sagar, and to Dr. (Smt.) Chandramani Singh who wrote the *Note on Paintings*, Published by D. R. Mehta, Secretary, Prakrit Bharati, Jaipur, Rajasthan, 1984.

I wish to thank the late Hermann Jacobi, translator from the Prakrit of the remarkable *Jaina Sutras*, from which I have sporadically borrowed in the re-creation of some of Mahavira's meditations and speeches; particularly the *Akaranga Sutra*, the *Kalpa Sutra*, the *Uttaradhyayana Sutra*, and the *Sutrakritanga Sutra*, first published by Oxford University Press in 1884, as Volumes XXII and XLV of *The Sacred Books Of The East*, edited by F. Max Müller, and re-issued by Motilal Banarsidass, Delhi, Varanasi and Patna, in 1980.

Special acknowledgment to *West's Annotated California Codes*, Penal Code Section, West Publishing Company, St. Paul, Minnesota, 1988, for its definitive summaries of legal cases and precedents, whose presence in this work is self-evident.

For ancient Indian cultural material, facts and details, I have relied upon countless works but am especially indebted to Jagdish Chandra Jain's authoritative book, *Life In Ancient India As Depicted In The Jain Canons*, Bombay, New Book Company, 1947.

In addition, I want to thank my dear friend, the great Jain scholar, Professor Padmanabh S. Jaini of the University of California at Berkeley for his two important works, *The Jaina Path of Purification* (UC-Berkeley Press, 1979) and *Gender & Salvation* (UC-Berkeley Press, 1991).

My gratitude to two Digambara monks with whom I once spent a moment of eternity in the village of Taranga, and—with the same felicitous memory—to the late Acharya Ram Suriji.

Much thanks to my friends Acharya Sushil Kumar-ji Maharaj and to Gurudev Shree Chitrabhanu.

A special note of appreciation to Carol Radin, and to my various friends downtown.

And, finally, my heartfelt gratitude to all vegetarians the world over.

In memory of Herman Hesse.

CHAPTER ONE

A Merchant's Dream

On that day there would be no beginning and no end. A pleasant south wind swept the Earth. Fields were umber green, stars were already beginning to glitter against the pale evening sky.

A teenager, Vardhamana was his given name, his long hair combed with an ivory brush and besmeared with pomade, his feet rubbed with sandstone, gravel and seafoam, his nails pared, his body having been delicately nurtured with lime that morning prior to a hot herbal bath, his teeth cleaned with a noothstick, his person clothed in an elegant golden double-silk kosseyam coat designed in chevrons, its warp woven with mashru satin, bounded home through the forest surrounding the village of Kundapura.

He'd torn the coat scrambling over the rocks, as boys will do, and he'd dirtied his nails in play. His best friend from school, Sakra, was just behind him, running and leaping with an equal air of total abandon. The boy in the lead jumped over a log. In an instant he saw the nest of cobras underfoot, splayed his legs apart and landed in a perilous position that ignited the half-dozen snakes from their coiled slumber. Electrified, erect, curving backwards, curving forwards, heads arched and hissing, they were now poised to strike with collective ferocity.

Far away, in Los Angeles, at the same time, and at another time, it was a strangely cold November morning, ominous, polluted and dry. Leonard M. Rosenbalm commanded his two hundred sixty thousand dollar midnight blue Continental Bentley at a safe fifty-five miles per hour past Vermont Avenue—where he took a deep breath which he held in for the rest of the day. He got off the 10-freeway at the Grand Avenue Exit, then headed to his forty-year-old three-story brick building in the garment district downtown. It was one of four warehouses owned by the Rosenbalms along Main Street. Bums wallowed in the alleyways, debris populated every cranny of the exteriors. Still, the Rosenbalms had managed to plant some grass and New Zealand poppies along the thin file of soil abase the structures. Today, Leonard sported a pair of eight hundred dollar loosely cut Armani slacks, the color of maple leaves, and a twelve hundred dollar matching cashmere sweater. On his wrist, he wore a fourteen thousand dollar Rolex watch. His Commes des Garcons shirt came neatly fitted with diamond cufflinks from Tiffany's.

Maybe it was the other way around; perhaps the car, the cufflinks, the buildings, the Rolex and Armani commandeered Leonard. Either way, he drove without the slightest doubt that he was in control, that the chaos and ugliness of downtown had been at least partially subdued.

In truth, he only leased the motorcar, a relative bargain given the fifteen thousand dollar write-off he could take each year. It was art, but it still had to be practical.

For his daughter, Denise, Leonard had actually broken down and purchased the much less expensive but equally seductive Bentley Eight, a three year-old model which he acquired for under seventy thousand dollars. It was cranberry red with a camel-colored interior. Denise adored its distinctive British grill. Leonard—who simply loved spoiling his one child—figured that with more people getting killed on the highways than in all of the Vietnam war, he wanted her driving a heavy car.

Both father and daughter kept a gun under their driver's seat. Downtown Los Angeles had its share of problems which even the eternally optimistic Leonard could not ignore. And, if ever he did, Leonard's wife, Miriam, a cateress specializing in Kosher foods, reminded him of them. She too carried a weapon in her black Jaguar. It was loaded. Illegal, but what did she care? Though she rarely ventured downtown, even Beverly Hills could be dangerous. She'd witnessed recently a terrible shooting, human blood, parts of a man's face, splattered all over a sidewalk, and shock never left her. That's when she went on her eating binge which led to her having half her stomach stapled to loose weight. She drove more quickly, now; offensively, always watching her rearview mirror for the worst, and when rear-ended just two weeks before, Miriam had reached for her gun and kept going rather than risk a setup.

Denise, aged nineteen, did not view life with anywhere near the same fears. She had gone to work for her father following two years at Cal Arts where she'd studied low-end woman's wear. She loved downtown; loved the diverse races, even loved the homeless, whom she often employed at five dollars an hour, whether to wash windows or sweep up the rear parking lot. One of their Mexicans, Ramon, had even graduated to maintenance supervisor. This was a mitzvah for which the Rosenbalms received a hundred thanks and occasional salted prunes and milk fudge from the grateful Mexican illegals.

Today, Denise was in the office early to negotiate a new loan with Mr. Hideyoshi, senior vice-president of their local bank. She met him over a plate of well-fried potato latkes at the local hangout.

"How ya' doin, Mr. Hideyoshi," she exclaimed. She planted a kiss on his cheek. Given Denise's sabra-like beauty and innocence, no Japanese businessman could possibly deny a mere hundred thousand dollar loan for two weeks, at twenty-three percent. The Rosenbalms were good for it, he knew that. Denise then conferred with Benny, the Rosenbalm's bookkeeper.

Benny was the calm lunar surface of money. The mummy beneath Egyptian sands, the bookmark languishing in unread tomes. He never exhibited any of the normal signs associated with money, like panic. Rather, he was solemnly devoted to year-ends, the calculation of water damage on blouses, the sorting out of countless garment-related minutia and financials. Money was slippery. It needed the Zen of Benny's dispassion. You can't do everything in one day, he was fond of repeating.

Like Benny, Leonard was also aware how ephemeral was money. He understood that real wealth meant a million a year in salary, a million in perks and a million in expenses. He dealt with plenty of fellow schlockers who earned such figures. While Leonard had been at it for twenty-five years (like his daughter, he started in the business as a teenager), and his father—now retired—for fifty years, the family's personal income rarely exceeded three hundred thousand in any given four seasons. And that included Miriam's income. She had only a minority share in Mazel Tov Kitchens. Still, the Jaguar and the Bentleys, the diamonds and the gold watches conveyed to the world a perpetual Rosenbalm bonanza. As Leonard's father, Ruben, always said, looks count for something while you're still alive. In Denise's young mind, three hundred thousand was nothing to be ashamed of, given the family's assets. Ruben Rosenbalm, her grandfather, had purchased nearly a city block during World War II for thirty thousand dollars. The buildings cost much less. The family had vowed never to touch them. Those four buildings, owned free and clear, generated over two hundred thousand a year in rentals, and had to be worth millions, even if the value of their leases had temporarily declined in the post-L.A. riots environment. But it was only a matter of time before the Koreans—who were condominimizing whole neighborhoods downtown—would attract stable tenants to Main Street.

Denise told Benny the news of her breakfast, and then went to inform Mr. Ti Ng, one of several associates most immediately affected by the Japanese loan.

"You've got your money," she said.

"You're my girl," Mr. Ng cried out, embracing her affectionately. He never doubted her abilities.

Mr. Ng—who once swam with his son in his arms through shark-infested waters to escape the Chinese—today oversaw the needlework and finishing of twenty thousand garments a month. The 2500 Overlock machines, Brother Exedra computers and Juki Robotic sewing apparatuses whirred. All the material had come from the dye house. Mr. Ng's five dollar-an-hour employees would then lay the cloth out in stacks, take electric cutters to it, do the sewing work, the quality control, the thread and button work, even the manufacturer's labeling. Leonard Rosenbalm financed his operation for a thirty percent cut.

Mr. Ng's patterns were knock-offs from far-away France, Japan and Italy. Every piece, from the frontneck to the bra back came from far away. This was the Berlitz of underwear, of two-for-five dollar leggings, jumpsuits, linen summer shifts, rayon blouses. A vernacular shared by some one hundred thousand merchants downtown. The great goal? To become another LA Gear, the company that went to nine hundred million overnight, from nothing.

Leonard pulled into his parking spot, adjoining the ramp where goods were slid down the cable. Despite Ramon's efforts, the small lot which adjoined a back alley frequented by bums was always filthy.

A bum put out his hand. Leonard ignored him, as he had for years.

—'I only give to blacks'—he thought. This man was white, red-haired, freckled—a drunk.

Inside, on the first floor, Leonard entered his partner Hal's office, which rather resembled the back alley. Hal was finishing up on the phone.

"Eddie, I can't sell those boys' briefs, not at that price. I'm trying. I want to deal with you. You won't come down to my price. I'm coming up to yours. I don't know what to do. What do you want me to do? It's a three seventy-five item . . . I'm telling you. Ahh—Now that's the sound of reason. Wonderful. Wonderful! You're a genius! I love you! Dynamite. Sounds great. See ya'."

Denise walked in. "Hi, Dad," giving him a big hug.

"She's worth living for," Leonard swooned.

Hal, in his fifties, had first worked for his famous uncle, Alvaro Spendetti, in shipping in New York from the time he was fourteen. He pushed hundred fifty pound carts filled with ladies dresses from Thirty-Seventh Street and Seventh Avenue, to Eighth Avenue, for fifty cents an hour. "I always wanted this," he told Leonard when they first joined forces. Hal knew Leonard's father, Ruben, who had also worked briefly with Hal's uncle in New York before migrating to the West Coast. They were all distantly related by marriage, somehow.

When Spendetti died, Hal also migrated to Los Angeles. Ruben Rosenbalm was by that time doing extremely well on Main Street, about fifty thousand dollars a year. He'd begun like other jobbers in the New World. "I need three yards of cloth for an overcoat," the client would say. Or, "I'll give you eight hundred dollars for the entire load." "For eight hundred I'll burn all of it," Ruben would grovel, in tears. "Alright. Eight-hundred fifty, I don't care how honest you are!" The business was a killer.

When young Hal first came to Los Angeles he was broke. His beloved uncle Alvaro had dropped dead of a heart attack at the age of fifty and to everyone's chagrin was discovered to be in the red, not the black. Whatever happened to all those millions of dollars of his which had been written about in Look Magazine? Or those expensive showrooms sporting all the blonde dames who put on pantiless floor shows for the out-of-town buyers that were more—candid—than the best of Broadway? Where was all of Alvaro's fortune? Only the blondes knew.

And so, Leonard M. Rosenbalm, an engineering student at USC, and Hal Spendetti, a thirty-year-old broken schlocker from New York, were brought together by Ruben Rosenbalm in nineteen sixty-nine. Ruben now looked pretty good. He had real assets. He seemed to play by the rules. Ruben put the two boys into business, thus perpetuating a tradition which was more blood and soul than money. The shirt off one's back, Ruben would say philosophically. Leonard, though somewhat younger than Hal, had his father's money behind him. Hal had the experience. It was never an even partnership. The money (Ruben) always controlled the business.

"It's Brian," Hal said, handing the phone over to Leonard, shifting in his big-man swivel chair, his feet propped up on his work table.

"Dickies, what about them?" Leonard importuned, his mind seized by the clarity of a hunch. They lived by hunches.

Leonard grabbed a pen and pad off Hal's desk and took some notes. Then he said, "I want to see a sample. Bring it over," and hung up.

"What's he got?" Hal asked in his feverish tone.

"Brian has a client who wants to blow them out at four twenty-five a unit." Brian was one of their buyers.

"Four twenty-five? Jesus, that's low."

"Very low. Brian says they need to move them yesterday."

"How many units?"

Leonard paused before the impossible suggestion. "Two million."

Hal sighed resignedly. "That's the kind of deal my uncle would have snapped up. You know what they say about Dickies? The Mexican wears a size twenty-eight Dickie but takes a thirty-eight for the fullness. That way he figures he's getting a thirty percent discount!" He laughed, then wondered, "Will they break up the sale?"

"Nope. They want a single order."

Hal lamented for half-a-second, condemned by habit and truths greater than himself to the other side of the tracks, at least in this respect, and headed out the door for lunch at Massoud's. He had a craving for an Iranian charbroiled steak. Even if they could find a buyer, there was no way they could get that kind of credit.

"I'll see you later. Remind Benny about that deposit." Hal left.

"How much can you sell them for?" Denise asked her father.

"They retail at sixteen ninety-five." He was trembling. The figures were like some horrible, wonderful premonition.

"Why would they sell so cheap?" she asked, a reasonable question for a nineteen year old.

"They need the cashflow, sweetheart. Two million units is pilpel to them."

Manufactured in Fort Worth, Texas, the Dickie was the best work pant in America, the star of stores like J.C. Penny's and Montgomery Ward. Pre-washed, many thought it outshone Henry Valdise or Cosmo. Normally, you'd buy them at fifteen dollars and sell them at sixteen. But Brian was talking about an unconscionable profit potential. Assuming there was a quick buyer for the lot.

Hal was right, of course. This deal was way over their heads. A hundred thousand dollar loan was one thing. But eight and a half million was impossible.

Leonard went up to his office and sat back in his recliner, weighing the fantastic situation.

His mind drifted, eyes inwardly attuned to . . . something?

Vardhamana remained calm and motionless. The cobras were ready to strike. But in his own heroic manner (as Sakra would later re-count the adventure to his parents) Vardhamana had already struck. Even now the snakes were settling back down, had ceased hissing, had relaxed their windpipes.

"Get away, NOW!" Sakra whispered frantically to his childhood friend.

"It's alright," Vardhamana said, not lifting his focus from the large glaring eyes of the female who must have reached a length of twelve feet and a diameter of six inches.

Vardhamana kneeled down in the dirt.

"What are you doing!" his friend screamed, backing away.

But it was too late to alter what had been ordained tens-of-thousands of years before. Vardhamana felt an attraction to the animals, and at the same time, experienced pain at having agitated them. Sakra was bewildered. What did it mean? There was his friend asking the family of King Cobras for forgiveness, extending his hand, slowly, imperceptibly, until he had made contact with the female. It was incredible!

Insanity and superstition clouded the air between the two boys.

Vardhamana stroked the animal's thick slender body which glistened in the twilight, murmuring words of the Prakrit dialect of Ardhamagadhi. He felt the black and white spectacle-shaped marking on its hood, coddled the region of its poison-glands, its windpipe, even putting his fingers to the fangs, utterly at one with the lethal beast.

The hamadryad crawled onto his arm, around his neck, proceeded down his chest and back to its nest of dried leaves where the eggs had hatched no more than a week before.

To Sakra, the scene was like something out of the *Mahabharata*. A dream. Impossible.

"Let's get out of here," he begged his friend. These snakes could spit their poison several feet. People went permanently blind, or were killed almost instantly.

That night, Sakra told his parents, Devananda and Rsabhadatta, about his friend's remarkable encounter. Devananda did not seem at all surprised and when Sakra asked her why she was not, her answer was oblique and mysterious.

Her own memories were flooded with that night, many years before, when something indescribable had happened to her. She had been a few months pregnant when she dreamt that a spirit, half goat, half god, carrying in its hands an unborn fetus, entered her and her husband's bedroom, got under the covers of their bed, and proceeded to do something to her body which she never dared talk about.

Leonard sat with his pen in his hand weighing his options, if any. These were dire and determined calculations with virtually no chance of surviving the test.

There was a knock at the open door. "Mr. Rosenbalm?"

"Yes, come in Brian."

"Here's that pant." He laid it on the table.

Leonard felt the Dickie's rough, durable weave.—I'm staring at five to six million dollars in profit—he thought to himself. And, as his fingers toyed with all that money, his mind began to sweat.

"You say they want cash?"

"Yep. Once the goods are counted and on the truck. They don't trust nobody," Brian said.

"Or course they don't." He considered his next words: "How much time can I have?"

"If it was anybody else, a half hour. For you, Mr. Rosenbalm, on account of we go back–"

"Brian, how long?"

"Look, I've got a window of time here, see."

"I understand. Will five o'clock do?"

"Three-thirty. You know how early everyone leaves to beat the traffic. I'll need to make a number of calls if you decline this remarkable, once-in-a-lifetime opportunity."

"Three-thirty." They shook hands.

Both men knew the reality here. Dickie was not going to wait for Brian, but Brian would have to wait for Leonard.

He headed out the door. Leonard called to him. "Oh Brian, one more thing. If I decide to buy, I want you to get them down to three seventy-five. You think that's possible?"

"I'll try."

When Brian was safely out of the building, Leonard got on the phone with his man, Julie.

"Julie, listen to me." Leonard was breathing heavily. "Here's the offering: two million Dickie trousers, new. I'm willing to let go of the lot at six and a quarter a unit. Who might want them?"

Julie was Leonard's chief seller who worked on a four percent commission. He knew everybody in America. That's what he intended his epitaph—soon appearing at the rate he was working—to read and there would be some truth to it.

"Brand new, you say? All sizes? Let me call A-to-Z. They could blow 'um out at eight ninety-five. I'll get back to you."

"Like right away, Julie. This is big. I can't take it."

"You're right."

Julie was also breathing hard. Damn right it was big! He immediately went to his buddy who was one of the buyers at A-to-Z. Instinctively, he knew they were the right fit. At the same time, within the space of one minute phone calls, he went to competitive contacts at Penny's and Sears.

Meanwhile the sweat drenching Leonard's innards cloyed like a damp wartime apparition. If he could buy the lot at three seventy-five a unit times two million, or seven million five hundred thousand, and sell for six twenty-five, or twelve million five hundred thousand, he'd be five million dollars richer less Julie's four percent. Those few numbers left him wan. He sat back in his recliner. The transaction would take a few phone calls and a few weeks to collect. It was too good to be true. He'd never had such an offering in his entire career. Nor had his father.

"What is it Dad, you look pale?" Denise said, plumping down on the white couch beneath the wall of photographs, images from the Rosenbalm family vacations to places like Mazatlan and Israel.

"Dickie." He ruminated out loud.

"Is it a good deal?" she asked, innocently.

"Maybe."

"So, we should do it."

The "we" was touching.

"Denise, I want you to call Maynard Rubbs over at Ali Baba's and find out how many Dickies fit in a shipping container. Work out the arithmatic. Two million pair. Then call Saulie at Consolidated and find out how many trucks and trailors we'd need. Do it quick, sweetheart."

"You got it." She jumped to the challenge, kissing her father on the cheek as she did a dozen times a day.

Assuming he could find a 5(A)(1) account, where was he going to find seven and a half million dollars? For two or three weeks? Leonard's brain addled and gulped.

He explained the situation to Benny, the bookkeeper, and, as he was doing so, Julie called.

"Yes, Julie?" Leonard's heart was beating like a captured wild bird.

"Great news. A-to-Z agrees to buy the lot."

"Jesus. How much?"

"Seven dollars a pair."

"Uh-huh . . . " Leonard's mind was operating outside of itself, now. Like some Einstein. "Tell them we'll do it!"

Benny's eyes opened wide. He didn't say a word.

Leonard reached Brian at his office five blocks away. "Brian, you get Dickie down to three seventy-five and we're in." Leonard already figured that twenty-five cent saving would pay Julie's commission plus the interest he'd be looking at on the loan.

"Let me call you right back," Brian said.

"Leonard, where are you going to get the money?" Benny said, thinking it wise to infuse a moment of sobriety before Leonard slit his own throat.

"I don't know. We'll raise it somehow. It's only for a few weeks."

Minutes later, Brian called back. "Three dollars eighty-five cents a pair and it's a deal."

"OK. Three eighty-five. Fax the details over. Congratulations. You're a real shot!"

"That ten cents just cost you two hundred thousand dollars," Benny said.

"Yeah? We're still looking at a mark-up of three dollars fifteen cents times two million, less Julie, less interest, less shipping. I'd say we're five and a half million in the clear." Leonard's face remained rigid. Benny followed his example. But, Leonard was also thinking—Who needs five and a half million dollars?—looking off towards the wall of photographs where he saw an image of himself, as a teenager, free and easy, standing in a bathing suit beside a mountain lake and looking off, in turn, beyond. Ready to dive into the cold water.

As Sakra finished telling the story, Devananda got up and went into her bedroom and wept silently.

Leonard felt the slightest ache, somewhere. An intangible instant, born upon invisible waves that had nothing other than oblivion to recommend them.

Then the spell broke. Leonard stood up, driven by autopilot, putting his pen on the table and both men in unison cried out, UNBELIEVABLE!

Denise walked in the door. "What's unbelievable?"

"You're father just etched the Rosenbalm name into the history books."

"That's my Dad."

"What did you find out?" Leonard said.

"Maynard says you can get up to forty pairs of trousers in a case. That's fifty pounds. One foot by two feet by one and a half."

"How many trucks, I don't have time for math exams."

"He said forget the Bobtail. It's a smaller truck, twenty-four feet. But, you can get a thousand boxes in a forty footer. Where are the goods going?"

"Across town."

"Fine. Figure on ten eight-by-eight-by-forty footers, all eighteen wheelers, twenty drivers, twenty-five dollar an hour packers, five trips."

"Twenty-five dollars?"

"Hey?" she threw up her hands, the big expert.

"Two six-hour-shifts throughout the night. Piece of cake."

"How much for the job if Saulie does it?"

"Twenty-five thousand."

"Tell him for fifteen he's got a deal."

She objected. "Dad? You know Saulie."

"Tell him. He'll come up to twenty and you'll keep the difference."

Leonard, Hal and Benny sat down with the Rosenbalm financials and examined the situation.

Later on, Leonard would know that all this was meant to be.

The situation was clear: Leonard had a few days to raise seven million seven hundred twenty thousand dollars. Forgetting the value of his own home, he had roughly half-a-million in bonds and treasuries which he converted to cash with a phone call. Hal was good for a quarter-of-a-million, though his wife wasn't to know. Benny asked to be counted in for ten thousand, his available savings.

Leonard then went to Mr. Hideyoshi with the facsimile confirmations of the deal from both Brian's and Julie's ends of it. Mitsui Bank would loan him one million. Money was tight in a recession. It was not right for Leonard to ask for more than that, especially on account of the hundred thousand Denise had gotten earlier in the day, which had already been consigned to Mr. Ng.

Leonard then went to Union Bank, which his father used. They were good for another million, but he had to attach two of his four buildings. He would have attached three of them but to his surprise, one had already been attached. Leonard had forgotten. The fourth building—his and Denise's offices—he would not touch. That was Denise's inheritance.

So that left four million nine hundred forty thousand to be raised.

Leonard called on Morris Feldbach, one of his unofficial partners. Morris was of Ruben's generation, a great legend downtown, and Leonard's friend and confidant. Unlike Ruben, Morris had gotten caught in Germany during the war. He was an Auschwitz survivor who still went to synagogue. Many survivors did not.

In his seventies, he worked seven days a week, owned two dye and finishing mills, two knitting mills, and the largest cloth printing shop in California. In Morris' world, one linear yard equalled one garment. K-Mart, A-to-Z, Target, Walmart—they all knew Morris. A thirty-six inch by sixty-two inch garment times eight hundred fifty thousand people a year. That's what Morris had accomplished. In ten years, he must have clothed the equivalent of the whole State of Florida.

"I need your help, Morris," Leonard appealed, explaining his situation. Morris thought about it for thirty seconds, then said "Sure," lending Leonard two and a half million of the nearly five million which he still required. He was glad for Leonard Rosenbalm. And, happy for his own fifteen grandchildren, all in Yeshiva, who stood between them to earn three percent in three weeks on Grandpa's shrewd loan.

Bolstered by commitments now amounting to four and a half million gathered in the course of an afternoon, Leonard visited his father in Beverlywood, a house he and Leonard's Mom had lived in for forty years, after their first few seasons in Boyle Heights. A little crooked swimming pool in back they never used, dark rooms heavy with the scent of rendered chicken fat, polished teak and damp carpets. Jewish, turn of the century, punctuated by an eight-foot tall television screen on which his father incessantly watched basketball and boxing.

"What do you suggest, Pop?" he asked, having layed out the deal.

Mom was in the bedroom, napping. She had suffered for years from an irritable bowel syndrome that left her enervated and depressed. In addition, her rheumatism was bad these days.

"Don't you do another thing. Stop right now. It's too big for you."

"No Pop, it's too big for YOU! Goddamnit, this is a mitziah, the deal of the century!"

"It's cockamamy."

"You must have a patent on that one."

"Oh?"

"You know exactly what I'm talking about."

"I don't know."

And Leonard recalled the bitter years, self-inflicted. Mom had had to cope and cover up. "Two seventy Riverside Drive. Remember? Sure you do. Jose and Impara Iturbe right next door, you used to listen to them practice. Robert Oppenheimer below. You two used to exchange trade secrets. They went places. Where did you go? Down, Pop! Remember? How the Metropolitan Life Insurance Company of New York foreclosed the whole goddamned thirteen story building from under you—ten years of hard work—because you were too proud to go out and get yourself an unsecured loan, the way Alvaro Spendetti would have done, a mere hundred thousand to save a lifetime of work!"

"You know nothing. Spendetti was a putz."

"Who was worth a half-a-billion dollars by the age of forty. Mother told me everything!"

"Your mother doesn't know beans. Don't tell *her* that. A hundred thousand during the height of the Depression. Do you have any idea how much money that was?"

"She knew if you'd borrowed that hundred thousand you could have held onto that building. You'd be rich today."

"You never carry an expensive building for a small building. And anyway, money isn't everything, son."

"Right." Leonard grew quiet with resignation.

"Where's your guarantee?" Ruben finally asked, questioning whether or not A-to-Z would even pay up?

"Guarantee? What guarantee? A-to-Z's a 5(A)(I) account."

"I suppose you think that's next to God?"

"Pop, it's Dunn and Bradstreet's best rating. Like the Federal Reserve. Like Bullocks!"

"Your mother stopped shopping at Bullocks years ago."

"Look, I know exactly how much money you've got stashed. This is going to allow you and Mom a comfortable retirement. Do you understand what I'm trying to do here?"

Ruben got up from the living room couch, with its lavender tulip prints, poured himself a soda water and sat back down looking sick.

"How much do you need?"

"One million. I'll pay it back within a month, plus twenty-five percent."

"Big spender all of a sudden."

"You put me into this profession. I've worked hard. I'm not sure why—"

His father stopped him. "I once bought twelve million yards of basic cloth on spec—in the thirties—eleven and a half cents a yard—"

"I know, Pop. Right up there with Spendetti."

"Sold the contracts out at thirteen cents. One hundred eighty thousand in profit. I know exactly what you're feeling."

"Those were pennies, Pop."

"Pennies, dollars. A question of a few zeros. What was my point? My point, son, is that money is not love, it's not children . . . " He meant to say more. "I'm so tired . . . "

"Will you help me?"

"Have you seen the goods?"

"No. But they're new."

"What if there's water damage."

"There's no water damage."

"How do you know?"

"If there's water damage I'll get a refund."

"You'll get nothing. What are the terms, cash on delivery?"

"Net ten days."

"What's that?" Of course he *knew* what it was.

"They're a huge company."

"So? All the more reason to pay on delivery. Never take an IOU."

"It's a signed contract."

"The nerve! I don't like it, so much gelt, so much stress."

"Will you help me? I need you, Pop."

" . . . Alright. I'll call Joe. But, don't be so greedy."

Joe was Ruben's banker of twenty years.

Leonard felt badly for himself and his father. Two generations caught so clearly in the spellbinding allure of profit that could be won and lost, or lost and won.

"Go say hello to your mother."

"I thought you said she's sleeping."

"I won't hear the end of it if you leave without saying hello to your mother. Go."

Leonard stepped lightly into his parent's bedroom. Ida was softly curled up amid a contagion of Russian down pillows, the slips embroidered in another era.

"Lennie, that's you?"

"Hi, Mom."

"Come, sit beside me. You'll stay for dinner?"

"Miriam and I have got plans. Another night."

It always pained him to have plans that excluded his parents, that brute slap in the face of affinity and longing. Some families managed to defy the forces of nature. There were times when he imagined it differently. A Third World enclave of three, perhaps four generations, all living together.

On the other hand, his parents usually drove him crazy within the space of one meal together.

Ida used to brag that when Lennie was still in her womb, he was such a good boy that he never kicked or moved, afraid of agitating his mother. But Ida got so scared she finally went to the doctor.—"He's not moving"—she said. Lennie must have heard her, or figured out that she'd taken him for dead. Even before the doctor could listen to her, he started making a ruckus. Ida cheered.

That same Doctor was witness to the fact that when Leonard was born, he laughed.

—"It's true. He never cried. It was a miracle. Imagine! Right out of the womb and my baby's giggling!"—Ida would tell her poker club and young Lennie would be awakened by all their noise and wander in his PJs from his bunk bed into the TV room where the boisterous gang was playing. And, he'd slip up to his mother's side, rubbing his eyes and protesting in half-sleep.

Leonard almost remembered, and as he kneeled over to give his mom a square kiss on the cheek, his head becalmed by the odors of antiquity which permeated this ancestral hearth, a strange thing happened: the whole room began to echo her motherly murmurs—the sonorous sound of a word *Kishatriya*, no meaning—the sense that merchants had occupied this same space in some other time, for a reason that he now came to embody; had felt the same pressure building in his heart. . . . The walls of the room drifted apart to reveal a kingdom, palatial, an abode in the ancient tropics that he'd never seen before, and the bedsheets scintillated, as other textiles flushed his temples in a congestion of patterns and designs—silver gilt thread, lozenges and quatrefoil, concentric rounds of cyclamen, a weft of loosely spun, unbleached cotton, tie-dyed satin, selvedges of dark green, bound and piped—as his surroundings were transformed and his mother became all mothers, her face, all faces, her tenderness, the world's tenderness, and Leonard fell into what might best be described as a nostalgic spin . . . somewhere?

When Vardhamana returned home following his experience with the cobras, his mother, Trisala, took the occasion of their dinner to tell her son of a marvelous recollection. For some reason, both she and her husband, King Siddhartha, felt that it was time the boy heard of these matters. Vardhamana seemed to know what was coming, though exhibited every sense of surprise.

Trisala described how, after nearly three months of her pregnancy, she began having these wonderful dreams. They lasted for a fortnight.

"I remember a mighty elephant," Trisala began, "whose trunk extended out to help all creatures in need. And a bull whose powers of intimidation were always turned towards good, rather than evil. There was a fierce lion with a soft spot in its heart who protected a beautiful princess whose body was anointed in aromas of the jungle. She lived in a palace of fresh flowers. At night, sometimes, she'd roll up her dress and step barefooted through the creek beneath a full moon. I see a festive occasion garlanded with prayer flags that rippled in a breeze, born along by currents of the warm noonday sun. And, in the center of the palace, there was a dark urn, thousands of years old, in which the waters of immortality would soothe the most troubled soul. I saw myself bathing in a lotus pond, in a wild sea, travelling through space on a heap of jewels, and finally, I dreamt that my very consciousness was a raging inferno, visible for miles around. And that fire was the joy of my creation, my little Vardhamana!"

The teenager gazed upon his mother feeling neither happy nor sad. He knew she had left something out. How a creature, half-man, half-goat, had crawled into bed with her and performed what could only be described as spiritual surgery, between her legs. She felt nothing. His friend Sakra, half-twin for a few moments while the surgery took place, had been spared any knowledge of these primordial happenings. But Vardhamana knew everything.

And, his father, Siddhartha, continued. "When your mother told me of these dreams, I ordered all of the diviners brought from town to interpret the wondrous visions, and to explain why the fields of corn throughout the territory of Videha had suddenly grown so tall and white; why good fortune had come to so many who least expected it. Thus it was decided that you should be called, among other things, Vardhamana, the Increasing One!"

"And then what, Father?" Vardhamana, feigning innocence, inquired.

"And then? And then, at midnight, during the third week of the first month of summer—the skies azure calmed—you arrived. The first thing I did was order all prisoners freed, the whole city swept clean, messages of good-fortune painted on every door, rice scattered for the poor, incense generously burned throughout the land. All debts were cancelled, all offences, big and small, were pardoned. Your mother and I invited dancers, wrestlers, acrobats, clowns, storytellers and ballad singers to perform. For twelve days the festivities went on. After which time you were bathed in a mountain stream . . . "

Leonard regained his balance, gazed upon his mother one last time, then left. He knew she felt lousy and had put on a courageous show for his benefit. She'd always had that kind of character. Nothing ever bothered her, or not that she'd admit to. On his way out, he took Ruben in his arms and awkwardly placed his lips to his father's grizzled cheek. He felt shakey on his legs as he climbed into his Bentley and put the top up.

That night, Leonard explained the deal in some detail to Miriam over a barbecued brisket, leftovers from a catered affair following a funeral earlier that day at Sinai Cemetery in the Valley. Leonard hardly ate.

Miriam was cool about the whole thing out of superstition. She trusted Leonard. They'd been married for twenty years. College sweethearts.

"If you say it's a good deal, then I'm overjoyed for all of us," Miriam declared, less intense about the actual machinations than her husband, who hadn't exactly told her about the one remaining problem, namely, one million four hundred forty thousand left to be borrowed. And, that's because Leonard had already figured out what had to be done. The momentum was driving him. He'd already forgotten what it was all about.

Miriam wanted to make love. She and Leonard fiddled for ten minutes but nothing worked. Leonard's mind was not complying.

"We don't have to make love," she said finally. "Just touch me."

He stroked her quietly and far away in the dark, as if looking back over a lifetime. A strange thought entered his mind—the notion that an ejaculation killed tens-of-millions of sperm. Where did the thought come from?

The next morning Leonard borrowed half-a-million against his life insurance policy. He then went to his appraiser to examine what would be involved in refinancing the fourth, supposedly inviolable, building. He hated to do it. The arithmatic was complicated—data involving the last three sales in the ten block vicinity, the building's income—which was down—the parking, location, square footage, date of original construction, that day's short-term interest rates, etc. . . . In the end, Leonard was still approximately half-a-million short.

"You gotta' be like a Spalding tennis ball in these situations," Hal ruminated out loud, his way of advising Leonard to go after street money for the shortfall. If you failed to pay it back, you usually got hurt, which is to say, killed. They knew of a merchant who plunged from the thirteenth story of the California Mart the year before, an alleged suicide during one of the market weeks. Fellow merchants had their doubts. But Hal, like Leonard, had no doubts about the deal. This was an Alvaro Spendetti kind of deal. Foolproof.

He went to the Iranians who, for four percent, made him a solid offer, though the terms suggested a horrible execution-style murder in the night if he failed to repay the debt, a threat veiled in such warm humor and apologies, over so festive a table, and the money in the leather case being so fresh and crisp, right out of the mint, that he could hardly turn it down, under the present circumstances. He walked out of that restaurant carrying the final half-a-million in cash.

Now Leonard started to really sweat it out.

At noon the next day, Leonard and Hal met Brian and the Dickie representative at a loading dock downtown. Leonard's people made a cursory check of the hundreds of cardboard boxes, prior to loading, for water damage. There was minor damage to a few of the cases which was duly noted. Each packing slip was carbon numbered.

All in all, it was a great dump. Hard to imagine an encore. Leonard signed the paperwork and handed over a cashier's check for nearly eight million dollars. In his possession was a facsimile copy, and signed original—messengered to him earlier that morning—guaranteeing payment on the other end within three weeks. This is how it was done with so big a company as A-to-Z. No problem.

According to the banks, to Leonard's broker, Hal's broker, the rating services, and the "buzz" on Main Street, A-to-Z was in great shape, with assets in excess of five billion dollars. Their stock on the American exchange was trading briskly. Benny's ten thousand investment would be worth thirty to him when it was all over. Hal would walk away with eight hundred thousand. Ruben and Ida, Morris Feldbach, Union and Mitsui banks, the Iranians and the mortgage companies all stood to make a bundle.

The trucks were loaded and sent on their way. Throughout the night the loading continued. By dawn the deed was done. Bills of lading signed.

Exhausted, Leonard hugged Hal, kissed his daughter, told everyone to take a day off, and drove home feeling oddly uneasy. Why? he wondered. He owned his home free and clear and though the value had dropped disastrously, it still had to be worth two million dollars. They owned an 1860s Corot that graced the dining room—one of the painter's Villa d'Avray landscapes—and several valuable signed etchings by Chagall. Not the fake lithos for ten-thousand dollars that flooded the galleries on Rodeo Drive. The two maids, Gloria and Juanita, kept the home immaculate, save for the rats which were endemic to the neighborhood. Actually, Leonard liked rats. Perhaps for the very reason that Miriam hated them. Someone had to like them, he'd say.

Leonard pulled up into his driveway, pushed the garage opener button and slowly pulled in, like some Odysseus back from years at sea. It had been a long and triumphant night. He stepped out of his Bentley at eight-thirty in the morning, stepping on air, his thoughts bathing in a paradise of cool reprieve, financial stardom, when he heard a strange squeaking; detected a frantic breathing and upon investigating the source of these cries, discovered a rat. It was alive, struggling, desperate, encintured in glue.

CHAPTER TWO

The Crash

Miriam must have asked Gloria to set the traps. Gloria, who came from Guatemala, had a thing about rodents, and would have been only too glad to rid the household of them. Leonard had never seen a glue trap before, nor any trap in his household, for that matter. It had been placed in a sneaky corner of the four-car garage, adjoining the six garbage cans and two yellow recycling buckets. Those proud buckets were otherwise rather contradicted by the volume of weekly Rosenbalm wastes.

Leonard approached the trap with trepidation.

The animal was small, perhaps not even a rat but a mouse. Its chest was sunk into the glue, as was its chin. All four fragile limbs were mired in the eighth of an inch of conglutinate, inescapable, an unimaginable death. As mastodons in tar, gazelles in African quicksand. He saw a fumbling evolution laid out before him, with its red tooth and claw. But the cruelty was greatly increased in Leonard's mind because this had been deliberately engineered.

His own body jerked with every feeble spasm of the little creature. Leonard's whole frame, weary from the long night of supervising the loading and shipping of two million trousers, knelt down beside the animal and was overwhelmed by unexpected feelings.

He lifted the tray of glue and carried it to the back patio through the house, stopping to get a roll of paper towels and a scissor in the kitchen. He encountered one of the housekeepers on the way. She scowled, backing away. Leonard said nothing.

Out back, the two animals—Leonard and the rat—stared at one another. The mouse, or rat, or whatever it was, had been entrapped for hours by the look of it. The creature had nearly given up, lunging with no slack, its minute mouth half covered in glue, its breathing frantic and incomplete. Its pitiful stare pierced Leonard's brain, flooded his heart.

Leonard proceeded to cut through the glue around its frame, surgically excising one paw at a time. The animal whined and rasped. Leonard ran to the medicine cabinet in their bedroom, found an eye dropper, filled it with water and returned to the animal, which was too frightened to drink. So Leonard dissolved several grains of white sugar in the water, and refilled the eye dropper to make it more palatable. But the creature was clearly in no mood for either force-feeding or mouth-to-mouth. By noon, Leonard had removed, more or less, the entire little guy. But its body was utterly covered in a tenth-of-a-millimeter-thick carapace of intractable sealer.

"Gloria!" he shouted, furious. She had remained far away from the patio throughout the operation.

"Yes, Mister Leonard?"

"Kerosine. Find me kerosine. I mean Turpentine!"

"What, Mister Leonard??"

Out of sorts, Leonard ran into the tool room where he did his carpentry. In the shelf above his ten-inch Powermatic table saw and eight-inch jointer he found the rusty container in question, raced back to the animal which he'd left on the kitchen table, lifted it, and began delicately dousing the critter over the sink. The glue readily dissolved.

Holding the animal with its pounding chest in his gloved gardening hand, he then rinsed it carefully in luke warm water and went back into the garden area with it where he tried again to entice it with something to drink. He tried lemonade. He tried some red wine. He even tried skim milk.

The mouse or rat didn't move. Leonard waited, like an expectant father. He nudged it towards the inviting grass and protected umbrage.

After a while, Leonard realized that his friend was dead. The ordeal had been too much for it.

Leonard Rosenbalm sank down on to his knees before the gaping, unendurable truth. He saw an altar,

Before which Vardhamana, clad in fine white cloth, himself knelt down on all fours, reciting a prayer of his forefathers, learned by heart, before a sculpture of a seated man. He then walked around this image, which had been roughly hewn from a serpentine stone, washing it with goat milk, water, sandalwood and—what was it, saffron?—arranging grains of rice on the marble temple floor in a symbolic swastika, dabbing three dots of rice atop the little pictogram, then fashioning a crescent-like moon above that. None of it made sense. The shrine was painted in white.

And Leonard heard the words, meaningless to him . . . *Namo arihantanam, Namo siddhanam . . .*

It was after twelve o'clock. Leonard had spent nearly four hours in the rescue operation.

"OK, Mister Leonard?" Gloria called out from the door toward the patio.

"NO, IT'S NOT OK!" he cried out. "Are there any more traps?" he demanded.

"Yes, Mister. Five more," she replied, her feelings hurt. "Mrs. Miriam, she says OK put traps."

Leonard ran to the other sites on the property. To his horror, one of them had succeeded in catching a second animal, a large one that had already suffocated in the glue.

Its body was locked in its final seconds of agony.

Leonard threw-up adjacent to the tennis court, where they kept additional garbage cans.

His portable phone rang. He didn't answer. He was crying.

He went indoors, sank into a hot bath and fell into troubled sleep.

He heard dogs straining at their leashes of hemp, yelping in a fever pitch. In a far field, Leonard saw a hundred peacocks tied to individual stakes. A huge crowd of villagers were betting on individual birds. Now another hundred peacocks were set loose upon them. The fights were to the death. Feathers rose up in a flurry. Cries, blood-stains, horrors. The dying birds collapsed beneath the weight of attack. Heads were chewed off. Legs ripped apart.

Champion birds were gathered up, thrown in gunny sacks, while the dogs were unleased to finish up the dead and dying. A feeding frenzy ensued. The birds were shaken, tossed, chewed to smithereens. These dogs were themselves beings trained to fight captured bears which would, in turn, be staked and tormented for the amusement of the locals.

On the edge of the clearing, Leonard saw Vardhamana, crumpled beneath a tree, pulling at his hair.

Leonard awoke to the sounds of Miriam getting undressed.

"Hi. How did it go? Oh, there's a number of messages you better listen to," she said.

Leonard's heart skipped a beat. He played back the machine.

It was Morris, it was Hal, it was Benny, it was Hal again, and there was a call from Ruben, his voice almost inaudible.

Leonard sat down on the bed. He reached Benny, who was the least volatile of the lot.

"What is it, Benny?"

"Julie called at ten-thirty this morning. I was just leaving the office. He said there were weird vibes at A-to-Z. Their stock plunged in New York."

Leonard stared, frozen in time, at the photographs of his family on the bedside table.

"Why did it plunge?"

"Did you speak to Morris, yet?"

"Not yet."

"Hal?"

"No."

"Morris heard something through the grapevine. You better call him, boss."

Miriam sat at her dressing table letting down her long black hair. She always kept it in a bun during working hours. "What is it?" she said.

"I don't know."

He called Hal. "Hal, Lennie."

"Jesus. Did you hear? What are we going to do?"

"Wait a minute. Back up. Did I hear what? About the stock, yes. What happened?"

"Not just the stock. D'you talk to Morris?"

"What's he going to tell me, Hal?"

"A-to-Z's in trouble."

"What do you mean?"

"Rumors they're headed into Chapter 11."

Leonard's insides shook.

"You know that's impossible."

"I don't know anything anymore. Remember Macy's?"

"A-to-Z was rated 5(A)(1) forty-eight hours ago, Hal."

"That was two days ago."

"The company's thirty years old."

"Macy's was older. So was Pan Am."

"Look. We've got a signed deal. So the stock went down. Have you looked at IBM lately? I suggest you calm yourself. There's reason to celebrate."

The other line rang. Miriam tried not to pay attention, taking off her make-up.

Leonard picked up. "I was just going to call you, Morris. What's up?"

"Did you ship yet?"

"Yes, last night."

"Too bad. Who were you dealing with?"

"I have no idea. What's this about?"

"They're in big trouble."

"How? I spoke with the banks, the brokerage firms—"

"Nevermind that. Banks will tell you anything to protect their largest clients."

"And the rating services?"

"They get the same information from the banks."

"Morris, what did you hear?"

"One of my sons-in-law works for Melankof, Ovitz and Gautama. He heard that their credit rating started sliding two days ago. I checked it out. Nobody's saying much but it's clear the company's got too much debt, interest rates have gone up—you know that—and their business has dropped way off."

"We've got a signed deal."

Morris uttered a pained laugh. "How old you are, Lennie?"

"Forty-two, Morris." Leonard was emphatically annoyed by all of this.

"You probably forgot about Standard Brand Paints? How they defaulted on one hundred forty-five million, delaying all credit? Not to mention Macy's."

"I know about Macy's."

"Then you know that Prudential got its money out, lawyers got their money out, preferred creditors who had liens got their money back. Non-secured creditors, they got raped. My point, Lennie, is this: Rosenbalm Textiles is no Prudential. Your deal was unsecured, right?"

"Well . . . yeah. But, have they actually defaulted?"

"Nobody knows. Maybe tomorrow you and I, we'll read it in the newspaper."

"Do you know anybody at A-to-Z?"

"I'm checking. I'll call you with any news. You'll sleep. The world will be the same."

"Thank's Morris."

Ten minutes later Morris called Leonard again. "I spoke with my son-in-law's boss. They're doing the paper work."

"What paper work?" Leonard's chest was heaving.

"A-to-Z defaulted two days ago on payments to the bank in excess of ninety million."

"OH SHIT! Nobody said a goddamned thing! I'll SUE!"

"You'll sue! So sue. You and a hundred other schmucks."

"It's not LEGAL!"

"Legal? What's legal? Tomorrow they'll be seeking protection under Chapter 11. Is that legal? Of course, it's legal."

"What do I do?"

"Plead with them to give you back your pants. Otherwise, it could be years before you see a dime. Maybe never. Frankly, you're timing stinks. We'll stay in touch."

They ended their conversation. Mercifully, Morris said nothing about his two point five million dollar loan to Leonard. He could afford to be patient.

"You look pale, dear," Miriam volunteered, ignoring the obvious.

"A-to-Z's going bankrupt," Leonard exclaimed, thinking it better to bring her into the maelstrom while the information was fresh.

"So I gathered. What does that mean?"

"I'm not sure," he choked.

Leonard called his father. There was no answer. Odd, Leonard thought. It was dark and Ruben had vowed to stop driving after dark on account of his impaired vision, the result of cataracts which he had stubbornly put off taking care of. He had always harbored the strongest feelings about doctors. He hated their guts. Ida had stopped driving years before.

"I'm going to light the fireplace," Miriam said.

She then went to the cellar for a fine bottle of Cabernet and threw together a mushroom pasta with garlic bread. Her intention was to provide her husband a quiet meal to get his mind off everything.

But as they were sitting down to eat in the dining room, before a crackling blaze, lights dimmed, the room looking as romantic as it ever had, the phone rang again, and this time it was from a nurse's station at the emergency room of Cedars-Sinai. There'd been an accident.

Within an hour the whole family was assembled at the intensive care unit. Ruben was dead, Ida scarcely hanging on having just gotten out of surgery.

It would be discovered later that Joe, Ruben's banker, had reached Ruben on his car phone late that day and warned him about A-to-Z. According to Joe, Ruben had taken the news more philosophically than might be expected, but was worried for Leonard. He had already driven Ida to see her chiropractor, which was halfway to Holmby Hills. He'd then evidently decided to continue to Leonard and Miriam's house. The accident occurred during the sunset hour, bright and blinding. Ruben was heading west at fifty in a residential neighborhood, and collided head-on with an enormous Chinese silk floss tree on a curve. He was not wearing a seat belt nor did his vintage Porsche come equipped with airbags.

Ida had been wearing her seat belt. But the impact had somehow managed to break her neck.

Leonard fixed his look upon her. She was inaccessible beneath her oxygen tent, hooked up to various wires and tubes, all bruised and purple. Her face was bandaged, the veins in her hands exposed to the life-rescuing fluids being pumped into her. She was unconscious.

Denise, who did not yet know about the family's other problems, was strong and tearless. Inwardly, she prided herself on being a survivor. She held on to her father.

Later that night, Ida passed away.

There was sobbing all around Leonard who stood steadfast, almost serene, in the midst of destruction. And, once again, his mother's bed-sheets began to scintillate, surrounding voices grew vague and distant—nurses over the intercom, a doctor consoling a granddaughter, shuffling strangers, technological beeps—and the walls and adjoining beds in the intensive care unit began to drift apart . . .

And Leonard stood before a Rabbi, surrounded now by friends on a hillside where his parents were being laid to rest. The Rabbi read prayers of astonishing beauty and everyone remembered things about the couple—how Ida had smuggled flowers across the Russian frontier during World War II, how Ruben had once beaten up three hoodlums who tried to take advantage of him. Hal Spendetti remembered how Ruben and Uncle Alvaro had made their first big killing together. Leonard, of course, knew that Hal was just being sentimental. Ruben never made a killing, or not Alvaro's kind. Hal wept with memories of Seventh Avenue, the bravado of all those years and deals, extinguished in an instant. Memories which only served to heighten his terror before this demon that had gotten inside him, had sabotaged his own personal affairs.

Hal had already been on the phone with A-to-Z's overwhelmed underlings in accounts payable that morning. The prognosis was desperate. The Los Angeles Times and Wall Street Journal had each run stories diagnosing what went wrong, blaming the global recession, cheap labor in Mexico, cheap fabrics from Korea, and so forth. The company's debt was forty-nine percent so their reference had remained high, while the company's bank had perpetuated the myth of viability. Nobody had mentioned a third-quarter loss of two hundred million.

The Chapter 11 petition had been filed following a meeting between the chairman and key bondholders and unions to pave the way for A-to-Z's emergence following bankruptcy protection. They wanted time to make the company attractive for a merger partner. The prepackaged bankruptcy evidently had the blessing of its major creditors and the Securities and Exchange Commission. The Rosenbalm Textiles of the world were not privy to these high-minded affairs. He had not structured a preferred credit deal and was thus out of luck. It didn't matter whether he was owed fourteen million or a hundred million. It was all in the deal and Leonard should have known that. Later, in a fleeting glimpse backwards at his former life, he would realize that he had deliberately, if subconsciously, sabotaged himself for reasons soon to be apparent.

Two men with a winch lowered first Ida's, then Ruben's casket into a single large hole, with the Ventura freeway off in the hazy distance below. A procession of some sixty well-wishers (half of their friends had already died or were too sick to make it to the funeral) then took up the shovel one by one, and tossed dirt into the hole so that no strangers should have to do it, and so that the caskets not be exposed for very long, according to Jewish tradition.

Dispensing with the shovel, Leonard squeezed a clod of soil in his hand and dropped it onto the caskets. "Good-bye, Mom. 'Bye, Dad." He squeezed his eyes shut, and heard the word "Parsva," uttered with great depth.

And there were Trisala and King Siddhartha, reciting their own prayers before the statue which their son had earlier knelt before. Incense rose to the summit of the high vaulted shrine.

Outside, cries of turmoil could be heard, the wailing of mothers who'd lost their sons, and sons who'd lost their mothers. A pestilence had stricken the region and funeral pyres were everywhere clouding the horizon.

Siddhartha's royal physicians were in attendance on the sick and dying while his son, Vardhamana, saw to the distribution of grain and money to all the villagers, without respect to caste—the Brahmans of Vaisali, the Ksatriya of Kundapura, or the Baniya in Vanijyagrama. But in his heart, Vardhamana was especially aware of the poor and homeless, the untouchables, those with leprosy and elephantiasis, goiters and pneumonia, starving children and starving grandparents who had only trees for shelter. Many of these people were the same ones who had bet upon the killing of the peacocks. In the air, there was a sense of all things coming around.

Late in the day, when Vardhamana returned from this battlefield of human suffering, he found his parents stretched out on two beds of kusa grass. He knew what they were doing.

"Are you sure this is what you want?" he asked.

And they told him how much they loved him and how proud they were to have been his parents.

And, within a month both King Siddhartha and Queen Trisala had died from voluntary starvation. When Vardhamana's friend, Sakra, came to comfort him, he found a young man of unflinching strength. "It was meant to be!" Vardhamana whispered. But Sakra could not be so strong and he shed tears for a man and a woman to whom he felt a strange and enduring connection. The extent of his own grief took him by surprise, though Vardhamana understood completely.

The late Trisala and King Siddhartha's son, Vardhamana, then had the corpses taken by royal bullock carts to the banks of the sacred river Ganges where, according to ancient tradition, they were cleansed with honey and clarified butter and burned with sandalwood. Ashes were sprinkled among lotus flowers in the river, where lordly vultures preyed upon any morsels not completedly consumed by the fire and blind porpoises careened upstream against the currents with smiles on their faces.

The bones were picked out of the embers and tossed upon a heap of elephant, camel, donkey and other human bones, near the river. This is where those paying homage would venture for years to come.

Leonard Rosenbalm drove more slowly now past Vermont Avenue. He no longer held his breath. In truth, he no longer worried about anything. There was no hope of reclaiming a dime from A-to-Z, let alone the Dickie trousers, which had already been swept up by other standard and preferred creditors. Denise had taken the news with utter contempt for reality. At nineteen, she could afford to be philosophical.

"Just as well," she said bitterly.

Leonard wandered with his daughter down Twelfth Street, known as Santee Alley with its thirteen thousand styles of apparel, hundreds of mannequins lining the narrow Old World chaos like Ming Dynasty sentinels.

The garments were low-end, a miasma of the world's veneer, modesty, sex appeal, local custom. Judy and Kevin Sportswear, LA Action, Jennifer Sandals made in Taiwan, Le Corinne, Vittorio Ciano, Kosher Star, Haddadin Gita International, Ali's linen, Habib fashion. . . . Jews, Indians, Persians, Chinese, Koreans, Thai, Latinos, foreigners changing the name of their company every three months to confound the IRS. If you were looking for quilted crepe, Georgette sleeves or triple voile of chiffon, you were in the wrong alley.

Leonard felt a profound nausea overtaking his nostalgia. They reached Julie's headquarters by foot on account of the parking which was impossible. They found him hunkered down and cowering behind a stack of invoices that would never be paid, all Net ten days, or Net thirty days. Try Net Never. All A-to-Z disasters and reading like a veritable conspiracy.

"Yes, it was my territory. And, I'm the last to know," he protested before Leonard could get a word out.

But, Leonard had not come to argue his claim. That would be left to lawyers out in the dark sea. He had come to inform him that, under the circumstances, there would be no commission.

"Naturally," said Julie.

Julie had heard about Leonard's parents. He conveyed his condolences.

"I also want to thank you for what you did," Leonard voiced, the curve ball coming from depths he himself had not expected.

"Thanks for what?" Julie asked, a little confused.

But, Leonard couldn't say, or, not yet.

At the office, Leonard and Benny studied the situation, going through financials. The street money had to be paid back first, since these people lived outside the law, then the banks, and then the remaining money—Hal's, Morris's and Benny's—had to be obtained without losing the main building. The Holmby Hills house, Ruben and Ida's house, the fancy cars and three of the four buildings were gone, poof, just like that. Two generations of sweat and tears. He had not intended to ask Denise to sell her car, but she insisted. Miriam had had the presence of mind to get to the bank immediately and remove all items from Ruben's vault. And the elder couple's will had fortunately been set up to avoid probate. But with each added calculation, Leonard was swept again and again by the same nausea which had overcome him in the alley.

Something was happening to him. Something extraordinary.

That night he remained alone in his office. Benny, aware that his life was going to change now, had caught his bus back to Pomona. Hal had left early, nearly catatonic with depression. For the first time in his life he felt like one on the outside looking in, whereas previously, Hal Spendetti had known himself as an insider, connected. Nobody could kick his ass because he had several hundred thousand more dollars than the next jerk. Hal's wife was sure to fall apart when she learned of their loss. Any excuse to down pills and take to drink. She'd been struggling with her obsessive behavior for years. This was not going to help it.

Leonard had sent Denise home to be with her Aunt Sarah and Miriam. It was a small family. He told her that he intended to spend the night in his parents' house. He wanted to soak up the last tangible memories, alone, uncluttered, immersed in the contemplation of familiar things. He didn't say it exactly like that, but that's what Leonard was thinking.

Already Miriam was beginning to organize for the move. It was simply a question of determining what was left. She was not at all happy about leasing a condominium in Culver City or wherever, but that seemed more than probable at this point. It all depended on how patient Morris was willing to be. He was a very rich man, but two and a half million dollars was two and a half million dollars.

Still, things were not so bad. The thirty thousand square foot building on Main Street was worth, according to the appraiser, nearly three million, though the leases were proving to be sporadic, at best. If Leonard sold the main building—which he did not want to do—he could pay off the second mortgages on the other three and make a good profit which would solve the situation with Morris's debt. The buildings all had balloon clauses which allowed him to do so. But, it would leave virtually nothing for his wife and daughter. And, the problem was compounded by the market. It was the worst time to sell downtown in decades.

Leonard sat alone in his office of twenty-five years contemplating his circumstances. Out of his complicated entanglements arose a clear sensation of his deliverance, inarticulate and inward. Like the image of that odd statue, twice repeated, in his thoughts. Of a lone seated figure. The image did not invoke the idea of escape, but of embrace, dawning upon him with the vigor of a treatise enshrined in law, bolstered by blind history, by precedents in every art book, literary saga and encyclopedia he'd ever thumbed through. It had no name, was wild and free, without possession or aspiration; it glided silently through whole centuries, born aloft by a message, or prayer, of liberation. Whether for the mouse or Ida, Leonard or the night janitor.

What was he thinking? He didn't have a clue. It was college philosophy class-type contemplation, long-haired hippy thoughts, or old retirees feeding pigeons in the park-type ruminations. Or maybe it was classical music, or a self-portrait by Rembrandt with tired eyes and penetrating look, or sheer deja-vu with no classification at all. Perhaps, it was the very essence of nostalgia. But, for what?

The building was dark save for his desk light which cast a glare on the plastic frames of all the photographs of his past life. What did a man need, after all?

Suddenly, he heard a noise down the stairs outside his office. "Ramon, is that you?" Leonard called out.

Leonard stood up and walked to the door. The side of his head was met by the cold, pressing steel of a gun.

"I gonna kill you, asshole!"

The gun pressed harder. Leonard could see nothing as the assailant stood to one side. The voice was desperate.

"Your money. Hurry up!"

A twinkle galvanized Leonard's frame of mind. "You're a little late, my friend."

The words came with the relief of one who'd left nothing for death, who'd burned down his fields of wheat rather than letting the advancing enemy get at them.

"You got one minute before I gonna kill you. You gonna be a dead man."

"We keep no safe here. No cash. Take my car. My watch. Take everything."

Leonard motioned towards his pocket with his upraised hands.

"Don't move!" and the man, shaking violently, the gun touching Leonard's left temporal lobe, reached into his pocket crudely and ex-humed the keys to the Bentley. He then ripped Leonard's Rolex watch from his wrist and pushed Leonard down on the floor.

Leonard knew he was going to pull that trigger any second. The man was out of his mind, and so was Leonard. And, perhaps this was the very deliverance he had envisioned moments before. Perhaps the violence of the universe, with its Big Bang and unceasing birth of stars, its treacherous Serengetis and cellular armageddons had decreed that Leonard Rosenbalm come back into the waiting fold this night.

He lay flat on his stomach, his face squished to the oak two by fours which he himself had laid one weekend long ago. The psychopathic voice kept howling, "I gonna kill you!" Like a caged monkey rocking back and forth, knocking its head against the bars. A filthy boot stiffened against the back of Leonard's head, execution style. The man, whom Leonard had still not seen, kneeled down. Leonard dreamt of Miriam and his daughter, of the Milky Way, and heard the heavy breathing and smelled the acrid whiff of one who had been living on the street. Leonard's body was limp and compliant.

"Hey, you! You sonofabitch!" a voice called out.

It was Ramon at the top of the stairs. He'd seen the light on and come for his weekly paycheck and without hesitating threw his only weapon—a mop—at the man with the gun.

The man freaked out, shot once at Ramon, missing, fled down the stairs, firing again, and again missing, before lunging out towards the back alley, where he tripped, dropping the car keys and watch, got up and fled.

Leonard slowly stood up. His mind was not right there, but far away. He did not want to call the police. He'd had enough official business for a lifetime. He thanked Ramon and paid him his week's salary, emptying his wallet.

"It's too much!" Ramon objected.

But Leonard insisted.

"You're sure you alright?" Ramon probed.

"I never felt better," Leonard said, crazily.

Ramon left to meet Carmelita, his wife, at a bowling alley somewhere.

For a moment, Leonard did not know what he was doing. His memory converged with identities and cajolery from places he'd never been, times in which he hadn't lived. His whole living body was as an invocation, vibrating, bewildered, full of wonderment. Perhaps the shock of his parents' death was just settling in, or the fear and apprehension of losing most of his wealth, or having just survived a brush with death. It could have been many things, of course. There had to have been a strong element of guilt, even shame in his present condition.

And yet, he was smiling radiantly, uncontrollably. Was it that the assailant's insanity had infected him? Or, perhaps Leonard was simply glad to be leaving downtown, for that was the sense of it. He knew he'd be leaving forever, though exactly by what means he could not say. And he started to walk away. . . .—'Where am I going?'—Leonard wondered.—'What am I doing?'—But, he had no answers. He just kept going, down the stairs, out into the darkness.

It was the tenth day of the first fortnight of the first month of winter, a day known as Suvrata, when this reversal reversed itself; when a sense of success overshadowed the man-length shadows; and melancholy turned to joy, distraction to insight, terror to confidence, the world of violence and pain to a dream of reason. And Vardhamana heard a voice hailing the great bull among his clan, repeatedly shouting the word, "Victory." And he knew that the voice was calling to him. That it was referring to the victory within, the conquest of oneself, of one's desires and impulses. There was much more to the voice than that, but Vardhamana understood.

And, he set out, at once, to renounce the immense wealth he had inherited from his parents, the palace, the heaps of gold and precious stones, his rubies and pearls, which he distributed to the debt-burdened with indifference, as his beloved parents had done. And, he bid adieu to his wife and his daughter, though this was especially difficult, involving an awkward scene—she screamed, she wept, she flung her fists at his chest . . . 'Please, don't abandon us!', but he could not easily console her in this matter and, finally, when it was obvious that nothing else would work, when the fates or gods or whatever demons had possessed him had worked their spell, she set aside her shame, her desolation, and blessed her husband, wishing him the very best in this life.

And he said farewell to all those comforts of his home, his village, his status, his friends, everything, and set out on a journey by foot across India that would take the rest of his life to complete.

CHAPTER THREE

The Great Renunciation

It was after eight o'clock in the evening. A moonless night and very cold. As Leonard walked out into the parking lot he noticed a huddled figure seated against the brick wall fumbling for cover with pieces of cardboard and layers of newspaper. Had he seen the figure before, a hundred times, a thousand times? If so, he couldn't recall. But this night, for the first time, he saw a human being beneath those newspapers. Los Angeles was in the grip of a cold spell. The man's plight went to Leonard's bones.

He walked over to him.

"Excuse me, are you OK?"

"Do I look OK?" The man wheezed. His teeth were chattering. Leonard still had a lingering image of the Milky Way in his thoughts. You could not see the stars from downtown Los Angeles due to all the city lights. In his wool Armani pants and jacket, Leonard was quite comfortable.

He stared at the man who stared back at Leonard.

"If you have nothing better to do, at least sit down," the homeless person offered.

"I'm sorry. Certainly. Yes. Why not."

Leonard took a seat. It felt like the right thing to do. To have declined the invitation would have been to dishonor the person, to have made him feel low. Among Jews, charity—if given as charity—is dishonorable. Charity must be extolled so as to uplift the spirit, as well as the physical circumstances, of the beneficiary, such that the joy of giving and the joy of receiving become the same thing. That usually translates into anonymous giving. But there was no anonymity in a back alley.

As the two men sat side by side, the homeless person's chattering increased until to Leonard's ears it was a cacophony.

"Here, wear this," and Leonard removed his jacket and draped it over the man's shoulders.

"The name's Henry," the man garbled.

But Henry's incessant carrying-on only escalated until Leonard felt that he had no choice but to give up his shirt as well. He helped the man out of his own festering shreds and into the three hundred dollar shirt.

"Hey man, that fits real good. Thanks. What about you?"

Leonard did not feel cold in the slightest, though he had no way to account for this odd fact. And anyway, his Bentley was right there and Leonard would be leaving soon. The car had a great heating system.

But, the night wore on and the temperature dropped and the homeless person's shuddering worsened. Until finally, inspired and feeling great compassion, Leonard turned over his pants, his socks, even his underwear to the now confused and embarrassed Henry. It was clear to him that his patron had some loose screws upstairs. Maybe he was one of those millionaires who you read about going crazy from time to time and giving their entire fortune to a pet cemetery.

Leonard did not feel the least self-conscious, however. Having become naked felt to him an astonishing relief. For one thing, the homeless person was so shaken by Leonard's gesture of goodwill, his teeth had stopped chattering. But the extent of Leonard's satisfaction can scarcely be known by those for whom nudity is only understood in the privacy of a bathroom, or under the covers. For Leonard's sudden nakedness there are few words. Yet, every physical body in the world, every birth and every death, every act of conjugal passion, each private net of hormones and lusts, jingling and blushing, thinking and longing, dreaming and desiring, stretching and self-touching, all hinge upon this centrality of Being, which surely exists in nudity and this hit Leonard with the force of an explosion.

To be rid of that nausea which had swept over his person, to bask in the night air, shorn of the day-in, day-out business of textiles.

His testicles quickly shrivelled up in the cold air to the size of button mushrooms. His chest puckered outwards in the darkness, sleek and muscular. And, for a man who'd driven a Bentley, he evidenced no aging, neither slouch, nor fatigue, but rather exhibited the agility of one who'd been naked his whole life. Indeed, as the minutes gathered, Leonard felt increasingly warmed from within. As if his very act of giving away his clothes had conferred on him some kind of immunity he would never have predicted. A sense of joy threatened to overwhelm him. How could this, this chaos of intentions, feel so good? So warm? So central to Leonard's being? His metabolism rose to the occasion.

He then invited Henry to sleep inside the building. He could have the white couch in Leonard's office. As the fellow made himself comfortable, Leonard sat down at his desk and took up a pen to write a brief message to Denise and Miriam. The words came with aching, slow care.

He had evidently made up his mind about something, but with as yet no premeditation.

Leonard left his keys, along with his Rolex watch in the same envelope, which he placed inside the top drawer of his desk. He was not thinking straight. He was not thinking. Everything was a blur.

He then walked away, dreamily.

"Hey, where are you going?" Henry called out.

"Out into the world," Leonard said, whimsically. "God bless you."

Leonard reached the parking lot and took one last look at the Bentley. He did not ask himself,—'What am I doing?'—He simply walked, his barefeet thrilling to the concrete slab and freezing grit. Each sensation was new.

A white cat raced across the street, stopping to look at the naked man.

A car drove by, accompanied by hoots.

Leonard knew exactly where he was going. To a palm tree down towards the freeway on-ramp. He'd planted the palm as a teenager, in front of the first building Ruben had ever purchased in California. Many years later, that tree had grown to maturity. A circle of fatigued grass surrounded it now.

More cars passed him, one slowing down. A face peered out the window. "Hey buddy, it's gonna fall off!" Trailed by laughter as the vehicle sped away.

It was sometime after midnight when Leonard reached the tree, and sat down. Within minutes, he was asleep.

And he dreamt that this place was called *Jnati-sanda-vana*, which referred to a park on the edge of the town known as Kundapura. And that the palm was actually an asoka tree, a sorrowless tree. He dreamt of the spirit of a person that kept haunting him, causing his vision to slide off the continent, out of time, into other dimensions, and then to become more lucid than ever before, that man called Vardhamana. No longer a teenager, but a grown man, who had stopped beneath the same tree, had undertaken vows of abstinence and austerity, had shed all his fine accoutrements, plucked out his very hair in five painful fistfuls, and become a wandering solitaire.

And, Leonard curled naked around a palm tree in downtown Los Angeles in the middle of a cold night, like a King Cobra coiled rapturously in the forest, his inner flame having been kindled the moment he'd ceded his possessions. His gesture of nudity was like some ancient emerging immune system, like the messener RNA, Cytachrome C, the call of a loon, or a dragonfly's aerodynamic. In an instant, he had acquired unthinkable fortifications. His seeming vulnerability had become a bulwark, his skin a palisade, his breast a bastion, his bones unfailing earthwork. These transforming pulses and fevers got into his blood.

A procession reverberated around Vardhamana, throngs of men and women and children who came forward from every walk of life to celebrate this earnest renunciate and to recognize in his convictions the condition of them all.

When Vardhamana left that tree, his hands cupped in the position of a begging bowl, of prayer, he had in truth given up his normal body, prepared to endure any and all calamity.

And Leonard's eyes rapidly quavered, he ground his molars like chaff, his fingers trembled and his toes dug into the remnant of soil surrounding the tree, where dogs and homeless people had urinated for years. For, it was as yet unclear what Vardhamana was really doing. These grand gestures, this pomp and ceremony surrounding so brutal a suicide.

In Leonard's dream, the day dawned over the jungle expanse of Kundapura, with its population of tigers and monkeys and parrots and water buffalo. He heard the riot of animal sounds, saw the myriad ellipses of smoke rising from the village, experienced the clamor of human settlement, ageless in its industry and self-interest, and then saw Vardhamana, like a jeweline pillar in the sun, shaded by his own self-control, spectacularly free from all inner turbulence. Or, that's how it appeared to Leonard.

Everywhere around him were the ferocious knots of destiny, cloying bonds and singular attachments—white gold, voluptuous girls, drinking halls, fancy chariots—yet this stranger, Vardhamana—Who Was He??—had managed thus far to rigorously banish every age-old enticement, as if such temptations were no more than dead skin cells. The word *"karma"* emerged in Leonard's brain.

But how?? He was a man, after all, a mortal being like Leonard. How had he done it?

The conjecture pursued itself . . . For there was Leonard.

In the darkest hour before dawn, produce and garment trucks heading down Main Street passed a creature entwined around a tree, its skincolor Semitic, hardly distinguishable in the diesel-scented night. The noise roused Leonard from his deep sleep. The shock of his reality further overwhelmed him.

"My God!" his head shrieked.

By instinct he thought to cover himself with his hands. He began to shiver in the cold. Tears involuntarily flowed down his cheeks.

"What's happened to me," he mumbled, frantic with indecision.

And he gawked at his bare legs, and at the tree which he planted, and then he remembered his dream.

The image of this man inside himself, as dark as the Earth, as white as the purest marble. Inviolate and compassionate, two qualities which most stood out in his hazy recollection. And, as he gathered his wits, his breathing of its own accord calmed down, his whole person stood up unashamed, as Adam in Eden, a sure-footed tribute to his parents, and their parents, and to a million generations unknown that preceded them. Not just human parents and human children, in Holmby Hills or downtown Los Angeles, but mice and rats and cats and peacocks. Even down to the annoying mosquito. Old ones used to fly into his house and die, every time he'd open the door. They'd come exhausted and proceed to crawl along the carpet. Leonard's insistent heart, unprepared for such generosity of spirit, avalanched with affection, wanted to shout in jubilation. Something in him had cracked, had opened up the floodgates, and it was all rushing in. He could not stop it for it had already happened.

They say the road to hell is paved in gold, the road to heaven unpaved. There was dirt in Leonard's fingernails, dirt that had been there for untold eons, as well as the remains of a dog's excreta, whose odor was incoming. Just a week before he'd had his nails manicured at John's in Beverly Hills for twenty-five dollars.

The tree was naked, the grass, the air and Leonard were naked, too. He heard his blood bursting through his arteries and veins, his heart and throat, down to his fingertips. Never had he felt so close to the ground, so involved in the palpable air, its molecules and odors, so aware of the sky, so at peace with this nature in tumult all around him. His head was spinning with the excellence of such company.

What was gone—wife, daughter, house, business, clothes—was gone. It was the beginning that shone before him now, rising out of the eastern sky like all of holy, sweet North America. And with it, one certainty which offered Leonard a paramount strength, remedied his lingering doubts, combated his fears, and ensured him of his dignity, of a universal truth that called to him.

The unendurable suffering of those two rats, the chattering teeth of homeless Henry, the forlorn and savage emptiness of a figure with a gun. Leonard no longer distinguished between them. How could he? Their respective pains had touched him. His nerve endings did not delineate, his heart asked no questions of suffering, a gasp was a gasp, the many cries in the night, undifferentiated. All creatures were blessed, there was no other premise by which to live, he now reckoned.

The turmoil and pettifoggery, the many mannered obsessions and cruelties which weigh down upon human life, all life, are nothing compared with the possibilities of this blessedness, thought Leonard. The very reflection was refreshing, even after a night in the urinated dirt. Did he fear the consequences? Knowing, even in his confused state that nudity would invite complications? That his situation was anything but liberating? That swarms of money lenders, realtors, officials, family members, society, moral avengers, guardians of the sacred trust, reporters, onlookers, cynics, professors, jealous gurus, disciples, students, seducers, pimps and prostitutes, women in love, men in love, lawyers, stray dogs, bandits, horrible people, good people, mocking children, astonished bystanders, angry merchants, bellowing traffic, gangs, Blacks, Whites, Yellows, Reds, bankers and judges, psychiatrists and jailers would all come after him?

Downtown Los Angeles with its infestation of lice, cockroaches, burglars, gangs, photochemical oxidants, nitrates, surface ozone, sirens, the overflow of races, the homeless staking out their pitiful hegemony, was certainly no pastoral Assisi, no mellow Indian tea plantation of prehistory. But, to Leonard, it was a magnet of vitality, where he knew by name Cuban messenger boys, Auschwitz survivors, Iranian chefs, Korean seamstresses, Japanese bankers, braless French girls, overbearing mobsters, and street people like Ramon, who'd saved his life, and Henry, who'd saved his next life.

Did he mean to set some kind of new example? He wasn't sure.

Against the oncoming headlights, at twelve minutes to seven, Leonard Rosenbalm started to walk East. It was beginning. The sun was rising.

At eight-thirty that morning, Denise Rosenbalm got in early to the office. She was surprised to see her father's car in the lot. But then reasoned that it made sense for him to plunge back into his work to keep his mind off the funeral and to address the most serious financial decisions of his career.

What Denise found, of course, was a sleeping bum on the couch in her father's office, wearing her father's clothes.

"Where's my father? Who are you? DAD!?" she screamed.

She frantically searched the premises for her father. Neither Benny nor Hal were in yet. She raced next door and grabbed Mr. Ng, who was in his own state of discernible shock, having to assess his entire business plan given the sudden catastrophic absence of any future cash infusions from Rosenbalm Textiles.

"Quick!" she cried. "Dad's in trouble!"

Together they marched back into Leonard's office. Mr. Ng carried a handgun. During the riots, in absence of any policemen willing to take on the mob, he and other proprietors had protected the building from the rooftops, their weapons aimed at the looters below.

"What are you doing here?" Mr. Ng exclaimed like a soldier, his legs braced, his gun hand at the ready. He, too, had seen the bum around, but they'd never spoken until now.

"My name's Henry and the Man (he pointed to Leonard's desk) left stark naked, he says to me, 'Here, Henry you keep these clothes until I come back.'"

His voice trembled. He was scared. He felt sorry for the Man. He also had a bad hangover.

"And he invites me up, says sleep right here. I could use it, that's the truth. And that's exactly what he said. He wrote a letter, too, it's in that desk right there. I'll just be going."

Mr. Ng would not let him budge, not until things were properly sorted out. Denise found the envelope addressed to her, with the keys and broken watch.

And then she read the letter to herself.

"Dear Daughter, I've given my clothes to one who needed them more. Everything else goes to you and Mom. It will all work out. I'm doing what I have to do. Please don't worry about a thing. Life is wonderful. I love you both. Dad."

At that moment, Ramon walked in the door and proceeded to explain about the burglar, and to assure Denise and Mr. Ng that the bum on the couch was not that same burglar.

Everyone was confused. Henry looked to Ramon, who looked to Mr. Ng, who looked to Denise, who looked at the letter.

Benny walked in the door. "Good morning. Whew!" He smelled the street person, then recognized Leonard's Armani suit. "Denise, what's going on?"

Ten blocks away, near Pershing Square, Leonard Rosenbalm moved lightly, steadfastly, looking directly before him, cautiously avoiding any bug. He did not want to inadvertently step on an ant. He walked a little strangely, in other words. On padded barefeet, in a tempo best described as careful. One of those you occasionally see, moving through traffic, into their own world. He was also careful not to make eye contact with anybody in particular. There was a sense of decorum about his shyness, a modesty or insecurity which wished to avoid familiar faces. Or a desire to disassociate himself entirely from the human race, at least for now, until he got his animal bearings right.

He vaguely planned on an eastward odyssey, the desert, the mountains, the Great Plains, the Eastern Seaboard and beyond. And one thought motivated this distant longing, namely, the blessedness of all creatures, a revelation that even now was rapidly reformulating itself in the authority of guises, words and images that were entirely new to Leonard Rosenbalm. Chemistry and physics were jolting his insides. Evolution was marching to his whistle.

Rush hour pedestrians tended to allow a wide berth for crazy people, for people with cooties, but Leonard certainly topped the list. He was not the first person to be seen naked on the streets of Los Angeles, and would not be the last. Nevertheless, it was admittedly a rare and unsettling sight to see a Caucasian so obviously well-groomed and well-fed trekking up Olive Street in his birthday suit. It was only a matter of moments before practical destiny should take notice. But, who could recognize that to walk naked through Los Angeles was to ascend Mount Everest, and beyond?

CHAPTER FOUR

The Arrest

Leonard stopped. There before him was a naked woman. Full-bosomed, bronze skinned, with lean hips and tight buttocks, cropped hair and a powerful expression, she was proud and her nobility was bathed in the golden copper glow of early morning. She stood upon the steps of Bunker Hill, near the Central Library and the Biltmore Hotel, between Grand and Flower streets.

Forty inches high, she was mounted atop a pedestal in a circular pool. Three large crabs clawed at her base. She was beautiful. The sculpture was named "Source Figure," by an artist named Robert Graham.

Leonard stared at her. Some might even describe his gaze as gawking. A photographer who happened to be there snapped a roll of images of the naked man peering at the naked woman.

There were angry taunts, catcalls and heckles from the large crowd that passed this way. A Jewish diamond merchant tried to help him, urging him off the street, pointing him towards a clothier and advising him to seek professional help.

Passers-by hurled angry denouncements and blaring lampoons. Leonard steered his way through this thicket of vilification, in each instance raising his hands in the gesture of prayer. An orange hit him in the head. He bowed in forgiveness and kept walking along with the stop and go traffic. A Greyhound tour bus crawled past him, as he strode up the perilous sidewalk. Forty eyes peered down from above. Smartly-dressed businessmen and women, runners in high-top Reebocks, blue collar workers in helmets, passed him on the street. More furious ejaculations and murmurs of profound sympathy.

"Poor bastard," one of them muttered, stepping far to the side.

Leonard was now speaking out loud to each and every passerby. "Blessed be all creatures . . . Peace be with you . . . " And then from his own inner voice came the invocation, "*Ahinsa Paramo Dharmah*." He hadn't a clue what it meant, or not literally. But it *felt* right. But, that wasn't the end of it. He then stated declaratively, "*mae samananam niggamthanam pamcamahavvaie sapadikkamane acelae dhamme pannatte*." He had no idea why, how, from whence these peculiar utterances had come, or what they meant. But he repeated them with the fluency of some exotic multiple personality disorder.

An East Indian passed by Leonard. His face was sculptured and aquiline. His hair jet black. Not just another face in the crowd. Leonard bowed before him and again uttered the phrase, *"Ahinsa Paramo Dharmah."*

The Indian cocked his head and smiled. "You must be a Jain?"

"A what?" Leonard said, his hopes consolidated in this one fragile query.

The Indian, who was not in the least embarrassed to be seen speaking with a naked man, did not know how to respond. "You don't know? Ahinsa means peace, non-violence, non-interference. It is the religion of the Jains." And, while speaking, he twisted his left hand into the air in a pan-Indian gesture of complete grace and equanimity.

"Are you a Jain?" Leonard implored.

"I am a Hindu. But many of my best friends are Jains. Good day to you, Sir," and he started to walk on.

A few blocks away from where Leonard continued on his strange and fantastic course, a mentally disabled woman was peeing into the street just as a police car was passing by. Its two occupants, Patrolmen Richard Davies and Edgard Washington, one white, the other black, stared forlornly at the nondescript woman. "I don't want to get involved with her," Davies groaned. He was wolfing down a grilled cheese sandwich smeared in mayonnaise. "It's sad," Washington stated. "Yeah, but it's life," his partner added.

They turned off Figueroa and headed South on Fourth Street. Up ahead, near the corner of Grand Avenue, Patrolman Washington was the first to notice something not quite right. First his eyes did not register the aberration. Then Davies saw it too.

"Why me?" Washington said shaking his head.

"Jesus, only in L.A.," Davies continued. "Here we go again."

"PCP or mental?" Washington wagered.

"I'll bet you lunch he's mental," Davies replied.

"Hell no. Look at the way he's walking. Man's high on something." Washington had seen other chemical abusers who thought they were burning up inside and ripped off their clothes to escape the heat.

"He's not staggering," said Davies. "He's keeping neatly to the sidewalk. Looks cool to me."

The patrol car slowly and silently followed Leonard for a hundred yards. They needed to determine whether he was, in fact, sexually provoking other people he passed.

An older woman who was walking with her young daughter, or granddaughter, attacked Leonard with her handbag, striking him once across the shoulder, declaring "You pervert!" before hastening across the street. Leonard merely bowed and uttered a prayer in an ancient language he did not know.

A shopkeeper shouted out at him, "Way to go, asshole!"

Leonard turned, apologetically, and said softly, "Ahinsa."

Davies picked up the CC unit in the vehicle. "We're Code six on a three eleven man at the intersection of Grand Avenue and Fourth Street. No back up needed."

Davies, who was behind the wheel, sounded the siren twice, skidded around a parked taxi, then pulled up onto the pavement, stopping directly in front of Leonard. People scattered.

The cops had already determined that he was neither agitated nor hyperventilating. Washington had also conceded lunch. They'd ruled out narcotics. Common sense. The naked man was *'firm in control,'* whereas most psychos tended to confuse the center median with the sidewalk. Half the time they get struck down by traffic before the police can get to them.

"How you doin' this morning?" Davies said, as both men got quietly out of the car, keeping their hands visibly away from their holsters. "What 'n the hell are you doing out here?"

Leonard stared at the policemen with relief.

"Where are your clothes?" asked Washington.

A crowd was now forming around the officers and their victim. Among the spectators was the Indian gentleman. He had seen the woman hit Leonard with her handbag, and then watched as the police arrived. He decided he might be useful.

"Come on, folks," Washington said forcefully. "You've all seen a naked man before. So move on about your business, please, let us do our job," as he went for a blanket in the trunk of the patrol car.

But, Leonard refused the blanket with a fast spray of words, spoken with the frantic charm of a wood thrush or song bird. He still had no idea what he was saying, or by what genetic loquacity of means. His head was burning up. He had a fever.

"*Mae samananam niggamthanam pamcamahavvaie sapadik-kamane acelae dhamme pannatte. Jaya yaya namda! Jaya jaya bhadda! Bhaddam te jaya jaya khattiyavaravasaha! Bujihahi bhagavam loganaha! Pavattehi dhammatittham!*" Leonard said, before falling down, flustered and dizzy with sudden exhaustion.

Deeply moved, the Indian in the crowd stepped forward to assist a friend in need. "He says that he upholds the practice of nudity for the sake of every living being in the entire universe. He says it will bring supreme benefit to all."

He helped Leonard sit up on the edge of the sidewalk.

"You know this man?" asked officer Davies.

"No. But, I think he must be a Jain saddhu," the Indian said.

"What's that?" officer Washington asked.

"An Indian religious figure. Some of the gurus walk naked."

"Not in Los Angeles they don't. In the car, fellow," Washington insisted, handcuffing Leonard.

They brought him down to the city's main police station at One Fifty North Los Angeles Street, five minutes away from the point of incident.

Davies and Washington liked to shock their colleagues, especially those of the opposite sex. Since Leonard refused a blanket, and because the religion business signalled the possibility of First Amendment hassles, the patrolmen had no problem escorting him in the manner to which he was accustomed.

They had not read him any rights. They didn't have to. He was already technically in custody for indecent exposure and creating a public nuisance, possibly lewd and obscene behavior and loitering. He might be mentally psychotic, endangering himself and others, they figured.

They parked some distance from their destination in the back lot and walked him with exhibitionist flare past the secretarial pool of the Record Bureau where six women were working—that got some chuckles—and into the underground garage, through a basement door, past the rollcall rooms and daywatch, past other patrolmen, traffic officers, narcs and assorted administrators. They then passed the Watch Commander.

"So, you boys caught yourself a real weenie-waver," the Lieutenant said, humored. "Give it ten feet!"

"We're taking him to mental eval," Davies reported.

In the hall outside Room 6-78, a black indigent who'd seen better days lay on a bench speaking eloquently. " . . . When Jesus delivers; when we're at peace; as soon as we are kind to each other; when a man gives you a drink of water; then he is delivered . . . " It was the right philosophy in the wrong place.

A sign on the door read, "Officers shall control their five one five zeros at all times."

Davies and Washington escorted Leonard inside the small room. They put a towel on a chair and sat him down before one of three desks.

Between threat management, missing persons unit, and mental eval unit, this was one of the busiest hallways at the police station. The chief, a supervising detective, third rank, had been down here since 1984, a cop for twenty years.

Leonard was one of over thirty thousand calls of intervention by the L.A.P.D. that year, and the approximately forty-six hundredth case in mental eval, according to the log book where they had him sign in.

"You think you've seen everything," the chief said. "Want some coffee?"

Leonard declined.

"You from the Mission?" the chief asked, casually. At least twenty percent came from the various missions.

Leonard registered a negative.

"Winegart detox?" That was the drug mission at Sixth and San Pedro.

Leonard shook his head.

This was the first weirdo who'd ever come in naked. There'd been one other, but he had welcomed a blanket.

"What's the story, gentlemen?" the chief asked Davies and Washington who stood by according to the rules.

"We found him wandering along the sidewalk, chief. Seemed to be minding his own business."

"Did he have an erection, or exhibit any other signs of sexual excitement or provocation?"

"None that we observed."

"Any victims?"

"One annoyed woman, had her daughter with her."

"Uh-huh. And at what point did you apprehend this gentleman?"

"A few minutes after we first saw him, chief."

"And what did he say?" The chief looked at Leonard and apologized for speaking about him indirectly. "It's just our routine," he said.

"He spoke in a foreign language. There was an Indian who translated."

"American Indian?"

"Indian Indian. From Asia, we believe."

"A friend?"

"Apparently not," Washington said.

"You speak English?" the chief asked Leonard.

"Yes," Leonard replied matter-of-factly, defusing the tension in the room.

"What's your name?"

"I've given up my name," Leonard responded.

"That's nice. What *was* your name?" the chief asked, patiently.

"Leonard M. Rosenbalm."

"B-A-L-M?" the chief checked the spelling.

Leonard nodded.

The chief looked at Davies who set to work on the computer.

"What did the M. stand for?" the chief asked.

"My parents never told me. My grandparents never told them."

"Sounds kind of mysterious. Is that why you gave up your name?"

"I've given up everything," Leonard went on.

"Why is that?" the chief pressed on, diligently.

"Having adopted the law, one should not hide it, nor forsake it. Correctly understanding the law, one should arrive at indifference for the impressions of the senses and not act on motives of the world."

The three police officers gave each other looks.

"I don't quite understand," the chief replied. "Let me put it a different way. Where do you live?"

Leonard thought carefully about his reply, searching through a region of memory for which he had no explanation. Yet his replies were there, on tap, completely worked out.

"He who does no acts has ceased from works; he who has ceased from them is called houseless. He who clings to his home is turned round in the whirl of pains."

"You're homeless, then?"

"Yes."

The chief was reminded of a case in which a homeless person actually had several hundred thousand dollars in the bank. Something about this fellow struck a similar chord, he thought.

"Where have you been sleeping?"

"I don't know," Leonard said. "Under the tree of life, I think."

"What the hell does that mean?"

Leonard flinched.

"I'm afraid I'm not very good at wisdom. Can you tell me where you were last night?"

"Under the constellation *uttaraphalguni*."

"That's great."

Davies, meanwhile, placed a couple of phone calls. On the first, he received an answering machine. He left no message, but handed the chief a slip of paper on which he'd written an address. On the second, he learned that a Mr. and Mrs. Ruben Rosenbalm had died two days before in an automobile accident.

The chief read the address to Leonard, a number along North Moraga Drive, in Holmby Hills. Ring a bell, Mr. Rosenbalm?"

"Yes," Leonard replied.

"Were you related to a Ruben and Ida Rosenbalm?"

"They were my parents."

So that was it, the chief reflected, suddenly given to a whole new level of sympathy. A clear case of extreme mourning, akin to a crack up. He'd witnessed similarly extreme reactions before.

"I can understand you taking it pretty hard. I'm real sorry. Who is your next of kin, Sir? Who would you like us to call?"

"No one," Leonard said clearly. "I told you. I have renounced everything. It's for the good of the world."

"World's a big place, Leonard," the chief said. "From my experience, it'll do whatever it's going to do, with or without us. Better you should concentrate on yourself, just getting through each day. Just managing to survive is pretty good."

"Survival is easy," Leonard said. "Conquering oneself is a whole other matter."

Neither the chief, nor his two cohorts were following Leonard very well. But one thing was clear. This man, in mourning, or shock, or whatever was bothering him, was picked up naked. And that wouldn't do.

"Do you know why you're here?"

"Certainly."

"Do you know what's happening to you?"

Leonard paused. That was not easily expressed.

"Do you know where you are right now?"

"Police station."

"Good. Do you know what day it is?"

"November . . . hum . . . ninth or tenth."

"Do you know what time it is?"

"Behind you is a clock which appears to be on time," Leonard said without a hint of sarcasm.

That rather addled the chief. "When did you last eat?"

"I don't remember. I'm fasting."

"Are you going to hurt yourself?"

"Do unto others as you would do to yourself."

"That's what I'm asking you. What are you going to do 'unto' yourself, or others, for that matter?"

"A righteous person does not torment, tyrannize, punish, harm, or kill another live being, ant, mother, shrimp nor elephant, nor cause or allow others to do so. Conversely, he does therefore neither torment, tyrannize, punish, harm nor kill himself, if he can avoid it."

Thinking him a learned man, possibly a lawyer or professor, gone wacko, the chief asked him his profession.

"Mendicant," said Leonard.

"Is that some kind of monk?" the chief wondered, looking to Davies and Washington for help here. Neither man was certain.

"Like a pure bronze vessel emptied of its water," Leonard began. "Like the unstrained mother-of-pearl. Free of dross. Like an unsullied lily-leaf, or a tortoise whose senses are withdrawn within himself. Like the Mandara mountain and the all-enduring Earth."

"Are you supposed to take any medications?" the chief continued, eager to get past this man's professional problems.

"No."

"Do you have a doctor?"

"No."

"Do you need or would you like to see a doctor?"

"Certainly not."

"What are your plans, what would you like to do now? How long are you planning to fast?"

"Recognizing the cause of karma, one should wander about waiting for one's death. Receiving alms, without fixed residence, careful to avoid harming any living being. You see, all creatures are blessed."

"That's very nice," said the chief. "But, you didn't answer my question."

"I believe I did."

"Well, then, that's not entirely promising, from our point of view, Leonard. You see, Sir, it's up to us to decide whether, in the department's opinion, you need professional help, right away. The State authorizes us to have you committed for up to seventy-two hours if we have reason to believe that you are likely to harm yourself, or are incapacitated. And from where I'm sitting, I'd have to say you've got a slight problem in both categories. I don't know, and I don't really care who your speech writer is, or what Church you belong to, but the fact is, you're plumb naked, man, and now you're telling me you plan to wander around until you die. Well, it's our job to protect you from the danger of yourself."

Leonard began, "Look, Sir, at birth and old age. Examine and know the happiness of the living. He who has right intuition, commits no sin."

"Words come easy to some," the chief allowed. "But the law has a very specific definition when it comes to indecent exposure."

Leonard was right there. "Many are attached to aspects of this world, be they clothes or jewels or a weekly paycheck. I too have been. Such attachment incurs great danger. But, for him who sees clearly the ebb and flow of life, who is aware of such attachments, and has the courage to let go of them, there is no danger. So it has been declared by the Sage."

"Who?" the chief let out, his fifty-year-old bushy eyebrows raised inquiringly.

"I only know him as Vardhamana. He has appeared in my dreams."

"Jesus," the chief muttered. "The last one claimed to be from one of the moons of Saturn."

"Not me," Leonard said. "I'm from right here."

"Look, Leonard. Here's the situation. I'd say we have probable cause to call your kind 'gravely disabled,' section five one five zero of the Welfare and Institutions Code. In my opinion, this is a temporary condition. But, I'm no shrink. I only know you do need help. That's clear. You're not allowed to go walking naked in public and I am therefore going to ask your old friends, Patrolmen Davies and Washington here, to escort you over to the Psych Ward, Unit Three, at County USC Medical Center. It's not far from here and they're going to take real good care of you. I promise. Compared with the shelters, it's a country club. You will be told your rights by the mental health staff there. You're going to get better. It's up to you. Hopefully, within a few days they'll cut you loose to your relatives and you can resume what I imagine was a very rewarding life. Do you understand?"

"*Michchhami Dukkadam*," Leonard blurted.

"Huh?" the chief said.

"I apologize if I have upset any of you," Leonard concluded.

CHAPTER FIVE

The Psychiatric Assessment

"Have a nice day, Leonard," Officers Davies and Washington both applied, as they released Mr. Rosenbalm to the custody of the hospital. Two dozen people stared at the naked man. An administrator told Leonard of his rights and offered him a luxurious white bathrobe and pj's. Leonard declined. Two large male orderlies were told to persuade him. They held him tightly and tried to place the garment over him. Leonard was ticklish and laughed hysterically. Then, he slipped out of their grasp.

"Hey, man, this ain't no straitjacket. Hundred percent Egyptian cotton. We're doing you a favor!" one of the orderlies explained.

They tried again and again Leonard behaved with a trickster's agility.

The orderlies looked towards the administrator who said, "What's the problem, Mr. Rosenbalm?"

"My nudity is a religious belief. This is a free country."

The administrator took a moment to consider the situation, no doubt weighing such matters as the other patients, most of whom were of extremely delicate minds. On the other hand, he was not unaware of that hazy realm of First Amendment business. He was not anxious to invoke anybody's wrath, such as the patient's legal defense—that invariably entered into these matters at some point. And, though he was not exactly sure what to do about Mr. Rosenbalm's legal claims, it was apparent that the patrolmen who brought him in had also observed that grey area. Which meant the L.A.P.D. had, as well. There were witnesses who would attest to the inmate's pacifity, or better stated, slipperiness. He had not struggled, only wriggled. And, wriggling was not ordinarily considered pathological.

"If we leave you unclothed, you promise not to bother any of the other patients? We have women in here."

"You insult me, Sir," Leonard proclaimed.

Frustrated, but making a specific show of his enlightened tolerance, the administrator nodded to the orderlies who escorted Leonard up an empty freight elevator to the third floor.

The orderlies explained the religious freedom business to the nurses on duty. Leonard was then asked to sign an MH 302 application for his seventy-two hour Detention, Evaluation and Treatment sojourn.

The doctor assigned his case, John Kushner, quickly surveyed the report before him, then discussed the situation with Leonard. They sat in an open and pleasant lounge. The doctor was very cool.

"Mr. Rosenbalm, how are you?"

"Fine, thank you."

"My name's Doctor Kushner and I'll be monitoring your case for the next few days. Your bed is being prepared. We're going to be giving you a hot shower and a hot meal soon. In the meantime, I'd like to discuss what happened for a few minutes. Would you like a glass of water?"

It had been two and a half days since Leonard had had any liquid or food. "Has it been boiled?" he asked, without understanding why it should matter.

"The water's filtered here. Are you worried about germs?"

"Unboiled water breeds microscopic creatures. I wouldn't want to kill them."

"I see." The doctor wrote down a note. He realized at a glance that he was dealing with no inarticulate indigent. He then called for a nurse to get the patient a glass of boiled water.

Leonard was unsettled by that exchange.—'What made me think of boiled water?'—his head spun, nearly out of control. Foreign words were flowing through his thoughts like so many boulders down a rushing cascade.

"I've never seen Rosenbaum spelled like balm," the doctor admitted. "Where's it from?"

"I don't know," Leonard said. "You would have had to ask my grandparents."

"Do you know why you're here?" the doctor asked.

"To determine whether I have any mental disorder. I don't."

"Good! Over the next three days a few doctors here, including myself, will hopefully concur. Please try to appreciate our situation. You were brought in here because, apparently, there was probable concern. I understand you were walking like this through downtown?"

"That's right."

"Would you like to tell me why? It's not that warm a day, after all."

Leonard's thoughts reeled back to the jungle. Before him sat not a doctor but Vardhamana, surrounded by a gathering of eleven men, dressed in tie-dyed white dhoti waistcloths, some in turbans the color of rose pink, violet, or green. The group was seated beneath a tree listening to the ascetic.

Leonard heard, and repeated Vardhamana's words:

"Those are called naked, who in this world, never returning to a worldly state, follow this path according to the highest doctrine which has here been declared for men. He will give up sinfulness. A wise man should lead the life of an ascetic by collecting pure alms. If the food be of good or bad smell, or if beasts inflict pain on other beings, all that happens to you, you will firmly bear. Thus I say. To a *ginakalpika* who is unclothed, such a one will be firm in control. The unclothed one who excels in this abstinence will often be molested. Nails will be hammered into his ears. Dogs will be unleashed on him. Villagers will stone him. They might laugh, or scorn him. Mosquitoes and midges will assault him. Sexual temptation may follow him. But, he bears these hardships like the worthy ones of former years. Endowed with perfect knowledge they had lean arms and very little flesh and blood, but they were enlightened, they crossed the *samsara*, they were liberated . . . "

The doctor listened admiringly to this patient who spoke with such charged and indisputable eloquence. He was a fanatic, alright, but not entirely irrational. That was clear by the correct, if archaic grammar. He thought,—'This will not be easy'—.

"You mentioned a word (he'd written it down)—*ginakalpika*, I believe."

"Yes."

"What language is that?"

"I'm not sure."

"But you must know, you said the word."

Leonard closed his eyes, probing backwards, or forwards, for, in truth, he was not sure where the visions were coming from. But the garment merchant in him knew that those textiles looked to be from India, and they were not modern. No computerized sewing.

"India," Leonard said.

"Have you ever been to India?" The doctor inquired.

"No," Leonard replied.

"Are you a member of some Indian religion, perhaps?"

"I was raised a Jew."

"A lot of people experiment with other religions."

"Is that a question?" Leonard asked.

"It might shed some light on your situation."

"I'm not a very religious person," Leonard said.

The doctor considered the situation.

"By your discourse a moment ago, I have to assume that you have either been brainwashed by religious fanatics, are temporarily out-of-sorts, what we call delusional—I understand your parents were killed two days ago and I hope you'll accept my profound condolences—"

"Thank you," said Leonard.

"Or, you are a clever exhibitionist with a well-worked routine."

The doctor let the statement linger, like a question.

Leonard looked baleful, not perverse.

"Or, and I say this advisedly and in some jest, you are what many spiritual leaders might call enlightened," Doctor Kushner finally said. "Some people see no difference between enlightenment and clinical dementia. Ezra Pound comes to mind."

"We read him in college," Leonard said.

"Which school?"

"USC."

The doctor was quickly getting his bearings with this one. The Chief Detective over at mental eval had indicated in his report, "Shellshock. Grief." And that was increasingly clear, even after five minutes.

"Whatever the explanation for your current frame of mind," he continued, "nudity is generally considered antisocial behavior. It also happens to be illegal, I believe. But, like various forms of mental retardation, epilepsy, drug or alcoholic abuse, such activities do not, by themselves, constitute a mental disorder."

"What does?" Leonard asked, curious.

"That's what we're all here to find out. There's no point second guessing the process," he said restrainedly. "If you want to know my gut reaction, I'd say you're having a nervous breakdown, nothing more. But I don't want to get your hopes up."

Doctor Kushner liked Leonard and had already made his preliminary diagnosis. There was nothing violent or otherwise disruptional about him, other than his mildly resisting the pj's and terrycloth robe at admissions. There was no senility, no evidence of malnutrition, though clear signs of self-abuse. The section under which he'd been admitted, namely, 'Gravely Disabled', referred to a condition, widely defined, in which a person as a result of a mental disorder, was unable to provide for his or her basic personal needs for food, clothing and shelter.

According to the detective's report, Leonard had indicated his desire to starve himself to death, or that's how it was interpreted. There was an easy way to test that.

The doctor led Leonard to his bed in a room with three other patients. A nurse brought him a tray with his lunch. It was a high protein, high energy meal consisting of a Salisbury steak, steamed brocoli, a garden salad, strawberry jello and iced tea.

Leonard stared at the section of dead animal and felt his insides turning over. Meat had never looked like that to him. Though the tray sat a good two feet before him, it seemed to be pressing against his face, forcing its way into his eyes and throat and nose, and in its gravy-covered appearance echoed the spastic cries of a cow being slaughtered, dangled by an ankle, the eight hundred pounds of its free suspension asphyxiating it, as blood rushed into its nostrils and its eyes boiled over in agony. While young men in rubber galoshes sloshing through knee-deep blood, listening to music over their head-sets, repeatedly bashed the animal with electric prods and carved away with machetes while the defiant cow still convulsed, clinging to a few more seconds of life.

Leonard's nausea had become terror. What was at first a distant analogy soon detonated into graphic panoramas of horror seething and distending throughout his skull. He could not separate the meat on his tray, offered no doubt in all humility and good cheer by the nurse, from the fact of an unbearable nightmare being played out by human beings around the world. People who had blinded themselves in the whirl of existence . . . *the whirl of existence?* The words themselves echoed in his heaving heart, words which Vardhamana had uttered. A teenager, long-haired, long ago; a man that had somehow entered Leonard's own being and now lived there, breathing, occupying his thoughts, re-directing his words and actions so that he seemed to speak in tongue, yet the meaning, the intention, the feelings, were not mysterious at all. Leonard knew exactly what was happening, in the sense that the message was clear. People had been killing animals since human time began. *That* was the whirl. And it would continue to spin like an insane tornado of cruelty until something was done.

Vardhamana had uttered the words "*Ahinsa Paramo Dharmah*," a new and lofty injunction in Leonard's life. And a man on the street had told him that it meant peace, non-violence, non-interference. A stranger out of time, who called himself a Hindu and had come to Leonard's aid when he was taken by the police. A man who came from nowhere and returned there. Was that merely a coincidence? Was the presence of Vardhamana's spirit a similar coincidence? His presence could not be described as *non-intervention*. On the contrary.

These questions weighed on him all in an instant, as his whole body grew faint with the revulsion and pain of that writhing piece of meat. The meat rose from the tray turning over and over like the butterfly in its chrysalis, transmogrifying and wailing, ascending and descending, from every pulse and deep precept of the life-giving, of flight and color and the love of its freedom, to the darkness of hell, with its unimaginable torments and cruel twists of biology. The meat scintillated before Leonard, its odor rank with a cavalcade of death, molecular ruin, every stagnant decay, every corpse, every pleading. Like the rotting, blood-engorged tissue of Ebola virus victims whose corpses can be poured, rather than placed, into their coffins. Heinous, ruptured, bellowing, the Holocaust, four million victims of Kolyma in Siberia, four hundred thousand tortured Chinese in Nanking, victims of the Japanese kill-all, loot-all, burn-all policies, untold millions of Meso-American martyrs whose young hearts were ripped out, sexes violated, bodies destroyed in the ceremonial pageants of centuries. Random winces. Ancient Rome. The Renaissance. All of human history, everywhere the same horror.

In every country, from Sweden to Peru, from Iraq to Germany, from Bhutan to Bosnia, from Canada to India—torture, mayhem, hell. The slaughter of innocents rising up before Leonard Rosenbalm in the palpating guise of dead flesh.

And, his whole lifetime of ignorance of these matters bore down on him; of complicity with the unspoken law of killing, maiming, degrading, separating, casting aspersion, insulting, of ill-deeds and ill-intentions, of silence and guilt, of greed and temptation, of every sin and every evasion, of comfort in the face of these transgressions . . . the massive, culturally sanctioned killing and consumption of meat and fish and poultry, of living beings, in other words who each have a face and a path and a destiny, a soul as indisputable as the soul which now cried out in Leonard Rosenbalm to be redeemed; that soul, which stared back aghast at what had been his unapologetic, unbothered apathy in the face of so much deliberate destruction . . . Somalian famine, Khmer Rouge atrocities, incessant fighting in South Africa, ethnic cleansing in a dozen parts of the world, torture in Guatemala, capital punishment in America, oppression of women and minorities and children in nearly every land, riots in his own downtown, and so on and so on and so on and so on . . . This hideous legacy of so-called humanity welled up inside an already desperate, dizzy and discombobulated biochemistry of a man and he managed at the last instant to fling the tray off his bed with a muted

scream from within the murmuring horror of a hemorrhaging heart before puking all over the sheets and passing out in violent relief.

The nurse ran in, then the doctor. They assumed he'd had an
allergic reaction to something he'd eaten—"What flavor was the jello??"
the doctor cried. "Strawberry!" the nurse declared—and they got him
down immediately to emergency, where blood and urine samples were
collected. They needed to locate a past medical chart or determine if he
was drug-impaired.

Miriam had called to Ruben and Ida's house repeatedly during the
night to speak with Leonard. She flew out of the house at eight-thirty
when Denise had called to tell her something was amiss at the office.
Miriam entered the flow of rush hour traffic and made one of her rare
appearances downtown. They were all baffled. Between homeless Henry
and Ramon's story and the sealed letter and abandoned Bentley, the keys,
the transfer of clothes, the grief and hysteria which surrounded the whole
building, Miriam sensed the makings of a suicide.

But these wild imaginings were set straight when she called home
for any messages and heard Patrolman Davies' voice.

By noon, Denise and her mother were led upstairs to the psycho
ward at the hospital where they were seated in the lounge, awaiting
Leonard.

"You have visitors," the agitated nurse informed the still trembling
patient, who had been brought back up to his room, following the medical tests. He remained naked.

Miriam scarcely recognized her husband, who wore a plastic ID
bracelet on his wrist, the only piece of "clothing," and whose face was
unshaven and eyes deeply disturbed, highlighted by rings she'd never
seen. His hair was matted. As Leonard had not yet taken a shower, his
odor, too, was telling. All six feet two inches reeked.

"My God, Lennie, why haven't they given you a robe," Miriam cried
out angrily. "What the hell is going on here?" And, she rushed to comfort
her man and hide him from her daughter's somewhat astonished gaze.

But Leonard kept his distance. He sat down shakily.

"Dad?" Denise uttered, with a direness of embarrassment and conjecture. She had not seen her father naked, maybe ever.

Leonard did not know what, or how to say the things on his mind.
He fumbled for explanations. And this ungainliness harkened back, in his
mind, to some other awkward event that surfaced now with unexpected
precedent. A woman by the name of Yashoda, a daughter whom he had
named Anuja. Both had felt forsaken, but could say nothing, bound by

dictates of the community, of a destiny long-ago engendered, to live with their sorrow, to bury it in the larger gladness of something incredible taking place.

But, precedent or not, this did not make it easier for Leonard, who was swimming in uncharted territory.—'What am I doing?'—rang through his innards and the whole enterprise slid into self-doubt.—'How can I do this to my wife, my daughter?'—the opposing voice beckoned. Reasons to rebuke this madness multiplied. All he had to do was wake up, cease this drug, this prehistory of antecedents, go on as he had gone on for more than four decades. Resume life, with its compromises and small comforts. His finances, though devastated, were not going to leave the family penniless. He could probably still take that sailing trip to the Marquesas which he'd promised wife and daughter; there would still be money to lease a nice car. He wanted to renounce possessions, fine, the houses and buildings were gone. Fate, bad luck, had taken them away, saving him the effort of doing so.

—WAKE UP, LEONARD!—the voice stampeded, championing his former self.

It was that easy. Two adoring women in his life stood ready to take him home.

And yet, all he really wanted to do was to start walking away. Into it. Into the mass of needy people, needy animals, into the mires and whirlpools of pain that had cast the tray off his bed, the clothes off his body. There was no other way to exorcise that vision of cows to the slaughter; no other manner in which to exercise his soul's pure expression. That soul was clouded with things, karmic connections, churning passions, emotional flotsam, his whole life.

But it was over, now. He'd been down that path. His soul, which had waited millions of years to express itself, to glory in its unfettered singularity, now boldy declared another volition, a new country of the mind, a new nation of nudity upholding itself, with no questions asked, and none needing to be answered. He was accountable only to himself, now. His soul, timorous and untested, had finally leapt its bounds, had probably been urging itself in this direction for years, imperceptibly, until the collective momentum, the ethical threshold, had finally forced this Columbus out into a new world and not even the heartbreaking perplexities of family, God-given, necessary, and wonderful though they be, could snuff it out.

He quickly resolved to tell all, unfalteringly. It was a far more difficult task than taking off one's clothes. Finality was in the air. Leonard's fear of the consequences of his behavior. Yet it was not merely fear, nor merely behavior. What was happening to him exceeded the furthest peripheries of common definition or parlance. He was alone in this, save for his phantasm, whose name and surreality infiltrated his thoughts with abundant contagion.

"Some things have changed for me," he finally got out. "I love you. I'm fine. But, I have to do this."

"Do WHAT?" Miriam put forth, able to restrain herself but little. "The detective said they picked you up like this, naked, in DOWNTOWN. Incoherent . . . Honey. It's called a nervous breakdown. And, we all understand. My God, what the family has been through . . . " And, she consoled herself with a handkerchief and commiseration from her daughter."

"We're taking you home, Dad," Denise said defiantly. "We're going to get you a new suit of clothes. Armani has a sale. We can still afford it." Nothing could impede her natural authority. No system of police and shrinks, and no extent of psychological turmoil was going to jeopardize Daddy's little girl. Her independence was summoned, her stability. Forget the income. Mom was falling apart. Grandma and Grandpa were gone, and now her father had become a profound liability to himself, debilitated and shrinking from the world. All of these events were ephemeral, soon to be erased from memory. She would see to it. Everything would be restored to its original balance.

"I'm not going home," Leonard said, modestly.

"This too will pass, Dad," Denise reiterated.

Leonard put up a hand so as to correct any misimpressions. "This is the hardest thing in the world for me to convey," he began.

Miriam's heart pounded. Denise, however, had it under control. Whatever her father said, there was an explanation—sort of like UFOs— and everyone, including her mother, should realize it. A man does not lose his parents and millons of dollars, and nearly his life, and not suffer mental hiccups as a result.

"A young man from long ago spoke to me. In a dream. In a vision. In myself. I can't tell which. But the result has been transforming. A man doesn't need possessions to be happy. Happiness depends upon the happiness of the world. Sadness hinges upon the sadness of the world. A man need only be honest with himself."

"Are you trying to tell us you're gay?" Miriam spilled with an appalling snicker.

Denise stared incredulously.

"Hardly," Leonard said with a grin. "But I have decided to become a monk."

"A monk . . . ?" Miriam, whose ancestors had all been rabbis in Vilna, in Odessa, in Kiev, had an image of her husband taking up the study of Talmud everyday, donating more generously to Israel, going regularly to the Yeshiva. Her parents—Orthodox Jews in Boston—would be pleased. But, what a bore!

"What do you mean, exactly?" she said.

"It has nothing to do with Judaism."

"Great. Dad's been born again," Denise applied, blowing air despondently.

"I'm in a bit of a dilemma here," Leonard continued. "I can explain everything. And, I can explain nothing. I don't know if it's a religious thing, or what."

"Monks usually are religious, Leonard," stated Miriam, flatly.

"A naked monk, sweetheart. Perhaps a better word would be ascetic. Alone. Homeless."

"He wants a divorce," Miriam declared out loud to their daughter. "But, I know better than to listen to this. You're not in your right mind and we understand. We love you."

Leonard paused, unprepared to address the practicalities of what he had unleashed. And the longer he paused, the more Miriam's sorrow increased, sorrow for Leonard who was so obviously in despair.

"I just want you to know," Miriam went on, "I forgive you in advance for everything you've done or thought or said. Honey, I'm going to take care of you." And then her old mirth managed to return and she added, "Just don't press your luck!"

"Thank you," Leonard whispered.

"Excuse me a minute," Miriam said and went to the nurses' station where she had Doctor Kushner called.

He soon joined her. "We're taking him home. He needs loving care, not . . . not this."

"I'm afraid that's impossible."

"No, you fail to get my drift, Doctor. Kushner was it? You're Jewish?" she said, neatly.

"Yes."

"A Jew should understand a Jew. His parents just died, horribly. This is a week for him to be with his family. Give him heavy tranquilizers. Fine. But, he needs to get out of this place." She hated downtown.

"The law forbids it."

"The law? Where was the law when a man nearly killed him last night?"

"I'm not aware of that. What happened? It could be relevant to his—"

"You don't know a goddamned thing about my husband. Relevant? I'll tell you what's relevant: his wife, his daughter, his life."

"We are in agreement on that point, Mrs. Rosenbalm. And, it is our sincere goal to restore him to that life, as quickly as possible. And, frankly, we're overcrowded here. We don't like seeing people on the third floor. But, your husband was found walking naked—"

"I know all about it."

"And technically, he was in violation of a law which forbids lewd and indecent exposure."

"He wasn't lewd. My husband? Hah . . " And she chuckled in recognition of a very conservative person. A man who had never cheated, never thought of cheating, she rightly assumed; a man who was even shy of much kissing. He was almost weird in that way. And, as she thought of these things, it dawned on her with a gnawing suspicion that Leonard's monk business was not so farfetched after all. And, she lost her brio.

"Perhaps you should think about retaining a lawyer," Doctor Kushner recommended.

It was all falling apart for Miriam. Nothing had gone right. There were not sufficient words or clear enough meaning, or the time needed, in an unpressured milieu, to banish this demon that had interfered in everything. In the last three months, business at Mazel Tov Kitchens had fallen by thirty percent—she hadn't even mentioned it to Leonard. Now, death, economic ruin, and a temporarily deranged husband added to her woes.

"The day after tomorrow, there will be a hearing here to determine whether or not your husband can go home, Mrs. Rosenbalm. There are numerous possibilities. If, at the hearing, he is deemed mentally incapacitated then he can be required to stay here, or at another facility, for a lengthier period. The legal standard is 'probable cause'."

"Who will be at that hearing?" Miriam demanded.

"I will be, at least one of my colleagues, a hearing referee, and we recommend the patient's lawyer be there as well."

"Have criminal charges actually been filed against my husband?"

"You'd have to ask the Los Angeles Police Department. Officially, however, he is not under arrest, as far as I know, but under the state's custody. A repeat offense would more than likely catapult his case onto the court calendar. A municipal court judge would make the determination if it's to be continued or dismissed. The judge might motion for a trial, or sentence him to fourteen, or thirty, or even one hundred days of intensive treatment, instead. Or, conversely, a judge could dismiss the whole thing, cutting him loose on good behavior. Anything is possible. It's up to Leonard, really."

This had made Miriam angry. She viewed her husband as a victim of circumstances and now things were getting quickly out of everybody's control.

"I'm calling a lawyer," she ignited. "What time is that hearing?"

He told her.

"I'll be there," she said.

She and Denise both hugged and kissed Leonard. Miriam encouraged him with assurances he'd be out the day after tomorrow. That she was hiring the best lawyer available and that he should just relax. The nightmare would be over soon. She promised.

That night, Leonard's roommates gabbed volubly. An Irish manic depressive who'd formerly been something of a baseball star and was arrested for destroying a pub; a pyromaniac ex-fire fighter implicated in several arsons, and a Japanese exchange student, not more than Denise's age, who had tried to immolate himself outside a sushi restaurant on a corner in Westwood, evidently in protest of chopsticks. Something about the Malaysian rainforests.

Leonard took on each of their cases, so to speak; engaging them in conversation with surprisingly therapeutic results: the men were soon sleeping like kittens.

The room animated by three sets of mentally disordered snorers, Leonard lay stretched out in bed wondering what the world had in store for him.

Before long, he found himself on a dirt path trailing behind Vardhamana. Avoiding all living things, having set himself up in exquisite, impossible isolation. He could not touch another's hand, and avoided even stepping on grass.

It came time for him to relieve himself. First he looked here, then there, then over there. Twenty-two places that were inappropriate. No peeing on a plant, on flowers, avoiding the dew, bypassing any living organism. No excrement in a place liable to breed creatures. Biologically exasperating. A bowel movement ordinarily waits for no man. Finally, he resorted to a dry, barren spot, covered in ash. Staying to the course.

That night they reach a cemetery. Vardhamana sleeps deeply. The next morning, off the side of a road, the young man is approached by two bulls that seem to know he is different. He has in his hand a large chunk of sugar cane which he breaks in two and offers to the animals. Attracted to his inner peace, the energy patina that enshrouds him, they lounge all day beside the naked man. He has testicles, like they do. They can see that. Late in the afternoon, Leonard witnesses an angry farmer searching for his animals, who, discovering them in Vardhamana's company, attacks the sage with his heavy herding stick.

Miraculously, just as the old fellow raises his hand to strike, the stick is jettisoned by unknown forces. Vardhamana has not flinched.

Leonard dreams of rain. The monsoons have begun, catching Vardhamana on the banks of a dangerously high river. Out in the middle, a family is trapped on their raft amid the raging torrent. The naked man swims to their rescue. He seems to course effortlessly through the current.

In a nearby village, Nalanda, where Vardhamana has decided to remain for the duration of the monsoon, word is spreading of his powers. And, he himself is formulating the principles by which he will live his life, adding to his argument, reinventing his persona, everyday. His literary skills are copious, his rules, 'fences', increasingly difficult to follow. Leonard sharpens his own mental pencils, taking note of everything.

"The living world is afflicted, miserable, difficult to instruct, and without discrimination," Vardhamana begins. And, he continues by relating how there is not one so-called 'all-soul' but rather individual beings, each embodied and in dire need of protection and reverence. He refers to earth bodies, water bodies, wind bodies, plant bodies, fire bodies, dust bodies; he speaks lovingly of bird eggs, an elephant fetus, an enveloping membrane in cows and buffalos, worm fluids, sweat from lice, coagulation in locusts and ants, butterfly and wagtail sprouts, and the regeneration of men.

He indicts all slaying, all harming, all wounding, all negative thinking. He wants others to know how much he loves this world, how much this world loves us. And, in his botanical and zoological frenzy, he enumerates hundreds of organisms, biochemical components, immanent souls ready to become living beings. His generosity is infectious. He refers to reciprocity. What is of the man, is the Earth. What is of the

Earth, lies waiting in man. All are entwined. Leonard is fascinated by the fact he speaks in both universals and details. His language—which Leonard somehow can follow without difficulty—soars in cosmic crescendos, then rummages in minutia. His speaking is presidential, not entirely humorless, guided by a nearly cubist sense of atmosphere and depiction. He outlines with a precise brushstroke, choosing decisive metaphors and similes, but sticking close to the organism. Vardhamana himself is experimenting, reaching, discovering new ground. Leonard understands.

Vardhamana simplifies the grand paradox by reminding his now hundreds of followers that they owe it to themselves to uphold that which they aspire to be in their dreams. To dwell on the positive side of human nature and make it live for others. It's simply a case of positive thinking. That's how Leonard interprets it.

"Why kill, if we can love?" Vardhamana summarizes.

"Why," says Vardhamana, because nature has allowed it. Man, woman, child, must not allow it; must create 'New Nature', consciously redoing ourselves everyday, every minute, beyond the conventional laws of brutality. We must become an island of conscience in a sea of tumult, he insists.

Is that possible, asks Leonard, ask others?

Only with discipline, replies the ascetic; only by applying this special love, this absolute forgiveness.

But, the tiger kills the muledeer, the pelican spears the catfish, a wasp paralyzes and feeds on the tarantula. Men kill men. Is not this the way?

By night, contemplating these matters, Vardhamana takes shelter in a weaver's shed. In the morning, he expounds on the holy path, which humanity must follow if it is to transcend the cruelties of nature, and alter its own course, its birth, nature and rebirth.

In essence, Leonard hears a perfect philosophy. As Vardhamana speaks, the rain pours down upon the village. Frogs are jumping, birds are huddling, snakes and worms are slithering through the mud lanes which wend between hamlets. Life is primitive. There are no cars. No electricity. No horses. It is a walked world. A slow world. A more natural world. Yet cruelty is everywhere about—the incessant slaughter and sacrifice of animals, each murder penetrating Vardhamana's heart, who weeps for the benighted ones, whose own tears mingle with the rain, and Leonard notes with irony how man has not changed, and how the message of Vardhamana has only gotten more difficult to follow.

All of these things affect him in his dream.

By now, Vardhamana is Leonard's age. They are staring eye to eye, shoulder to shoulder. Tear to tear.

Leonard hears a scream . . . not in the village of Nalanda, but down the hall. His eyes open. The screaming continues. Electro-shock therapy in the middle of the night. Or some other form of torture. Torture from within, torture from without. Leonard stares at the ceiling, his fingers clawing into the metal frame in which his mattress sits. Until the horror, or imagined horror, subsides. In the musty darkness, a siren converges outside. A megaphone orders someone to lay down their weapon. NOW! The sound is grating in the middle of the night. Overhead is the horrid wrangle of a helicopter's rotors, and the reflected beams of its search-lights penetrating the flimsy draperies of the hospital bedroom, a strobe light in search of criminals. A Nurse enters the room, checking. Leonard's roommates are up, peering out at the goings on.

A body shuffles to the bathroom, coughing asthmatically. Some-where, a phone is ringing. A red light is flashing. Its rhythmical pulses carry Leonard back into sleep.

Leonard's eyes are addicted to the brightness of Vardhamana's body. Like moths stricken with the light of the moon. This ascetic's inner impulses are spectacularly directed, clear, joyous. Simple, severe, austere, erect, and so sublime. The best of mountains, imperturbable, yet light on his feet. Like a bharunda-bird, a coming storm. This man's wild eye gazes upon excreta and sandalwood, a piece of straw, a precious gem, a clod of clay, a beautiful woman, with equal detachment.

A would-be follower shows up in the village. His name is Makkhali Gosala, an ascetic already known to many. His figure is wracked with obvious passions and ill-winds. He envies Vardhamana, wants something from him, expects to beat him at his own game. Leonard has street smarts, even in his dreams. He detects a crook, but is powerless to warn Vardhamana, who invites Gosala to study with him.

Walking side by side, the two men encounter a Brahman by the name of Vesiyayana who is at that moment in the depths of extreme penance, his hands raised high towards the sun. He has been in this posi-tion for days. His body is covered in lice.

"Are you a sage, or a host for lice, old man?" Gosala bridles him.

"Why are you speaking in this manner?" asks Vardhamana.

Suddenly, the old man discharges a powerful lance of psychic heat at Gosala. Without missing a beat, Vardhamana stares into the line of fire and somehow magically neutralizes it with his own cooling emanations. —'Get rid of this jerk!'—Leonard thinks. Gosala means trouble. But Vardhamana takes up the challenge. If he can convert Gosala, he can convert the world.

The monsoons have stopped. Mists are rising to meet the heat of the Indian subcontinent where the procession travels by day, stopping by night, always on the move. The numbers of followers are growing. Skeptics throw stones, but more and more are feeding the wandering band of ascetics. The feedings take place in standing positions. Villagers pledge that the food is pure, is vegetarian, is not this, is not that, and they merely place it into the ascetics' cupped hands. One meal a day is all they eat. Everywhere they go, Vardhamana urges local villagers to stop harming animals, to stop harming one another. It is that simple.

Vardhamana is gaining strength. His doubts have subsided. He knows who he is, and what he must do. It will take time. He is patient.

They are approaching the village of Kausambi. On its outskirts, the procession passes through fields of tumeric and long pepper, fresh ginger, linseed, safflower and millet. Sugarcane grows up intermittently. Paddies of kalamasali line the fringes of the forest. Sowers with rusted sickles thrash, winnow and collect their grains. Dried skeletons of water buffalo infested with flies are strung up on sticks like scarecrows to keep away the birds. Cow-dung fires burn all the way to the horizon. Bricks are being dried, chapatis cooked. Leaf-gatherers and grass-cutters bow before the passing entourage. Fowlers also pass by but the ascetics turn their heads. With spades and bamboos and baskets in their hands, these fowlers carry live provender. Vardhamana does not turn away, however. He sees the francolin partridges, the ducks and quails, and they see him. It is terrible.

But, even worse is Vardhamana's encounter with the *pulindas*, the elephant killers, whom he sees bringing in the tusks. Vardhamana is unstinting in his cautions, recommending alternative materials for the amulets. It does not need to be ivory, he says. Later on, he provides yet other suggestions for the necklaces of little girls which the locals have been manufacturing from the bones of monkeys.

Inside the village, Vardhamana encounters a chaos of tradesmen and craft peoples. Smiths working in zinc. Chariot makers and leather workers. Scribes writing commissioned letters on the leaves of the birch tree. Preparers of lac-juice are busy applying the inks to the stomachs and backs of those corpses which are to be given to the vultures.

There are tanners working hyena skins for the shoes of the sick nuns. This man manufactures toilet articles for woman, lodhra powder, myrobalans, collyrium boxes. This one makes the looking glass and hair-ribbon. And this one gathers cow-dung to smear along the walls of a local shrine dedicated to the Jakkhas.

Vardhamana and Gosala make their way past Vedic fortune-tellers, rope-walkers, pipers and prostitutes. The sick are already gathering before the naked ascetics. Gosala has his own chants and dead-animal cures, which Vardhamana rejects. He has new therapies the people have never seen. A co-wife comes to him with a flatulence problem. He recommends drinking monk's urine. Others come with piles, leprosy or acute headaches, for which he recommends the taking of nun's urine over the common practice of tying the victim to the leg of a vulture for a day. Vardhamana discourages the use of fly droppings to curtail vomitting or horseflies to soothe a seeping eye. He reviles the use of pearl oysters for the storing of medicine and suggests that the cool mud from ant-hills can cure fever, dog bite, trembling, humpbacks, and overweight.

All of these measures he recommends for laypersons. For the true monks, disease is deemed irrelevant.

But, it is precisely the lay community that challenges Vardhamana wherever he wanders. And, while his followers are growing in number, the vast majority of locals dismiss his outlandish insistence on non-violence.

"What good is it in time of war?" he is mocked. "In the presence of one's enemies, or one's neighbor if he covets your wife? Or steals your cattle? Or slanders your daughter?"

Vardhamana's obsession with sparing all life forms is positively heretical in a land, and at a time, accustomed to devouring almost anything that moves. Violence is a way of life. Anything else is for dreamers, they say. For a time when the camel becomes your barber and a locust the king, not until then.

Some consider him soft in the head, or a coward. Local politicians think he may be a spy, or a conspirator whose goal is the political demise of the entire kingdom.

Vardhamana himself has not yet worked out many of the details. He, too, is struggling with first principles, causes and effects. And since he himself is not keen on using ink, because, he says, it disrupts the Earth body, he is memorizing everything. Others, if they wish, can eventually write it all down.

A pregnant nun has come to him prepared to kill herself. What should Vardhamana do? What should he say?

A father comes to him whose daughter has been raped by three brothers and she has died at the hands of her wretched tormentors. He demands vengeance and expects Vardhamana's blessing.

A jailer with a whip in one hand and a pitch fork in the other looks at Vardhamana and simply shakes his head. "You don't know about life yet!" he says.

A rasavanijja, a manufacturer of the local kayambari, the wine to which everyone is addicted, is deeply troubled by Vardhamana's rejection of alcohol. Would he expect to put a thousand growers out of business? How dare he malign a tradition venerated, even, in the *Vedas*!

And a butcher, from a long line of animal slaughterers, raises a similarly bitter complaint, when Vardhamana enters the village of Kausambi, where the residents have feasted for centuries on everything from frogs to tigers, and asks them to dine on pulses and rice, instead. —"Who the hell is this spoiled dilettante to come in here and tell us what we can, and cannot do!"—he shouts, rousing the mob.

In fact, Vardhamana has not told anybody what to do, or not to do, exactly. He has set by strategic example a pattern of restraints which many have found baffling. And when asked why, he has not hesitated to explain his point of view.

People have angrily besieged him. "But, how will we live?" they ask.

And, at night, Vardhamana agonizes over these many earnest queries. They are essential concerns, of course. Because if the people are discouraged by the magnitude of the task at hand—before they even begin—then there is no hope. Not everyone was raised in a palace and has the luxury, or frame of reference, or strength of character, to renounce basic comforts, or to adopt a philosophy that would radically alter one's habits. Indeed, he appreciates his peculiar situation. But, none of it is worth a damn if he can't answer the questions.

He begins to formulate two sets of vows, greater and lesser, for those on the road to monkhood, and for those lay persons who have no intention of renouncing their families or their wealth and status, but can, nevertheless, practice the basic tenets of non-violence.

The trouble is, the locals have little patience for new gurus. These people are constantly being solicited by a steady stream of them, each presiding over an alleged spiritual empire; each preaching a vastly different world view; each one offering salvation.

Vardhamana has a real problem in terms of the prevailing competition. All the other ascetics in town are offering greatly marked down salvations; powerful gods who will promise to keep converts outfitted in the finest clothes, bedecked in jewels, smothered in kisses and supplied with drink, for eternity. Indeed, some of the local shamans have gained converts by advertising a religion in which the God and his consort—the most beautiful seductress in the world—are immortally locked in a shocking sexual embrace atop a Himalayan peak.

So what does Vardhamana have to offer which can compare? He comes into town bereft of even a pair of shoes, or a cloth to cover himself. Proffering no God, giving away no discounts or special prizes, and promising not one lurid enticement now or in the afterlife. Furthermore, he speaks ad nauseum about the "soul" which is like discussing blue sky.

Not only that, Vardhamana has the bad taste, the gall, to suggest that people—poor people, rich people—give up many of their already meagre comforts, to change all their bad habits, ill intentions and deeds, ill feelings and corrupt practices—all those things, in other words, which give them a modicum of pleasure in a world that is short-lived and difficult.

Hunters and fishermen would be unemployed. Certain farmers would go bankrupt. Whole communities could very well lose their financial base and collapse. Even armies would no longer have the mandate to rape and pillage, if this dissident, Vardhamana, had his way.

On the other hand, nobody has ever seen so beautiful a young man, nor experienced one so gentle and true. He is, in those respects, a phenomenon. In spite of their angry and jealous husbands, women flock to him. Perhaps there is sexual attraction on their part, but if so, it never emerges beyond their hearts. What does come out is their grievous condition at home. Vardhamana is the first ascetic to pass through their village who rejects all subordination and maltreatment of women, calling instead for equal status among the sexes. He says this is basic.

Furthermore, he rejects the caste system, inviting untouchables and brahmans alike to journey on the road with him. Not towards any tangible paradise, just on to the next village, the village after that, all the way across India and back, until people behave decently to one another, and to all other life forms. That, says Vardhamana, is paradise!

"But how are we to survive?" the people demand. "You've cautioned against cutting down trees, or harming animals, even insects, or keeping cattle, or burning fields in the Spring. What is left?"

Vardhamana has carefully suggested possibilities, measures taken step by step, one at a time, day by day, in a logical effort to make this a painless world. He refers to several hundred local species of plant which he has observed on his journeys to be growing in abundance. "Eat the banana, but spare the monkey," he advises.

To some, this young man actually makes good sense. Who would doubt that a grain of wheat feels less pain than a water buffalo?

But to others, pain is good; babies are born in pain, virgins impregnated painfully, men of valor decorated for their pain. Hard work is painful. Growth is painful. Every adolescent will tell you that. So what's wrong with pain? To such men, Vardhamana is stark raving mad.

"And, what about the economy!" he hears everywhere he goes.

In the course of these encounters, Vardhamana discovers a young woman named Candana who has been enslaved by a lecherous merchant. He had rescued her from a rapist in the forest but then repeated the crime by installing her in his house and forcing himself upon her every night, while his wife watched.

The woman, certain she'd be pursued and killed, fears to escape. Her beauty is admired by all, though she is clad in filthy rags. In the market, where she has come to purchase goods for the merchant, she is considered an outcast, Vardhamana sees her and, at once, detects her predicament. Leonard is unclear how Vardhamana perceives these things. There is magic about his person. He seems able to predict the future, to know the past.

Vardhamana intercedes and rescues Candana, adhering to a belief that pacifism or indifference in the face of evil is tantamount to conspiring with the offender.

Gosala falls sickly in love with Candana. Her thighs tantalize him. He can't keep his fingers out of her robes. And, he is compelled to throw a white robe over himself to conceal only the most blatant sign of this lust. But, he cannot conceal it anymore than a dog can.

As for Candana, she is not revolted by this imposter who calls himself an ascetic. Vardhamana's message has reached her. She has renounced everything in gratitude to him.

On the road, the group is attacked by ruffians who attempt to kidnap Candana. She means trouble. Men of this world crave her and will stop at nothing to have her. They sick their ferocious dogs on the party, dogs who have been trained to attack men, not women. Gosala and the other ascetics fight to save themselves, but Vardhamana does nothing. He will not raise a finger. Nor will the dogs go near him.

"What magic is that?" demands Gosala.

"No magic," Vardhamana says. "Only the power of ahinsa."

Within minutes the anger in the dogs, the cruelty that has altered their nature and unleashed a vicious storm of fangs, has been utterly reversed. Vardhamana has miraculously transformed their temperaments. Even their masters have been somehow becalmed, and go away.

But this magic—this *ahinsa*—has no apparent power over Gosala. At night, a local potter woman, Halahala, takes the party under her roof. Gosala is at once attracted to her, too, having been rejected by Candana. He slips out of his bed in the middle of the night and deflowers her.

Vardhamana lies awake in the dark shed listening to the violent lovemaking. His eyes are fierce with thoughts, desires, self-pity, the memory of his own nights in bed. He is a man, after all, who cannot help but be affected, in such close quarters, by a woman's heavy breathing, her sighs, and the sight of her breasts caught now and then in the platinum moonlight. He struggles with this, but wins.

At dawn, Vardhamana, Candana, and the others depart. The wildly priapic Gosala does not go with them.

It is an unhappy time for Vardhamana. Man's nature is not so easily conquered, he realizes. But, Gosala has only increased Vardhamana's zeal to make things right in the world. Adversity is what gives us our strength, he alleges.

The sun suddenly strikes the edge of the window, glancing onto Leonard Rosenbalm's face. And, within minutes there are yawns and groans and expletives all around him, and the sound of the hospital waking up. A nurse comes in with a tray. With medicines.

"How are we this morning, Mr. Rosenbalm?" And she takes his pulse, looks at her watch, asks him to stick out his tongue, and inquires whether he's had a bowel movement.

"Give me monk's urine," he says.

"You *are* sick!" the nurse replies.

Everything about Leonard's person suggested a dilemma at that point. He was a living testament to transition between species, between ideals, from one world to the next. His unshaven face belied the purest marble of his insides. He did not want a shower, or breakfast, or sedatives, and they could not legally force him to comply.

Doctors Kushner and one Jason Rampart, a psychiatrist, arrived slightly after eight a.m. on their morning rounds.

"Good morning, Leonard. This is Dr. Rampart who's going to sit in on our conversation."

Prompted by one question after another, Leonard finally launched into a discourse upon life as an animal, the joys of homelessness, the exquisite feeling of air moving freely about his genitals and nipples; the sweet sensation of fasting, of stepping outside evolution and remarking with all one's might upon the possibilities for compassion. He reminded them how the act of giving was far richer than the act of taking, an old and valid truism, and swept them up in a physics of verbal fluidity, until they too might have been tempted to join Leonard in his odyssey. For here was a man who clearly believed that the greatest freedom came neither from riches nor from health nor political arrangement. The greatest freedom issued from an inner voice which had succeeded in recognizing that not even that inner voice exists; in other words, a self that had the willpower to renounce everything.

"I want nothing, I fear nothing, I am free," Leonard declared with passionless passion.

His convictions were conveyed without ornament or shade. There was neither subtlety nor zeal. He had never communicated more pellucidly in his young life. Whatever irration might have been detected in the previous day, had now evaporated. Leonard had become acutely objective, analytical. And, this made the doctors's task all the more difficult.

They took some notes, conferred and nodded agreeably. They asked him repeatedly if this was a religious conviction. And Leonard said it was, though "religion," perhaps, needed clarification. When asked if what he really meant was simply that he was a nudist, one of many who populate "clothing optional" hotels in Las Vegas, and colonies up and down the West Coast, like Elysium in Topanga, he said not. His nudity was the nudity of a St. Francis, or of a St. John the Baptist in the desert, of a young man named Vardhamana to whom the possession of clothing represented guilt, fear, inhibition, the lack of honesty. Leonard asserted that for himself, nudity was a first step towards confronting the liberation of the soul. The body fell away from this deeper consideration, was like dust beneath his feet.

In the end, Leonard concluded that nudity, for him, was indeed part of an ancient religion, though he did not refer to his dreams, in which dozens of holy men wandered naked about the plains of India.

That same afternoon, Miriam, having taken two weeks off from work in order to deal with these tribulations, called Morris Feldbach for the recommendation of a lawyer. Morris had always been a true friend and she knew he had an attorney son-in-law.

"Morris, Leonard's had a nervous breakdown," she began.

"I heard," he said. "Hal told me. With his schmegegie dangling up and down Main Street. Miriam, if you don't mind my saying so, this is state of the art mishoogina."

He dialed a number and put his son-in-law, David Ovitz, the one with Melankof, Ovitz and Gautama, on conference call.

"David, how are you?"

"Hi, Morris. What's up?"

"I want you to meet my dear friend Miriam Rosenbalm. Her husband, Lennie, a close associate, has had a nervous breakdown after losing his parents, Ruben and Ida Rosenbalm. You must have seen their touching obituaries in the Jewish News yesterday. Wonderful people. A tragedy."

"I'm sorry, Miriam," David said.

"Thank you," she said.

Morris continued in his dolorous and plodding Old World manner. "Leonard also had some business problems. But, they will take care of themselves, eventually. I'm calling you because Lennie is in trouble. He flipped out. He gave his clothes away to a homeless person and was picked up by the police walking downtown. Now they've got him for three days in a mental institute. But, let her tell you."

"I saw the picture," David immediately replied.

"What picture?" Miriam cried.

"In this morning's *L.A. Times*. I assume it's the same person. There was no name but there was a naked man in front of a statue of a naked woman. That beautiful Robert Graham piece. Near the Biltmore. I guess the photograph was taken just before he was picked up. Must be the same man."

"My god," Miriam mumbled. She hadn't looked at the paper. "He's not that way. And, this isn't about us, our marriage, I mean, if that's what you're suggesting?"

"No, no . . . I'm not suggesting anything. Is there a hearing?" David asked.

"Day after tomorrow," Miriam told him. "I don't know the time yet."

"I'll be there."

"One more thing, David. He thinks he's become a monk of some sort. An aesthetic."

"That's *ascetic*," Miriam enunciated.

"You sure they're going to let him out so soon?"

"That's why I need you to be there."

Over lunch, David mentioned Miriam's problem to Indrabhuti Gautama—most of his colleagues and clients called him Gautama, for short. Originally from the city of Patna, somewhere between New Delhi and Calcutta, his family had moved to New York in the early 1980s, via England and Antwerp. His parents were diamond merchants. He chose a very different career and had distinguished himself in the field of constitutional law, graduated with honors at Cambridge before migrating to Los Angeles five years before.

"What is it?" David said, surprised by Gautama's pronounced show of interest in the case.

"Where I come from, naked Jain ascetics have been wandering the backroads for thousands of years."

David knew that Gautama was himself a Jain. A vegetarian, though David had seem him drink milk. Beyond that, nobody in the law firm had much of a clue what Jainism was—whether it was a weirdo low-cholesterol religion for people from India allergic to leather, sort of like the Breatharians, but dark-skinned, or a subsect of nonviolent Hindus, a secret cult for rich businessmen who all had fortunes but drove Hondas and refused to wear belts or Gucci shoes, an ancient hippy philosophy without the long hair, an offshoot of Greenpeace in conservative drag. Something about Gandhi. But there were too many Jain diamond merchants to qualify it as a religion of poverty or simplicity. They never cracked jokes, according to Gautama. David didn't really know, or care. Whatever Jainism was, or wasn't, it seemed harmless, and it really didn't matter, anyway. Gautama was clearly no spiritual fanatic. He kept his Jainism at home, never bringing it to work with him. In fact, he hardly ever talked about it, which led David and the others to suspect that there must be quite a few skeletons in Jainism's closet. Things you might not want to know. Maybe they performed grisly ritual tofu sacrifices by the full moon? The point was, Gautama was a superb trial lawyer. That's all that counted. And, that's why a soft-spoken Indian had been made the junior partner in an otherwise all Jewish law firm of considerable power and prestige in Beverly Hills.

"This is no backroads of India we're talking about, obviously. Furthermore, the guy is Jewish. Textiles. Wife's a Kosher cateress."

"I want the case," Gautama stated emphatically.

"Sure, take it." David was glad to be let off the hook on this one.

Gautama called to introduce himself to Miriam. He asked her about Leonard's religious beliefs, which made her nervous. He explained that in the event any charges should actually be filed, religious beliefs might be useful.

"He's not a religious Jew, particularly. I just want it to be over," she said.

Gautama procured a copy of the written files from the mental eval unit at the L.A.P.D.. It was not a transcript, but a loose summary, as interpreted by Patrolman Davies and the Chief Detective.

Gautama then spoke with Doctor Kushner, who relayed seminal facts from his own discussions with the patient. Gautama finally called upon Leonard himself.

There is an old adage that American cows in captivity, when introduced to the sound of an alpine cowbell, become delirious with yearning for the Swiss Alps. And, much the same could be said of Leonard when he laid eyes upon Indrabhuti Gautama.

As Gautama, clad in a three-piece suit, extended a warm handshake, Leonard shed a veritable tear and declared, "But, I feel as if I already know you!"

And, Gautama felt much the same way.

CHAPTER SIX

The First Disciple

Leonard and the lawyer spent a brief time together.

"If released, as we expect you'll be, what are your plans?" Gautama asked candidly.

"To continue heading East," Leonard replied.

"When you say 'East' what do you mean?"

"All the way across America."

"And then?"

"By then I'll be seventy-two years old. A good time to die."

"I hope you didn't tell the Doctor that?"

"Not in so many words."

"And your wife?"

"I told her. I know it's not easy for her, or for my daughter."

"Why are you doing it, then?"

Leonard paused. Gautama shifted on the couch, suddenly uncomfortable.

"I have no intention of returning to my previous life," Leonard began. "Neither home, nor business, nor family, nor friends. I've renounced everything."

"When you say 'renounced' . . . ?"

Leonard thought carefully before speaking.

"I am not what I used to be. Sometimes, in my dreams, I feel certain that I've had a past life, or lives, and am being given glimpses of it for some purpose."

"Have you ever traveled to India, Mr. Rosenbalm?"

Leonard pondered the query, greatly disturbed, or fascinated, by the proposition. "I don't know," he finally said. "In my dreams."

"Surely, one would know?"

"You'd think so."

"According to the police report, you spoke words of some Indian language. Are you familiar with Hindi?"

"No. But words have come to me, into my head when I have these —what should I call them, dreams, visions—and also, words sometimes when I speak. A language I somehow understand. But, I really don't, you see. I don't understand a word of it!"

"So you've memorized Hindi?"

"I have no idea. It's just gobbledygook. I'm fluent in it for short bursts. I mean, it's like a fluttering tongue that locks into some grammar and vocabulary otherwise unknown to me, then dissipates just as quickly and mysteriously. When I try to get it back, all I hear is static inside me. But, when I'm not thinking about it, not trying, in other words, the phrases and sentences come out of me, on their own. I'm sorry I can't be more helpful."

"Could you say something for me now, in this fluttering tongue?"

"No. I mean, I don't think so. I can't control it. That's the whole point." Leonard stared away.

"Try."

Leonard concentrated. His insides twitched and grappled. Languages, like genes, mounted towards self-expression in a halo of incommunicable desire. What was mute and dark began to burn off, like mist from an ancient sea, giving rise, nearly, to hidden reserves. But just as quickly, the impulse passed and Leonard remained locked out, unspeaking.

"It doesn't matter," Gautama said. "I just thought that—"

"It's coming . . . " And there, right before him, was his phantasm, like so many jewels spread out in a procession, traipsing through the sunlight, words repeated over millennia, memorized by untold generations of devotees who registered their emotions in a persuasive recitation before all of nature.

"*Ahinsa Paramo Dharmah*," Leonard began gently, unwaveringly, like some medium whose very nudity was his Ouija board, his unmistakable link to a spirit.

The lawyer's whole body trembled, congruent with Leonard's own apparent revelation. He repeated the words, in translation, astonished. "Nonviolence is the supreme religion . . . That's Sanskrit! That is the fundamental Jain prayer. Surely, you know that?"

But, Leonard was transfixed with his verbiage. He kept going. "*Parasparopagraho Jivanam.*"

"All life is connected," Gautama intoned, his eyes bright with incredulity.

"*Khamemi savva jive, Savve jiva khamantu me, Mitti me savva bhuesu, Veram mazza na kena i.*"

"But really, you must know what it all means?" pressed Gautama.

Leonard came down, slowly. These speaking bouts were fantastically draining. A spasm of saliva leaked out of the corner of his mouth. It was an unnatural white, the color of ectoplasm.

"I want to say it has to do with forgiveness. Of all beings forgiving one another. Something like that. To be perfectly honest with you, this scares the hell out of me. I don't know how I'm doing this. You're telling me it's a real language, and you understand it?" Leonard felt exhausted. His ears were tingling.

"Mr. Rosenbalm—Leonard—of course it's a language. One of the oldest in the world. And the sentiments are Jain to the core. Mahatma Gandhi himself spoke them. Are you . . . do you know about, I mean, where did you read or learn of Jainism? Surely, in school?"

"I studied engineering," he replied, almost by way of a joke.

Leonard could not explain the transformation, not all at once. "I know nothing about this Jainism," he said. "Honestly. I don't profess to know anything, anymore. I only have these unstoppable feelings, the images that keep gnawing inside me. That's who I am. Who I always was. It's just that this week, something happened to me. Something grand. This is hard for me, Mr. Gautama."

The lawyer felt a profound sting of sympathy for Leonard.

"In these persistent dreams of mine, I have seen ascetics and have even followed conversations, and gleaned some principles. But nobody has said anything about 'Jainism'. Yet someone on the street asked me if I was a Jain. What is it? Please, tell me?"

"What is a Jain?" The young lawyer sat forward, re-shifting, taking stock. He was enlivened with the possibilities of describing that which was his proud birthright. But, the arena was heated, the stakes unbelievably high. From the moment he'd laid eyes on this Los Angeles Jew something far-off and impossible had clicked in his gut, something he himself had dreamt of. The fantasy of every Jain, in a sense —to actually do it! To separate from the world of possessions and wander off through the streets preaching peace and love, if that was truly what Mr. Rosenbalm had been doing. Adopting the solitary gait of a monk, the word *ahinsa* reverberating on his lips. Yet, how could he reconcile an ideal with so imperfect an incarnation as this bumbling man who spoke in tongues and, for all Gautama knew, was perhaps a con artist of some sort, a virulent fraud determined to win disciples, glory, notoriety; or to swindle his wife out of an estate, or escape creditors and family responsibilities, or perhaps Leonard Rosenbalm was truly an exhibitionist of the subtlest and most consummate sort, a sexual pervert, fabricating these blurry revelations so as to invoke First Amendment rights. It could be anything. And yet, everything suggested that this man was authentic. Spiritual. Crossing a most tenuous, razor-sharp bridge. He needed help. And, Gautama felt up to the rescue.

"Where does one begin," the lawyer sighed, nervously. "It is the oldest religion in India, possibly in the world," Gautama suggested. "There are at least seven million of us around today and we have no God —but we're not atheists either. I suppose we've replaced the idea of God with our concept of the soul, which we were all raised to believe exists in every living creature."

"But this is common knowledge," Leonard broke in.

"We think so. But then, if other people agreed, why is there so much killing? Why is so much cruelty inflicted? This is the quintessential nut every Jain must confront, knowing that he does not have the right nor the means to crack it for others. He can only hope to attend to his own salvation."

"Which is?"

"An imperishable soul, though it suffers constant change, some good, some bad."

"And, one can distinguish good from bad?"

"Oh yes. Awareness is not the problem. Habits, temptations, blurred ethical considerations, the pressures from that larger society with whom Jains have always peacefully cohabited. That's where the difficulties arise. You see, we have this strain of masochism in our blood which forces us to behave as if our actions matter. We do not subscribe to fate. Man's fate is in his own hands. That's what my parents, and their parents, always told us as children."

"I believe that as well," Leonard said.

"Not everybody does. Furthermore, we Jains try earnestly to live our lives with one foot in heaven, and the other on Earth. It means going out of our way to ensure that all other animals can also gain a foothold in that paradise. It means protecting them. It's not even their earthly bodies that are so important. Because reincarnation mixes everybody up. Today I am me, tomorrow I am you. It's the soul that matters, and it is our reponsibility as feeling, thinking humans to try and protect the souls of other creatures so that they might evolve spiritually in their own way, in their own time and become whatever they may become. My parents indoctrinated me and my sisters to live accordingly. To love nature with all our hearts, to thank nature in advance. *Ahinsa* is a code word for us that encompasses our total non-militarism, our vegetarianism and charity, our ideals of truthfulness, and our strong ascetic inclinations. We do a lot of fasting. You might say that Jains were the first ecologists. Because most Jain businessmen refuse any activities that exploit animals. Some of our monks, known as the Digambara, or sky-clad, live most of their lives naked. The others, Svetambara, wear white robes. The rest of us—all those millions of Jains who aren't up to monkhood–wear three-piece suits like myself. I mean, we're normal. We look like good Hindus or Christians or Buddhists. Or Jews, for that matter. But, when I heard about your case, I immediately assumed that something strangely familiar was taking place right here, in Los Angeles. It happens frequently in India. Though no businessman, to my knowledge, has actually gone to the point of disrobing all the way. Or, not in several decades. Only the monks do that. So, how is it that a Jew who drives a Bentley should have come by these same sentiments?"

Everything Gautama was saying crystallized Leonard's still waters. Reality was breaking in, and it was good.

"Perhaps, I have some long-lost Indian blood," Leonard speculated. "Although, I seriously doubt it."

"When were you born?"

"Are you an astrologer?"

"All Indians are astrologers."

"Nineteen fifty-one."

"Nineteen fifty-one, let me see. He rifled through his memory. "The year of the making of 'An American in Paris,' and 'The African Queen,' Ben Hogan won the Open, color television was introduced, and the first heart-lung machine invented."

Leonard warmed to the absurdity of this information. "Am I to assume you've been on the quiz shows?"

"As a student, at Cambridge, yes. That's how I earned my spending money. Now let me see, I gather from your wife that your family came from Russia?"

"My grandparents did. And, I suppose their grandparents, as well. From faraway Birobidzhan, in Siberia. A Jewish Autonomous Region. They were all scholars or poets, or dentists or doctors. Arrested, shot, the lucky ones forced, penniless, into exile."

"Any family tree?"

"As a matter of fact, there is a cousin of mine, I haven't spoken with that side of the family in some time. Let's see, his great uncle married my great aunt's cousin, or something like that. As I recall, there was some genealogical work done. They contacted the Mormons who are fanatical about such things, as you probably know. Miriam might have the fellow's number. Back East somewhere. He sent a flyer to all the distant relatives. They had a reunion. This is years ago. A hundred Rosenbalms. I didn't go. What does it matter?"

"All of it matters, it matters very much. And, I can predict that the medical referee will agree. You do realize that they could keep you here indefinitely if things went badly?"

"Don't worry," Leonard said.

"Don't you worry," replied Gautama. "I'll be at the hearing to help. And, once you're out of here, you can count on me to do what's right."

"What's right?" Leonard asked, his voice nearly pleading for direction.

"We'll find out," Gautama said.

Both men felt the queerest convolutions, incentives hidden behind hunches rolled up into enigmas. Leonard negotiated through stares in the hallway back to his room. There, his roommates—busy playing checkers—exercised remarkable restraint in ignoring his nakedness. There was pity in the air.

Gautama left the third floor, went to the parking lot and drove away in his Honda.

Later, Leonard was visited by Doctor Kushner. While they were speaking, the nurse brought Leonard a plate of fruit and vegetables and a glass of boiled water. It was his one meal in three days. In the calmest and most sensible voice, he told the Doctor he was feeling much better and looked forward to leaving.

In his thoughts, Leonard felt pain for his wife and daughter. It was Gautama—with his talk of this *Jainism*—who restored his waning confidence, absolving him from the guilt of having abandoned those closest to him.

He lay awake pondering his coming days. With drowsiness came more visitations. Nothing noteworthy cued the onrushing scents, the aromatic herbs, the sulking redolence of umber soil, the jasmine haunted air, or that boisterous mingling of kokila birds and macaque monkeys high in the deodar canopy whose vague tropical jabbering slipped over Leonard's naked sleep like a light cashmere blanket in the chilled night. No obvious invitation for crickets to jostle betwixt corn stalks, or bulbous frogs to burp adrift the lotus ponds. But somewhere across a river, buffalos lowed; and in the backbush a tiger with her cubs prowled silently in search of shade. These, and other sights and sounds entranced Leonard, as he lay across his hospital bed pastoral and paralyzed by the inward glow of other times and places.

Years, not hours, seem to have taken their toll on the walking entablature of Vardhamana. Exhausted, his bones showing through, the lone figure sits under a sala tree in the fields of a householder near an abandoned temple on the banks of a river. Beyond, Leonard makes out hills through the noontime haze. Vardhamana's heels are held tightly together. He sits akimbo, in the position one might adopt whilst milking a cow. Yet his eyes are wide open, his whole being attuned and radiant.

"Some water?" asks the owner of the property, who has come trundling a bucket. "It has been boiled."

"Thank you," Vardhamana says, taking a sip.

The heat is vibrating off the fields. Mirages have formed over the sala tree. Clouds begin to accumulate there, the distant hint of thunder. Mist rises, aggregates, drifts. A swirl of butterflies alights in the branches overhead sounding like a swarm of bees. By stages, the sun is obscured, then revealed. A penumbra of spectacular storm is forming there where Vardhamana sits upright, hour after hour.

The crickets measure time with their prosody. A thrum that causes all the meadows around to sway as in some delirium. In Leonard's eye.

The storm breaks. The rain pounds. In a swoosh, ten thousand birds burst skyward, while the rain turns to hail and the ground is covered in ice. Lightning strikes the very tree, narrowly missing Vardhamana, illuminating his bald head for just an instant. After-tremors rumble over the land, as if, in tandem, there were seismic confirmations that his inward gaze had struck gold in the outer universe.

Gold that now is transformed into a myriad of rainbows breaking cover. All the heavens are incandescent with their arcs and spectral hues. Prisms dripping into substance, revelation becoming soil. Ice turned to heat, and heat to air.

The man becoming his full potential. Spirit usurping biology. Dreams transformed to dew, and dew to fuel.

The householder has run outside to witness smoke left from the lightning flash, rising into the clear dusk from the ice covered tropic.

There stands a diamond of a man, tall, hieroglyphic-like, gleaming in the heart of rough nature.

The householder trembles, clutching a bush nearby for support. In his eyes, the ascetic has become a rainbow. Aware that demons or gods might be watching, he decides to set the record straight.

"I, Samaga, have witnessed this day—in the second month of summer, the month of Vaisakha, the—oh dear, what day is it?—ahh, I think the ninth or tenth day, and it is the fourth fortnight, the day being called, oh dear, it must be Suvrata, the year being, of course, five fifty-seven, near the temple of Vijayavarta, a temple of monkeys, on the banks of the

Rjupalika, the water being high, near the village of Jrmbhakagrama, beneath the Parasnath hills, on my very property, beneath a sala tree, a miracle!" blurts the householder, recording for the wraiths, for the posterity of nature, that stares and rejoices to either side, standing himself amazed in the center of a hail-burdened field of wheat and flowering mustard. "Blessings to you, oh Venerable Ascetic Mahavira! Obeisance to the Arhats! Obeisance to the Liberated Ones! Obeisance to the Religious Guides! Obeisance to the Religious Instructors! Obeisance to all Saints in the World!" And he kneels upon one knee, his hands raised in a gesture of prayer, his eyes closed, then kisses the Earth, and awaits whatever destiny has in store this day.

. . . Mahavira! The name itself, Great Hero, emanating like a drum —the sound of *divyadhvani*—from his body, from the lips of the householder, from off every blade of grass in the surrounding swale. A million eyes view his awakening. In the midst of circumstance, far away, his old friend, Sakra, feels a tremor and knows that the snake has shed its skin.

In a secluded courtyard garden, where time has been sleeping, the ashes of his parents sprout at that moment into mango trees. And, further away still, in a big city, a man listens, watches, follows in the night.

As Mahavira moves away from the tree, leaving behind his childhood name, as well as twelve years of trial and error which had led to this moment of *kevalajnana*, of final, unimpeded, all-embracing vision. Mahavira, aged forty-two, has conquered karma; has taken control, in other words, of his own life.

At once he comprehends the six substances and seven principles and proceeds to speak of them—of *dravya* and *tattva*—to the bewildered Samaga, a simple old man who has certainly not expected on this day when he planned to chop wood, visit his granddaughter, get drunk and take a long snooze, that he should instead be the fortunate first to confront the twenty-fourth Jina, or Tirthankara and hear his clear-speaking message.

"What can I do?" said Samaga, peeing in his pants.

"Be prepared to buy me a goat," said Mahavira, joyfully, and he departed for the nearest village, an hour's walk away.

Night-black water buffalo, grey humped brahma bulls, flittery hens, annoyed camels, mangey canines, flocks of copulating crows teem along the still-damp pathway into the village. The odor of the rain is redolent and fine.

In the dirt, a phalanx of ants is devouring a grasshopper that still jerks towards freedom, one leg having been severed. Mahavira bends down and saves it.

On the fringes of the village, an old woman and her grandson sit beside the road begging. Mahavira blesses them both.

Further on, he approaches a gang of vultures hopping and pecking atop the mangled ribcage of an ox. Tigers had gotten to it earlier in the day and only bones remain now. But bones, fur and the taste of blood will do, if you're a vulture. As Mahavira passes the scene of carnage, the birds cease their food carnival and seem—to Leonard's mind—if only for a moment, to give up meat-eating altogether. But no, not for a mere moment. Even as Mahavira has vanished from their sight, the birds have given up their quarry and circle high above the trees, agonizing, as if trying improbably to reverse their very nature. And, sure enough, upon closer scrutiny, Leonard realizes that these vultures are flying backwards!

A steady drumming of the dholak and the metallic shaking of timbrels, accompanied by much merriment, ushers the lone Mahavira towards the center of town. There, a wedding is in full swing and most of the populace is present to honor the newlyweds. Masked dancers are twitching their shoulders to lilting music performed by nomads on bamboo flutes. The air is bacchanalian with sensuous bodies cavorting under a rising quarter moon. Richly caparisoned elephants, dressed in brocades, peacock feathers and gold are paraded through the crowds while fireworks light up the evening. Thousands of clay images adorned with flowers and sweets lay scattered along the path the couple will travel. Gods and goddesses—Vesamanamaha, Lakshmi, Ganesha, Lord Jagannatha, Durga, Kali and Shiva, Nandi and Hanuman—are each represented by flower arrangements. Young balladeers harmonize on the many-stringed ravanahatta, while jugglers and acrobats perform for all the guests, kicking up dirt, miasmas of coursing flesh spinning wildly through the brilliantly-robed arrays.

Rhapsody and the night . . . A poetess dances the sapera, circling in languid serpentine arabesques, the anklet bells on her owl-skin boots tinkling as she recites a paen to Lord Krishna—"Sweet the speaking, Sweet the doing, Sweet the wearing, Sweet the stance, Sweet in going, Sweet in roaming, Honey sweet, The honeyed Lord . . . " And now she roams through the congestion of bullock carts and joy-makers seducing young boys, whose time, like that of the groom, is one day coming.

People stuffing their mouths. Rhapsody and the stomach . . . Rice with saffron, sweets, vegetables and fruits have been amply placed upon painted trays and spread across dozens of tables carved from betel nut. There are delicate cakes layered with gold and silver foil, and creamy milk in abundance flowing from red earthen pitchers. Children are laugh-

ing, screaming, running through the crowds. Old men ornamented in peacock feathers and the tails of scorpions, their boots fitted with ram horns,
their beards dyed purple, stroll with staffs in their hands, patriarchs out
for a good time, inspecting all their progeny.

Rhapsody and the coming wedding night . . . And now a Brahman
priest is feeding the sacred fire with clarified butter, seeds and grain and
preparing to join the couple as the bride, her eyes decorated with kajal,
her hands and feet painted with mehndi—the love juice of henna, a
lovely tint—her long gown tied to his, is led seven times around the
flames and women sing of the tightening of her bonds with each circle.

Mahavira stays clear of the comminglings, remembering back to
his own wedding, his heart skipping a beat, watching from a discreet
distance. Every snapping of a finger breaks through the subtle, subtle
essence of his hearing; every burst of giddy childhood enflames his
otherwise tranquil skull. Whereas the celebrations around him are
moving fast, he is standing slow; while eyes and fingers are flitting, his
glance is enduring; and, just as laughter streaks the night air with robust
energy, so his slow love drifts across the panorama, like the night itself.
And, what it focuses on, this adoration, is not the spectacle of pleasure, of
life's pageant, but rather, a goat tied to a short tether in the midst of this
communal elation.

The goat, frantic and straining with all of six inches granted its
remaining time on Earth. The eyes are black and terrified, its chest
pounding, the nostrils frothing. Dust is kicked up in its face. Nobody
cares. The playful effervescence all around it only accents its deepening
sense of doom. It knows. And Mahavira's heart is breaking.

And suddenly, the priest has stepped forth with a knife carved in
the shape of a parrot and is approaching the animal. He plans to slaughter
it. The goat flails and cries, struggling. Even now the fires are being
stoked—the goat's eyes are rupturing with foreknowledge—and the
groom will be the first to thrust a piece of hot goat meat into his mouth,
and stuff it with two fingers into the senseless death-conspiring mouth of
his bride.

Leonard looks on as the determined naked man strides quickly
through the crowd and without hesitating, blinking, flinching or delay,
deftly intercedes in front of everyone to curtail the butcher's knife. He
reaches up, gently staying the arm of the priest, evoking a tyrannical out-
cry from all quarters.

And, there is Gautama, the very lawyer, dressed not in a Brooks
Brothers suit, but in the white, festive trappings of the wedding. For the

bride is evidently a cousin of his and he, like all the others, is outraged by this outsider's audacity, ascetic or no ascetic.

"Who are you to intrude this way!" he shouts, threatening with an upturned fist and a gleaming sword which he has drawn.

And, Mahavira boldly denounces the sacrifice on the grounds that all creatures are blessed, that the life force knows no distinction. Whether atom, or vegetable, goat or man.

Leonard feels the full weight of Mahavira's argument, his reasoning power, his breath, the universal consciousness that animates him before this dangerous mob. Mahavira's eye circulates with an omniscient grasp of his circumstances. He is utterly at peace.

Indrabhuti Gautama's two brothers, Agnibhuti and Vayubhiti step forward to re-enforce Indrabhuti's show of force against the miserable, pompous outcast.

"What right have you to disturb this wedding?" they shout, the refrain echoing throughout the rabble.

"Let's sacrifice him!" a voice rings out. "Him and the goat both!"

"Grab him," screams another. "We got ourselves one tasty ascetic!"

But, Mahavira is undaunted and with the slightest gestures and presence, somehow manages to captivate the entire public before him. Leonard is dazzled. No statesman, no rock star, no beauty queen or philanthropist ever demonstrated such charismatic powers. From rage, the motley gathering is brought to attention, as Mahavira calmly speaks.

"All hurting is a reprisal against the self. Do you understand? A wise man, even a fool, should not act sinfully towards animals, nor cause others to act so, nor allow others to act so. Thus I say, by my love of each of you—and he pointed to individuals all around him—you, you, and you, this little goat, the honored bride and groom, revered guests, welcome cousins, venerable parents, the venerated deceased, and those blessed ones yet to perish; by my love of your loved ones, by my love of the memory of those who have come and gone before this day. I love all of you. I bless all of you. My friend, Samaga, the old one who tends the fields near the monkey temple on the edge of town, he shall pay you for the goat."

And, he bows before the newlyweds, before their parents and the priest, then unties the goat with steady hands and bewhispered reassurances, and leads it like a pied piper towards the woods.

The animal licks Mahavira's leg, its little tail wagging frantically.

It is as if another lightning bolt had struck Gautama. He stands, mouth aghast, eyes yearning and bright, totally agitated, confused, amazed. And the sword falls from his hand, and his fist collapses upon itself.

"Get him!" shouts another voice.

But Indrabhuti, and now his brothers hold back the mob with a marked restraint.

Indrabhuti bows before his relatives and follows the ascetic.

And, Leonard's mind fades from vapor and vision to deepest slumber. At peace now that that goat has been saved.

The lawyer, Gautama, meanwhile, calling from his office at home, has entered a very different forest, namely, the phone system in India.

"Hello?" he shouts. "Hello??" But the line goes dead. He tries the second number, and it is busy.

Earlier that afternoon, Gautama had made some calls to Connecticut and Pittsburgh and unearthed some interesting news about the Rosenbalms via subsequent fax. It seems that Leonard's great-great-great-grandfather on his mother's side was a Dutch Jew, not Russian, and he had worked for the Dutch East India Company back in the early nineteenth century. He was stationed in the British-controlled town of Cranganar for five years buying spices, gems, and rugs from the Jewish and Jain communities up and down the southwestern coast of India. It was at the Jootha Bazaar in Paroor, one of the most ancient Jewish markets in India (functioning to this day), the place where one seasick St. Thomas threw up in the second century prior to converting scores of Hindus; where Jewish descendents of the ten tribes during the time of Hoshea, Israel's last king, had once been fragmented by the Assyrians and shipwrecked nearby along these same sand dunes and tropical beaches, that Leonard's ancestor met, and subsequently married a young woman whose maiden name was Mahapadma.

Gautama knew at once that it was a Jain name. And no ordinary one, either.

It was late morning in Paroor when Gautama finally reached the local historian-cum-archivist-cum-genealogist, who sat on centuries-worth of documents and knew where every name was buried. He sounded like a very old man, as befitted his occupation, his voice frail but in command. Gautama's conversation would cost him plenty, because the man had to keep looking up things and Gautama was not about to call back and risk not getting through. But, the price was worth it.

Apparently the Jains had both a monastery and a nunnery in the village, along with a famous sacred grove of alstonia trees, where lovers used to meet. And it was probably in that grove where Isaac Benjamin (Essaji Benjami)—Leonard's direct ancestor—courted Kavita Mahapadma.

Since the Jains had no God, a Jew's fear of their being idolatrous—the basis of all traditionally closed Judaism —ceased to be relevant. Isaac, like the other new Jews to the region, had gone from eating northern European sausage to unleavened rice bread; from a five-story mansion on the Herengracht in Amsterdam to a modest dwelling with throw rugs over the thatch floor. His gentleman's dress of crimson and fashioned boot stood out among rough country muslin. And soon, like the Portuguese traders before him up north in Goa, he was wearing the local satin pajamas and sandals.

According to the archivist, the mixed marriages produced offspring known as Kala Bene Israel to designate those descended from non-Jewish mothers.

The couple was married in the ancient synagogue at Kunnamkulam by Rabbi Shalom ben Aaron, the first Baghdadi Jew from Aleppo, in 1790. The historian had photo copies of all Jewish historical records and while Gautama sat on the phone waiting, the old man rummaged through his documents and files and soon found a handwritten book with mention of the couple's *ketuba*, their marriage certificate, dated 1822.

Indian Jews and Jains were each looked upon as minorities, but they looked upon one another as equals. And, it was this familiarity and the extent of their business relations which cemented unique marriages.

The couple's offspring—two girls named Aka and Ambai—were known as *kala* or Malabari Jews, their skin color being more black than white. They would eventually join the ranks of other dark Jewish offspring whose family names included Sassoon, Praeger, Reading and Montagu. They spoke Malayalam and Marathi. *Havlaga*, Hebrew for restraint, became *ahinsa* in the local languages. *Rosh Hashana* became known as *Naviacha san*; *Yom Kippur, Darfalnicha san*. The last King of Cranganore was a Jew, Joseph Azar. And, by that time Essaji Benjami was one of nearly two thousand Jews who had settled in that area. Many had intermarried. This was the epicenter of India's *Galut*, its Jewish diaspora. A profusion of cultures and faiths and dialects interbred, according to the archivist. Cochini white Jews, Meshuachrim brown Jews, Baghdadi black Jews, Marranos, Dutch, English, Spanish, Portugese, Arab, Hindu, Cnanite Christians, and of course, Jains.

Remarkably, despite vastly different histories and migrations, the difference between the Jewish and Jain calendars was all of twelve hours. They were on the same wavelength. Certainly Isaac Benjamin and Kavita Mahapadma were.

The archivist admitted that Jewish-Jain marriages were few. Today, he said, there were less than one hundred fifty Jews in the area, and far fewer Jewish-Jain descendents. Many of the black Jews had left for Europe and America when India gained independence in nineteen forty-seven.

"Are there any Benjamis still living in the area?" Gautama asked.

"None," replied the old man. "The records show that the couple moved to Holland three years after they were married."

As for Kavita, the archivist was able to date her family name to the ninth century in that area. Jain scholars and merchants, all of them. Before that, her personal past simply trailed off into the vast geneological unknown. Her ancestors had probably migrated from some other region in the south like Karnataka. Possibly from the city of Gangavadi, where followers of Mahavira prevailed over the Ganga dynasty for seven centuries.

Though Leonard Rosembalm was unaware of this esoteric family history, Gautama now believed that it had some bearing on his particular mid-life crisis, or whatever it was, albeit genetical and distant.

Furthermore, Gautama marveled at how all things seemed to come around in life, a lesson his religion had stressed.

While Kavita Mahapadma—Leonard's great-great-great-grandmother—left no ancestral records beyond a thousand years, the family name itself possessed other important identifying characteristics. Gautama knew that in traditional Jain canons, that very name had been applied to the coming next Jina, Mahavira's successor, so to speak; a man who would achieve enlightenment sometime, somewhere, when the present *kaliyuga*, or age of vice, had subsided. Some Jains versed in cosmology figured it would take millions of years. Others reckoned on only another twenty thousand or so. Gautama did not know. He was never very good at science.

CHAPTER SEVEN

Redemption

A cynical lawyer, well-trained, Gautama did not expect to have such feelings for a client. Getting up the next morning, he aired this to his wife, Asha, "You know, I have this uncanny feeling that Leonard Rosenbalm and I are going to be close friends for the rest of our lives."

Asha had never heard him speak about a client that way. She went and brought him strong coffee and the morning paper.

"Better drink this," she advised.

Gautama had been up most of the night preparing for the worst case scenario, poring over legal precedents involving nudity. An article in the L.A.Times jumped out at him. "Best Clues Yet for Existence of Black Holes." He read of the new and revolutionary glimpse of the disc at the center of a black hole, seen by NASA's Hubble Space Telescope. The numbers were topsy-turvy. Physics, time and space were upside down inside that hole, whose mass was estimated to be ten million times that of the sun. The information settled in him. He opened the drapes onto the garden which they shared with an adjoining condo. The world seemed slightly different today. Something fundamental had changed in the universe—he could feel it—not only in the galactic cluster of Virgo, forty-five million light years away, but in Los Angeles, as well.

At three o'clock that afternoon, the hearing at the medical center got underway. Present was Leonard, naked, his wife, Doctors Kushner and Rampart, Gautama, and the hospital hearing referee, Henry Poindexter, all clothed.

It seemed to Gautama that Leonard was outnumbered.

Poindexter was aware of the hospital's decision to allow the patient to remain naked but this was the first time he had actually laid eyes on the man and it was clear that he was slightly flummoxed. "Before we commence this proceeding, might I hazard a foregone conclusion. If the patient is deemed suitable to leave these premises, he will not get very far in that . . . condition."

Gautama stepped forward quickly, "I am Indrabhuti Gautama, Mr. Rosenbalm's attorney. I would like to point out that the matter of my client's nudity is one that enters into a legal realm outside what I understand to be the narrow focus of this hearing. It should be taken up at a later time, and in a more appropriate setting. Thank you." He sat down.

Poindexter continued. "Mr. Gautama, your client's nudity is what got him taken into custody and brought here to our care in the first place. That and certain alleged comments by the patient suggesting the potential for causing injury to himself. May I remind all those present that this hearing has one goal before it, namely, the determination of Mr. Rosenbalm's soundness of mind. If he is judged to be of such sound mind, and his behavior corrected, I am advised by the DA that any possible charges against him shall be nullified. Doctor Kushner, you have examined the patient?"

"I have. Mr. Rosenbalm is a thoughtful, indeed inspired individual, in my opinion. He expresses himself in a manner which is somewhat mystical and provocative. I don't claim to understand what it is he is trying to say on a spiritual level, but in terms of his ability to articulate what is obviously a deeply-felt passion, he acquits himself well, or, better than the next man. He does not exhibit any conventional forms of psychotic behavior. I have witnessed no paranoia, nor delusional fantasy. Though he does worry excessively about animals and germs and I would ascribe this to some displaced form of anticipatory anxiety. In his short time with us, he has been courteous, alert, interested in others, and socially adept. I am aware of the recent tragedy that has struck his family and feel enormous sympathy for what he must be going through. In short, Mr. Rosenbalm is an intense but totally rational and healthy individual. However, all of that notwithststanding, it is my conclusion that Mr. Rosenbalm should not be permitted to leave this hospital until he has gotten over what should be obvious to everyone. And that is his insistence on wearing no clothes."

Miriam, who sat behind Leonard, felt the first sense of rage in her bones. Gautama turned round and gestured to her that it would be alright. Leonard, meanwhile, gave no evidence that he was upset.

"I should add," the doctor went on, "that Mr. Rosenbalm's nudity is tantamount to a blatant disregard for his own welfare. Medically speaking, his vital signs are normal, though he has refused all but one meal in the last three days, and that was hardly a meal—just some fruit and vegetables. In addition, he has steadfastly rejected any medication that might have relaxed him or eased the burden of his situation."

"Since when is the refusal to take tranquilizers a crime?" Miriam uttered, despairing of the irony.

"Please continue, Doctor," said Poindexter.

"He wouldn't touch his jello, he vomited at the sight of meat, and seems, in my view, to be unwilling to cooperate. It all boils down to this strange obsession with nudity. Inasmuch as it is the responsibility of this facility to ensure that patients not be allowed to harm themselves, I would have serious misgivings about letting him out until such time as he is relieved of this problem. He needs to dress like a human being."

"Doctor Rampart, do you have anything to add?"

"Not really. My brief visits with the patient suggest to my mind that he is simply grieving in an unusual manner. I would like to see him go home. It should be a small matter to convince him to get dressed. Once he's home, he can be as naked as the next man. I believe his wife has brought a fresh set of clothes for her husband."

"Is that correct, Ma'am?"

"Yes, it is," Miriam said.

"I'd like to hear from the patient. Mr. Rosenbalm, we recognize that you have suffered greatly in recent days and want to see you restored to what I understand was a prominent position in the business community. You have a loving wife, a loving daughter, many good friends. I don't know if you have a family dog."

"No," Leonard said, with a slightly peevish grin.

"Well, what can you tell us about the state of your mind at this point? Are you ready to go home?"

Gautama had a migraine headache and this moment only exacerbated it. He knew trouble was coming.

Leonard stood up.

"Please remain seated while you speak," Poindexter said.

Leonard sat down. "Friends, I appreciate your reasonableness. Everything about this hearing reflects a standard of civilization that is encouraging, even edifying on some level. But keep in mind that even as we follow the rules, other creatures are suffering the horrors of manmade hell. Cows at the slaughterhouses, chickens and turkeys on poultry farms. Abused children and their mothers. Last year alone, over one hundred thousand women were raped in this country. In other countries, political dissidents have had their fingernails ripped out and arms hacked off. Animals at the pound are being forcibly put to sleep as we speak. Millions of wretched creatures are trapped in medical laboratories. I am one voice. I can do little to prevent the rest of the world from killing itself. But, I will not allow myself to become either kindling, a pawn, or a party to that agony. Do you understand?"

"Is that some kind of threat, Mr. Rosenbalm?" Poindexter asked, utterly befuddled by this outbreak.

"Not in the least," Leonard said, mildly.

He felt good getting it out. For that mouse, or rat, or whatever it was. For every little thing he'd always noticed along the fringes of the surface roads, squashed and ruined in a final violent moment. For all those quivering seconds of apprehension, a newspaper article, a picture on the news, some mention of a distant agony that seemed invariably to strike Leonard down for a second and leave him feeling not only ashamed to be a member of the human species, but acutely aware of his own vulnerability.

Miriam was astonished. This was not her husband speaking. Not even remotely.

But, with that one speech, Poindexter had already reached the limits of his good graces. "Mr. Rosenbalm, I did not request a sermon. And a hostile and pompous one at that. Save it for a more appropriate pulpit. What I'm asking you is very simple. Are you willing to be an adult, get dressed, and go home, or do you intend to make this difficult for everyone?"

Gautama broke in. "I'd like a word with my client, please."

"Fine, fine! This is no trial, Mr. Gautama. Speak with your client. But, please make it quick." Poindexter was exasperated, looking at his watch. He hoped to beat rush hour traffic leaving downtown.

Miriam leaned forward and took hold of her husband's shoulder with one hand and produced a white box from Neiman Marcus in the other. She whispered, "I got your Rolex fixed and I've brought your favorite jogging clothes. There're fresh logs in the fireplace at home and Benny says we're going to be able to hold on to one of the buildings. And, Leonard, I love you, darling."

Leonard half-turned and vaguely smiled. "Thank you."

Gautama now leaned towards Leonard and, in a confidential voice, essentially reiterated Miriam's inducement. "Jainism advocates empathy, Mr. Rosenbalm. Empathy towards oneself, one's wife and children. May I suggest, at least for purposes of this hearing, you compromise. You're not here to prove anything to anyone. What you do tomorrow is another story. The way I read the situation, the courts can't touch you."

Leonard's agitation did not show. But, Gautama felt it. He had become this man's greatest fan. He wanted Leonard to succeed, though he wasn't sure what that meant, or what was even possible in this day and age, in America, in a big city like Los Angeles. His own confusion reigned. But what carried his reasoning was the order of priorities. Leonard had to get out of the system or the system would devour him.

Leonard quietly stated, "You have crossed the great ocean, Gautama. Why do you halt so near the shore?"

Gautama remembered the very words from childhood. Words spoken by Mahavira himself to his chief disciple, who could not bring himself to take off his clothes, lose himself to absolute clarity, in other words, because of the very love he felt for the venerable ascetic. Love which was appropriate to this world, with its passions and contradictions, not to the next. Gautama could only utter a frazzled, pleading few words, "Please, Leonard."

"What's it going to be, Mr. Rosenbalm?" Henry Poindexter stated. "We don't have the whole day here."

"Please," Gautama repeated one last time. "Don't throw it all away. Not at this stage."

In truth, Leonard was stumped at this crossroads. And, he sought that inward voice which proved to be his master and his guide. While it did not declare itself so brashly, or presume to control his actions, the voice nevertheless emerged, like a template. Leonard envisioned, or saw, Mahavira amidst a sea of great troubles. And, recognized twenty-two particular hardships which, as Mahavira put it, a monk must learn and know, bear and conquer, in order not to be vanquished by them. And they included hunger and thirst, cold and heat, stinging insects and erratic life, abuse and lodgings of all kinds, physical cruelty against oneself and others, the asking for something, the being refused something, the prickling grass on one's naked body, the dirt in one's eyes and mouth and nostrils, even the seemingly good things, like understanding and righteousness and respectful treatment—these, too, were counted as troubles because they had the potential for perpetuating pernicious attachment.

"Tolerate living beings, do not kill them, though they eat your flesh and blood . . . " the voice in him stated. "At one time, he will have no clothes, at another, he will have some; knowing this to be a salutary rule, a wise monk should not complain about it."

Conversely, Leonard also felt the urgings of a dispassionate man; one who would remove the obstructions to right knowledge and right faith in order to be free from hindrance.

At the same time, Leonard sensed that he who endeavours to recognize the vanity of all desires—even the desire for nudity and purity—will arrive at perfect indifference, which in turn will lead to liberation. By ceasing to act, he will obtain inactivity, and thus stifle the accumulation of *karma*.

Without flinching, Leonard at once realized that he had adopted nakedness in vain, if he could not let go of it.

And yet, he had let go of everything else just in order to become that very vacuum which was nudity, the law of his being.

An infinite number of times, these contraries waged philosophical battles in Leonard who had become a child in the world's library; an innocent lost in a labyrinth of ethical disputations and arcana. Whichever way he acted, he was bound to hurt somebody. And since this dialectic had no beginning and no end, he was not sure what to do, or how to stop the double-bind, this voracious illogic, from commandeering his ability to made any decision at all.

All eyes impatiently upon him, Leonard summoned the image of Mahavira, who had become his secret garden, that place of refuge for weary hearts.

At that moment, Leonard concluded that his tolerance in this instance was well-founded. The voice continued, "A pious man shows an island to the beings which are carried away by the flood of *Samsara* and suffers for their deeds. This place of safety has been proclaimed by the Tirthankaras."

Ever the pragmatist, Leonard looked up at Henry Poindexter and in the most agreeable voice stated his resolve to get dressed, at least for the time being.

A mighty sigh of relief went up in that room.

Papers of discharge were signed. Leonard got into his red velour jogging suit and Adida tennis shoes. His socks were white. His sunglasses expensive. Except for the tangle of hair and the unshaven face, he looked his old self.

Everyone in the hospital wished him well. The trio walked to the underground parking lot. There was Miriam's Jaguar parked next to Gautama's Honda. It all seemed to be over. Gautama wished Leonard the best. Miriam opened the door on the passenger side for her husband to get in.

But, that wasn't at all what Leonard Rosenbalm had in mind.

"Miriam, you will always be my college sweetheart. And you, Gautama, I think, my champion. Now, you may say I'm mad—it's been said before—or cruel, dim-witted or stubborn beyond words, but everything is different for me. This universe is different. I am different. I must go on." He was thinking, 'I can't go on.' "I must go on," he repeated.

Gautama's thoughts—those of the lawyer in him, and of his Jain childhood—raced.

"I have to continue on the streets, walking, naked, with nothing. That's just who I've become."

"Leonard, do not try my patience. Not for one more minute. I am a flexible person. But I have a breaking point. This has not been fun for me," Miriam decreed, in a raised and menacing timbre. "You have touched . . . or gone all the way over the deep end. I don't know which. Maybe you ought to stay in the hospital until this aberration is corrected." She looked to Gautama for re-affirmation.

"Miriam, listen to me," Leonard said calmly. "People change."

"You listen to me!" she cried, wrestling with his passive arms. It was a final, desperate act. It pained Gautama to see this. Had it been any other setting, a more poignant and romantic place, an historical place, like the Blarney Stone, or atop the Eiffel Tower, even the north rim of the Grand Canyon. But an underground parking lot in Los Angeles?

"If you're telling me that you prefer the insanity of what you've become, then to hell with you. You deserve whatever it is . . . " and she could not continue. She got in the Jaguar, put the keys in the ignition, hard-faced, and gave her husband five seconds to get in the car.

"I'm counting, Leonard! GET IN THE GODDAMNED CAR! NOW!!!"

Leonard looked to Gautama who neither cowered nor volunteered. "What does the law say about nudity?" Leonard asked.

Gautama had done his homework. He was prepared. "I think you have a better than fifty-fifty shot. There are some surprising loopholes and precedents. I would be honored to take the case, as one Jain to another."

"Go home, Miriam. This is not the end," Leonard resolved with an inadvertent air of ambiguity.

She bore down on Gautama—"You're a real BASTARD, you know that!"—and, to her husband, cried, "And you are a bloody fool! I HATE YOU!" her mascara carried by angry tears. The car squealed away, its burning rubber echoing against the concrete structure.

"Last night," Leonard began, not visibly discomfitured, "I witnessed a man named Mahavira at the moment of his emancipation."

"You WHAT??" asked Gautama, still shaken by Mrs. Rosenbalm's hasty flight.

"Yes. There was a storm. The tree was struck by lightning. He was pummeled by hail, fire, wind, even earthquake. Yet, he was suffused with confidence, because, in truth, there was nothing to doubt. Even when villagers nearby pelted him with insults and threatened him with stones, even when horseflies bit his cheeks, he did not waver. This same man I have been following night after night in my dreams, Gautama. I don't know why Mahavira. Or why me."

Gatauma was feverish. To Jains, Mahavira was all-important, the spiritual vortex of their faith. He was the Christ, the Moses, the Buddha, all rolled into one. Their twenty-fourth, most recent Tirthankara, or Jina, a great soul who lived twenty-five hundred years ago and managed to mould the oldest religion in the world. To be in touch with that man, as Leonard was professing . . . it was like some ecstatic blasphemy!

Leonard continued, "I only know that this phantom has imparted purpose to my life. I cannot stop now, just because my wife yells at me, or because the law, and the times in which I find myself, make it especially difficult to go on. Do you know what I'm talking about?"

"Of course I do. Not in the least. That is to say, entirely!" He smiled.

So did Leonard.

Gautama was terrified, jazzed, carried away by his own association with such self-importance, yet selfless at the same instant. It was the first time in his career of over a decade that he felt his entire life, even his next life, hanging in the balance. The sensation was incredible. The reality, daunting.

"They'll arrest you again. Revolving doors. I might get the case remanded to a superior court, maybe even the California, or U.S. Supreme Court. It could take months, years, to get on the court calendar. In the meantime, what will you do? Wait in a hospital, or in jail? We'd have to petition for solitary confinement to prevent your being sexually molested, to put it mildly." Gautama was thinking out loud. In his mind, he'd already considered the options.

"There is only one possibility," he then sparked. "Maybe I can work a deal with the City Attorney's office. They're going to fight to keep you off the streets. I'm not sure if it's a City violation, or a State violation, or both. It's unheard of, what you're proposing, Leonard. But I think I have ample ammunition to keep you *on* the streets, to make legal history in this country. It'll be up to a Judge in a closed session. If he agrees he can issue a gag order against the police to leave you alone. But Leonard, if he does, if we succeed in this, where is that going to leave you, practically speaking?"

"What do you mean?"

"I'm your strongest supporter. But, I'm not blind. You know downtown better than I do. This is not rural India. Even if the police are told to stay away, what about the people down here?"

"People are people, in all times, in all places."

"Where will you sleep?"

"In graveyards, in deserted houses, beneath a tree, in solitude, in a pure place. On gravel turn-outs. Along railroad tracks and river banks. In parks, in shelters for wayfarers, pilgrims, and the homeless. In vacant lots and atop hills, in mountain caves and potter's workshops; in a shed of straw or traveller's hall. Know that the unwise sleep, the sages always wake."

"Great. And what will you eat?"

"I shall fast, I shall beg. I shall drink dish-water, or water in which barley has been washed. And the food which is given to me shall be pure food, or I shall not touch it. Food derived from plants of no more than one sense."

"Such as?"

"Barley-pap, cold sour gruel, wheat, and sesame. Gram. Panic and leguminous seeds. Sugar cane and cucumber. Radishes and bread-fruit. Grapes and wood-apple. Citron and tinduka."

"What is that?"

"Why the fruit of the ebony tree, of course."

"Leonard, get serious, you're not going to find tinduka or panic seeds in the homeless shelters. And what about the cold weather? You're embarking in winter."

"I will be warmed by my inner discipline. Not minding heat and cold, free of sensation, I will examine and know only the happiness of the living."

Gautama was flustered. He knew that Leonard was somehow quoting, or paraphrasing the sutras, whose cadenzas and verse he had grown up with. In a morning puja they were appropriate. Now, taken to the level of action, such passages were terrifying.

"If you get pneumonia it's all over. They'll cover you with blankets. Will you take drugs, derived from animals? Antibiotics? Will you be driven in an ambulance which, of necessity, kills insects under its tires? Will you renounce your health? I'll tell you what could happen: the courts might decide that you are incapable of fending for yourself if you get sick. They will force-feed you. It is illegal to commit suicide, Leonard. And that will be the end of your grand gesture. Purgatory."

"There is no end of it," Leonard said, calmly. "I am not afraid. I have a message, for as long as it lasts. I . . . I just don't know any other way."

"OK. You're walking into a personal hell, Leonard." Gautama felt badly saying that, but Leonard seemed so helpless, so terribly innocent

for one who had survived a cutthroat business and (once) drove a
Bentley. And yet, it was really Gautama who was the innocent one, help-
less and afraid, wracked by duelling wants, torn by his fascination for
Leonard Rosenbalm, who rekindled twenty-five hundred years of
Gautama's own ancestry.

Leonard paused, considering his thoughts. Then, "he who knows
hell knows pain; he who knows pain knows birth and death; he who has
experienced birth and death knows all animal existence; he who knows
the animals knows himself; he who knows himself has found paradise."

"You're really going to do this?"

"I've already begun."

Leonard took off his jogging suit, folded it neatly, and handed it to
Gautama.

"I thank you in advance," he said, before heading out towards the
street, naked, so as to continue his journey East.

Gautama drove alongside at three miles an hour with his parking
brakes flashing to avoid being rear-ended. He was trying to get his
thoughts together. This was not an easy situation. Leonard was in a
trance. Gautama felt sorry for him. Yet, he envied his pure aspirations—
impossible, quixotic, misplaced. Or maybe not? Maybe they were central
to the future. Gautama deep down knew that Leonard Rosenbalm was a
hero setting out to ford the stream, to conquer reality the way a bird conquers gravity. His heart had become his monastery. He seemed all but
immune to the torture he was about to invite upon himself.

In truth, Gautama realized that he was this man's disciple.

Leonard paralleled the freeway. It was that hour of twilight when
nothing is truly visible. Headlights are brighter, noises more blaring, traffic thicker, the wind colder, reality harsher, certainly in downtown Los
Angeles. Smoke was spewn from the congestion above. Traffic ground
bumper to bumper across ten lanes. It was a grey November evening.
Pieces of dust and paper inundated the air, blown hither by millions of
Los Angelinos anxious to get home after a day of work.

Within minutes the real saga began as Gautama watched a patrol
car in the opposite lane convulse into a hundred and eighty degree skid,
siren blazing. Gautama slipped back and observed two officers approach,
handcuff and arrest Leonard on charges of indecent exposure and creating a public nuisance.

In the near darkness, they were taking no chances. Their guns were
raised and they adroitly pushed Leonard face down on the pavement
before reading him his rights. Gautama noted all the circumstances care-

fully. The city's district Attorney would have to determine whether this repeat offence constituted a verifiable misdemeanor; whether Leonard had offended anybody. Was there a victim? It was clear to Gautama that there was not. But, Gautama would have to prevent Leonard's case—Leonard himself—from being catapulted into the judicial system.

At that moment, Gautama stepped forward and explained who he was and what the situation was all about. He pointed out that this man was a religious mendicant exercising his First Amendment rights, namely, freedom of religion.

The cops were not amused. They'd been on their way back to the station to call it a day. Leonard's arrest meant overtime which neither especially looked forward to.

"Follow us back to the station," they told Gautama, curtly.

As Gautama drove, he called his wife, Asha, and explained why he'd not be home for dinner.

"You're both crazy," she said, about as unamused as the cops.

"You again?" the chief said, down in the mental evaluation unit. "And, who are you?" he asked Gautama.

"I'm Mr. Rosenbalm's lawyer."

"Is this some sort of joke? You're deliberately screwing around with the system, aren't you?"

Gautama explained the situation. There could be no bail because they were not about to let Leonard leave without his clothes. Not this time. And now there were actual charges filed against him.

Gautama advised his client to meditate, or take a vow of silence, or whatever he wanted to call it. Just not to talk. He did not want him leaving any evidence that might be used against a First Amendment case. And that's exactly what Leonard did, or didn't. The City Attorney's office was essentially closed down for the night. Leonard was led away to a private cell where he sat for hours in a state of deep samayika . . . *Equanimity towards all beings; self-control and pure aspirations; abandonment of every thought which is tainted by desire or aversion* . . . his mind sang. For Leonard, the cell was deliverance. Every person he'd passed along the way, every catcall from other prisoners, hands reaching out between bars to tease him, or reach towards his genitals, the officers who frisked his naked body and took his fingerprints, the guards and wardens and everyone else all seemed to him to be creatures in pain, creatures struggling with themselves. And this place was the microcosm, like Earth herself. No beginning, no end. The concrete floor was made of stellar atoms. The bars were the metallic condensate of physical forces billions of years old; *pudgala, samghata, bheda, paramanu, loka-akasa,* words that resounded in his mind, against his fingertips, in distant recesses of cognition. Matter, aggregation, disjunction, the elements, all floating in space-point dimension. What did it mean? What could these strange words, this primeval science possibly mean to Leonard Rosenbalm, who sat in Gandhian bliss within his jail cell on a Thursday night, two weeks before Thanksgiving, not two miles away from where he and his father had worked for two decades buying and selling schmata? While his former partner, Hal Spendetti, sat in his hospital room watching CNN and taking treatment for two ulcers that had gotten ugly in the aftermath of his financial loss? While Miriam Rosenbalm went systematically through Leonard's things at home, packing them up or tossing them. She was finished.

To Leonard, this was the first intimation that he could handle it. He had transformed a cloud of unknowing into purpose. His dreams were manifesting reason. The phantom, Mahavira, was materializing.

At ten o'clock the next morning, Leonard was roused from his contemplation by a guard.

"Emperor Rosenbalm, get your butt up. You got a visitor."

Leonard was escorted to a reception room where Gautama was waiting.

"Good morning. You alright?"

"Wonderful!" Leonard exclaimed. "I wouldn't have missed it for the world."

"Here's the deal," Gautama began. "I've spoken with Jack Winston, the District Attorney. I think he understands we mean business here. The good news is I was able to swing a session with the judge tomorrow afternoon at one-thirty, an *in camera* proceeding, as it's called. Highly unusual. Normally, the DA and a lawyer make their deal in advance and tell it to a judge at the bond hearing in court. But given the nudity issue, and religion issue, I was able to obtain this special meeting. I can't guarantee anything. She'll have had a long lunch and should be feeling good. Winston's staff is going to have to hustle to catch up. He wanted to wait until after Thanksgiving."

"You say the judge is a woman?"

"That's the bad news. Judge Newcomb is a sixty-year old conservative with three granddaughters, one of whom was raped several years ago. It was big news. I should add, she is *very* conservative. While it should bear absolutely no relevance to your case, I'm worried about your being nude in her chambers. It was either go with her or wait, possibly months, to get a more liberal judge. That was Winston's own trump card. I can't see you waiting months, Leonard."

Gautama half hoped that Leonard would relent and wear at least his jogging suit to the closed session. But, he also knew that this would, in its own way, invalidate the case. There was only one choice.

"You going to be alright tonight?"

"I'm fine, Gautama. You just do your homework and I'll pray for both of us."

The next day, Leonard was taken in his birthday suit by police van —bars separating Leonard from the two policemen up front—to the municipal courthouse a few blocks away. There, he was led up a service elevator to Judge Newcomb's private chambers.

On hand to meet him was the judge, Gautama, District Attorney Jack Winston and two law clerks from Winston's office, Blithe Harrisburg and Fred LeRusso. One of the two police officers remained outside the door for protection. The chambers were neatly crowded with impressive volumes of West's Penal Code Cases for the State of California. The judge wore black robes and sat at one end of a long oval table, suitable for a dozen people. Winston's associates carried large briefcases which spilled out onto the floor and each had small laptop computer plugged in, humming, ready to scan a hundred volumes-worth of data from the West's case summaries.

Gautama, also, had his own portable power pack. He turned it on and inserted a disc.

Now everyone was armed, except for naked Leonard who was introduced and seated at the far end of the table.

"I will confess that this is a first for me," Judge Newcomb said, gravity clawing at her voice. "There'd better be a damned good explanation. The burden is upon you, Mr. Gautama," she said. "Your client has now twice been picked up for indecent exposure and for causing a public nuisance. The law, and I'm of course referring to California Penal Code Section three fourteen, is very specific in these matters. I don't mean to pre-judge this session, but I think you're going to have to come up with something rather original if it's your intention to have the court system of Los Angeles arbitrarily waive criminal prosecution."

"More than that, your honor, I want you to grant my client the right to continue to walk naked in public places."

"When the DA mentioned that, I thought he was joking. Now I see he was not. I'll tell you right now, I think you're as crazy as your client coming in here and trying to make a deal with a judge. That happens to be illegal, Mr. Gautama. You could be disbarred."

"I'm not talking about any deals, your honor. I'm trying to draw your attention, and that of Mr. Winston, to what I consider to be a unique situation."

"Public nudity is against the law for reasons that scarcely need repeating. And, frankly—I shouldn't bring this into it, but I will—as a God-fearing Christian, I can't imagine an argument that's going to alter my point of view. I have some strong feelings about this, I don't mind telling you."

"I appreciate that, your honor," Gautama vowed.

She looked at Leonard and shook her head. "Frankly, this whole thing is embarrassing. I'm sure Miss Harrisburg feels the same way."

"I do, your honor," she said, not daring to cast her eyes towards Leonard.

"Why don't we start by examining Jack's summary of evidence, any precedents you care to summon to our attention, and what your office would like to see happen next. Then we'll hear from Mr. Gautama. I'm happy to entertain debate and, if necessary, to examine and cross-examine the defendant. Let me remind all of you that I've agreed to this session in hopes of resolving this problem before it can be dragged into one court after another, at taxpayer's expense. Now, may we begin?"

"Thank you, your honor," Jack Winston said. "Mr. Rosenbalm was picked up by two L.A.P.D. officers five days ago. They encountered him walking naked on the sidewalk, speaking to pedestrians at random. One woman, in the presence of her daughter or granddaughter, took offense, hit him with her handbag and called him a pervert. A shopkeeper, male, yelled at him. If the officers had not picked him up when they did, who knows what would have happened. According to their report, he went with them peacefully though refused their offer of a blanket to cover himself. He spoke in a foreign language, according to the patrolmen, which a man of Indian extraction who happened to be passing by was able to translate. The man claimed not to know Mr. Rosenbalm, though we have no proof of that, and he alleged that the defendant had said something to the effect that he was a religious monk and his nudity was part of that. Once in custody, Mr. Rosenbalm was cooperative. During his mental evaluation he indicated suicidal tendencies according to the detective in charge of the unit who interviewed him. He put on a somewhat happier face at the USC Medical Center where he was released after three days of observation. At the hearing it was determined by the medical referee, that Mr. Rosenbalm was grieving over the loss, last week, of his two parents."

"I'm very sorry," the Judge said.

"Thank you," Leonard replied, with a nod.

The DA continued. "Grieving and in shock. But it was felt that he was quickly coming around and his wife was ready to take him home and nurse Mr. Rosenbalm back to the living so that this sorry affair could be put behind him. It should be pointed out, however, that Mr. Rosenbalm insisted on going nude during his entire stay at the hospital, even during the hearing. It was only at the last moment that he agreed to get dressed."

"The staff complied with that?" the judge asked, somewhat astonished.

"Yes, your honor. The Doctors and hospital administrator decided, in his case, this was best. I imagine it was done to facilitate a swifter recovery."

"I'm very surprised," the judge said. "I imagine there were complications that resulted from this, in terms of the other patients?"

"Apparently not, your honor," the DA said.

"Go on."

"Mr. Rosenbalm checked out of the hospital. No charges had been filed. Approximately thirty minutes later, he was picked up by two L.A.P.D. officers. He was naked once again. The officers were not aware of Mr. Rosenbalm's history and as they read him his rights, Mr. Gautama—who had been evidently following Mr. Rosenbalm in his own car—identified himself, and followed the officers down to the station. It was the next morning, yesterday, that my office was reached by Mr. Gautama and he informed us that he wanted immediate arbitration to solve this problem, inasmuch as, according to him, his client's rights were being violated under First Amendment freedom of religion and that, given the unique nature of his client's form of religious expression, namely nakedness, any delay in legal response would pose mental agony to the defendant. Those are the facts as we know them to this point, your honor."

"Thank you, Jack. And what is it Mr. Gautama has asked of your office?"

"Just as Mr. Gautama stated a moment ago. That Mr. Rosenbalm be allowed to continue to live as a homeless person, naked, within the city of Los Angeles."

"Just so I'm absolutely clear about this—he's asking for this exception to the law on First Amendment grounds?"

"Correct, your honor."

"Is that correct, Mr. Gautama?"

"Yes, your honor."

She contemplated the proceedings thus far and shook her head with some degree of incredulity. "We've had our share of sun-bathers—worshippers of the sun, I should say, of prostitutes who tried to make a case that their profession constituted the deepest form of religious experience, of nudist colonies that continue to legally operate essentially uncurtailed on grounds of right to privacy. Same with strippers in nightclubs. But, to my knowledge, this is the first time a case has arisen where nudity itself was alleged to be fundamental to a religion. What religion does your client call this, Mr. Gautama?"

"It's known as Jainism, your honor. I, too, am a Jain."

The judge's brows widened. "But, you're certainly well-dressed?"

"There are major distinctions within the religion, your honor which I shall, in good time, clarify."

"This—how do you call it?"

"Jainism." Gautama spelled the word out.

"This Jainism, I believe I might have heard of it. It's an Indian thing, right?"

"Your honor, if you please, this 'thing' as you call it is among the oldest religions in the world. Traditionally, Jains come from India. But, there are some people from other countries who have become Jains. Currently in the United States there are approximately forty thousand Jains."

"How many Jains are there worldwide?"

"Somewhere between seven and ten million."

"There are Government surveys that will attest to that?"

"Government of India census records, your honor."

"I'll take your word for it," she said.

"Mr. Gautama, we'll get back to Jainism. But first, I want to know what the DA recommends from its own vantage. Jack?"

"The City is willing to drop the felony charge of indecent exposure and the misdemeanor of creating a public nuisance if Mr. Rosenbalm will agree to undertake one hundred days of psychiatric observation and counseling. I've checked with our friends at Atascadero and they do have room. If Mr. Rosenbalm resists this recommendation, we would have no option but to prosecute aggressively under the full latitude of the law."

"Why don't you spell that out for Mr. Rosenbalm's attorney."

"One year maximum sentence in a state prison for indecent exposure, three months for causing a public nuisance. A total of fifteen months without possibility of probation. The law is very clear. I should add that every offense consitututes a doubling of that jail sentence. With respect to a public nuisance, every day counts as another offense."

"Thank you, Jack. Your turn, Mr. Gautama. Get to the point."

"Your honor, firstly, I should like to draw your attention to a 1971 Superior Court of Cleveland judgement in which a Jain conscientious objector was granted immunity to the draft on the basis of his religion, which the judge, in that case, agreed made it incapable for its adherents to kill. I submit a xerox of the details of that case herewith."

"So nudity is not the only principle of this religion?"

"Correct, though the two are related, as I will show. But, I mention this case for obvious reasons. The judicial system in this country has already recognized Jainism as a distinct religion important enough to warrant at least one special exemption."

"Duly noted. Continue."

"But, even if my client were not a Jain, strictly speaking, nudity in the city of Los Angeles, or for that matter in nearly every other city in the United States and Europe, is not, of and by itself, illegal. Mr. Winston and his staff know that."

"That's news to me," the judge said. "Jack?"

Winston knew this was coming. "To be honest with you, your honor, I must confess that this came as something of a surprise to my office, as well. Mr. Gautama is correct, in the letter of the law. It is not illegal to be naked in the city, except on a public beach. The code was written to encompass such situations as, say, running naked from a burning house, or if someone stole your clothes."

"Your honor, it is precisely for that reason that the Penal Code under question, number three fourteen, defines lewd and indecent exposure as sexually motivated conduct, or a desire for some other explicit purpose to direct the public's attention to one's genitals. Public nudity not so motivated—which is precisely the case of my client—has been sanctioned by the law, as in Savery versus Donaldson and the People versus Bradford."

Gautama gave his colleagues time to call up those opinions on their own computers and study them.

"I would also submit a case from twenty years ago in which even sunbathing in the nude on an isolated beach was not construed as indecent exposure given the fact there was nobody else on the beach and thus the defendant in that instance could have had no sexually motivated intention with respect to said public."

"Your honor, this is academic. We're talking about downtown Los Angeles," the DA stated, firmly.

"I quite agree. Mr. Gautama, please stay to the task at hand."

"Your honor, a conviction under Penal Code three fourteen places the burden of proof that the defendent willfully and lewdly exposed himself for sexual purposes upon the State. All that Mr. Winston has is a naked man in public. The officers observed no provocative behavior and have said so. Nor have any witnesses come forward to file a complaint of any kind. Furthermore, I will prove, beyond a reasonable doubt, that sex is the last thing my client has on his mind."

Gautama assumed that was true. He realized that he hadn't actually discussed the matter with Leonard and if the DA were of a mind to, he could probably establish that Leonard and his wife had made love within the past month. He pushed forward on blind faith. "Quite to the contrary, Mr. Rosenbalm has become a celibate, renouncing sex entirely."

"Wandering around in his birthday suit is one hell of a way to prove it," the DA said, mocking the seemingly flawed logic.

"Go on," the judge stated. Her level of respect for Mr. Gautama had risen one notch.

"Furthermore, your honor, with regard to the public nuisance offense, we all know how difficult that is to prove. When was the last time you actually saw a nuisance case filed?"

"That's not the point," the judge hastened.

"Considering the law was enacted in 1872, I think it is relevant. More so is the fact that a public nuisance, defined under Title ten, number three hundred seventy, stipulates that the prosecution must prove actual injury to the public's health."

Mr. LeRusso broke in, "You've left out that a public nuisance unlawfully obstructs the free passage or use, in the customary manner, of any public place, and that includes a street. Mr. Rosenbalm was clearly creating an obstacle on the sidewalk."

"Excuse me. There was no such indication in the report of the arresting officers."

"It can be assumed," stated LeRusso. "Furthermore, a public nuisance is also defined as one who is offensive to the senses."

"I'm sure Mr. Winston is aware that what is offensive to one, is not to another. And I would draw your attention to the People versus Findley, nineteen seventy-six. That was a case involving a prominent billboard that displayed a naked body which the prosecution deemed offensive. But offensive to whom? John Q. Public? The state of California did not agree, ruling that the terms 'public morals or decency' were unconstitutionally vague."

Miss Harrisburg was typing on her computer as fast as Mr. Gautama was speaking. She got into her computer window, called up a second, conflicting case, and spoke out. "Your honor, that same year the courts ruled in the People versus Martinez that lewd, dissolute and obscene were all consitutionally sufficient and synonymous terms."

"You're straying from the focus of this discussion," Gautama struck back. "In the People versus Nelson, nineteen seventy-nine, once again it was determined there must be specific intent to create sexual arousal in those persons observing the defendent. The court, in that case, stated emphatically that the element of sexual intent had to be there. Merely offending their sensibilities or even troubling their deepest moral conscience was insufficient. In the case of Riley versus the U.S., both willfulness and lewdness had to be proved by the prosecution. According to the very definition of those terms, handed down by the California Supreme Court, there is absolutely no evidence whatsoever to suggest that Mr. Rosenbalm either set out to offend, or did, in effect, offend, anyone."

"Mr. Winston?" The judge looked to the DA for a rebuttal.

Mr. Winston whispered something to Miss Harrisburg.

"This is not a courtroom, Jack. Whatever you have to say, I'm sure, is of interest to all of us," the judge went on.

Leonard sat gazing upon these proceedings with indifference. He suffered no hope, endured no doubts. The outcome had already been ordained.

"I am not going to argue about the sufficiency, or insufficiency of terms that have long been understood by every one of us, by the lawmakers, and by the public. Mr. Gautama knows as well as anybody that you can cite cases until kingdom come to justify or oppose a law or point of view. That's what we all did for two years in law school. It is the consensus opinion that finally matters. And, in the case of indecent exposure and obscene behavior, all that's necessary for the determination of wrongdoing is the most basic appeal to prurient interest or general offensiveness in the face of contemporary community standards. There are limits of candor, there are fair standards and practices, there are such things as redeeming social value. A naked adult male flaunting his penis in public, strutting unconcerned before young girls, and old women, and

little boys—I don't care what the motive—is, in essence, spitting in the
face of civilization and my office will not be a party to it."

"This is not an election year, Jack," the judge reminded him.

But, the DA was determined. Gautama was not clear what his
motives were in presenting so adversarial a point of view. Maybe he was
trying to prove something—a macho thing—to Miss Harrisburg. As for
Leonard, he could not have looked more benign, sitting there in an almost
bewildered inward state, a melancholy—Gautama thought—that belied
an otherwise radiant, sterling temperament.

"Look, your honor," the DA continued, "does this—this exhibitionist under any other name—promote the general corruption of morals?
That is the question. And, the answer must be an overwhelming, 'Yes.'
Does it exceed the limits of customary candor? Absolutely. Would you
want your own children bumping into this man on the street? I think not.
Are there any contemporary standards that would validate such morally
repugnant behavior? None that I can imagine."

"Mr. Gautama?"

"Your honor, the whole point of my citing past cases is not to dem-
onstrate that I have done my homework. It is to remind those present that
the law has already spoken to these issues. We are not groping in the dark
here, or exploring altogether new territory. There is ample precedent in
the State of California for reaching a fair decision under the law regarding my client's right to express his religious beliefs."

"Mr. Gautama, how long have you been in this country?"

"Eleven years, your honor."

"I presume you have read the U.S. Constitution?"

"Your honor may not be aware of the fact I have written two books
on the U.S. Constitution."

Judge Newcomb coughed into a handkerchief. "I was unaware of
that. But since we have an apparent expert here, I'm sure you are the last
person I need to remind that the constitution guarantees its citizens the
right to believe and to think and to feel whatever they darn well please.
But with regard to the actual expression in public of those beliefs and
feelings, the law comes down hard. And, well it should, or we'd have
Neo-Nazis fire-bombing synagogues under protection of the First
Amendment. Smitten versus the U.S., eighteen seventy-eight. Celebrated
case. Polygamy deemed illegal. The First Amendment protects religious
liberty, but not immoral acts, Mr. Gautama. That was the outcome and it
hasn't changed. In this State, if conduct is considered obscene under Sec-

tion three eleven of the Penal Code in question, then there is no First Amendment protection. Are you aware of that?"

"Your honor, I am. But I am also quite familiar with the fact that the Federal court will interfere with State criminal prosecution if the statute upon which that prosecution relies can be shown to be a bad faith enforcement, or have what is termed a chilling effect on the exercise of a defendent's First Amendment rights, with no adequate remedy in sight."

"And you are sure that your client's behavior falls under his First Amendment rights?"

"Absolutely, your honor."

"It's not credible," Miss Harrisburg averred.

"Pathetic's the word," LeRusso seconded.

"Look, I think I have already indicated that my client had no obvious or implicit sexual motivation for his behavior."

"You haven't proved that," retorted LeRusso. "Let me just remind you of the most important case ever judged along these lines in this country. I'm referring to Justice Douglas's dissention in Mankewitz versus the U.S., in which he stated emphatically that the First Amendment does not—I repeat, does not—go so far as to permit nudity in public places. End of story. If we're going to argue cases, that should provide all the precedent needed to come to a sober conclusion in this matter."

Gautama was shaking his head.

"What? What?" LeRusso testily invited.

"I am familiar with that case," Gautama said. "Douglas was only referring to sexual misconduct. Once again you are making an erroneous presupposition that my client had a sexual intention. He did not. And in addition, I could cite Thurgood Marshall who acknowledged that the notion of 'sexual misconduct,' and the term 'sexual promiscuity' were examples of loose and flawed ascriptions, unacceptable under the law. Even if they were not flawed, Justice Brennan reversed an obscenity charge in Van Der Meer versus Illinois—remember that one?—by stating that 'patent offensiveness' was negated if any redeeming social value could be shown. I can show it."

"Then do so," the judge stated. "We don't have all day."

"In India, the contemporary standard allows for monks, like Leonard Rosenbalm, to walk naked. People actually revere such figures."

The DA rolled his eyeballs. "Mr. Gautama's native homeland is not relevant here, your honor. He is diverting us from the task at hand."

"How many such men, or monks, are there in India who walk naked?" the judge asked.

"But your honor, this man is no monk and this is not India!" the DA applied, barely able to control his frustration.

"I'm just curious," the judge went on.

"Among the Jains, fifty-six, your honor, as of this time. They are called Digambaras and their tradition dates back at least five thousand years. It is known, for example, that Alexander the Great confronted a naked Jain monk during his attempted conquest of Asia. The monk persuaded the young Alexander to take off his own clothes, to sit in the dust naked with him and quiet his heart. Alexander was apparently so moved, so humbled by the experience, he quit his expedition to the East, and brought his troops back home to Greece. The history books would have been entirely different, if not for a naked Jain monk. I can provide you a bibliography of several hundred scholarly books, encyclopedias, and articles by many of the world's leading historians and theologians, all of whom refer to these naked ascetics."

"Oh, for God's sake, we're talking about a Jewish jobber in the garment business," Winston railed. "He's no more a monk, or a historian, or whatever the hell his lawyer would try to have us believe, than I am! We know about Mr. Rosenbalm. We want to protect Mr. Rosenbalm. And, we want to protect the public. The American public. Whatever they do in India is their business. If he's so enamored of a Third World country, that's fine. Let's help expedite his emigration papers."

Gautama stayed utterly cool. "Your honor, in nineteen seventy-four in Briant versus the U.S.—an obscenity case tried in Federal District Court—it was determined that the jurors could admit evidence of contemporary community standards existing in a region or country far away from the particular district in question. Precisely to avoid any personal or regional biases, racism, sensitivities, insensitivities or opinions on the part of the jurors. A year later, in the U.S. versus Dudley, once again outside community evidence was deemed admissible. If my client had desired to move to India, he would have done so. But, America is his home."

"Sustained. Go on," Judge Newcomb said.

"Hindu law, the law of India, recognizes the practice of naked monks. The Government of India recently supported a cultural program for celebrating the twenty-five hundredth anniversary of Mahavira, the most recent and revered of the historical Jain holy men. He was a contemporary of Buddha and spent the latter part of his life wandering through India, naked. Part of that cultural program included the prominent display on public monuments of various images of the naked Mahavira. Such blatant displays of male genitalia in public were not considered in contradiction with India's many obscenity laws because community standards in that country recognize that Jain monks constitute a national, even a world, heritage of extreme importance. My client is such a monk—in spite of what Mr. Winston would have you think—and the significance of his being allowed to perpetuate an ancient religious practice is of utmost importance. The fact that he has chosen to do it in this country should be viewed, in my opinion, as a real plus; something the city can be proud of and rally behind."

"He's grasping for straws, in my opinion," the DA advised. "Furthermore, it's obvious that these naked people have had no impact whatsoever on curbing the horrible outbreaks of violence which continue to plague India." Everyone in the room was aware that even as they spoke, Moslems and Hindus were battling each other throughout India.

"Why must the monks go naked," the Judge asked, her interest clearly perked.

"Your honor might recall that Christ and Saint Francis both went naked at times."

"They did?"

"According to everything I've read, your honor. In fact, Saint Francis actually took off all his clothing, renounced his family, all of his possessions in a Church before an image of Christ. But, he was actually following a much older Christian tradition. Many of the Desert Fathers in the Sinai Peninsula went naked. But this tradition was actually begun in India by the Jain monks thousands of years ago. Such renunciation is the expression of a religious conviction which holds that mankind's existence should be pure and simple, unfettered by the vanity and illusion of material possessions. Once stripped bare of these things, the Jains believe that a human being is in a better state of mind to concentrate on the salvation of his soul."

"And, what does that mean?" the judge asked.

"It means different things to different people. But, I suppose you could summarize it by saying that such salvation refers to enlightenment, here on Earth. To be enlightened is to become truly merciful, compassionate, caring for all other creatures. To go beyond the mere trials and tribulations of physical evolution. To become spiritual. To help one's neighbor. To cherish all life forms. Jains are devout vegetarians and nudity represents an honest man's attempt to rid himself of possessions and to become, in essence, as pure as an animal. Symbolically, it is very important. And, it is not an easy thing to do, as you can imagine. Harder in our times than in any other. In fact, I would think it one of the most difficult things to do. How much easier for Mr. Rosenbalm to simply put on his clothes and go home. That he has demonstrated the courage to resist that easy temptation is a remarkable triumph that few could equal."

"Mr. Gautama, I appreciate your explanation. But, I fail to see why it is necessary for Mr. Rosenbalm to be naked at all times, and in public. The State has no problem with him maintaining this nude condition in his home, even in a private shrine or monastery, or even on a trail in the State wilderness areas. Nobody's going to complain. Why downtown Los Angeles where he's just asking for trouble, not just from us, but from the citizenry? I don't get it."

"Your honor, you should ask Mr. Rosenbalm that question."

All eyes turned towards the naked man.

Leonard's impulse was to stand but Gautama motioned him to remain seated.

"Downtown is where I am, where I have been. Eventually, I plan to travel across the United States," Leonard said, plainly.

"Naked?"

"Yes."

"They'll arrest you everywhere you go, if the local rednecks don't tar and feather you, first. I'm simply advising you of that as one who appreciates the dilemma you must be in," the judge said. Gautama sensed she was turning around. Leonard knew she was.

"Ma'am," continued Leonard, "the city is turned round in a whirl of pain, if you ask me. Between six p.m. yesterday and six a.m. tomorrow there will have been a spate of human murders in this city. Drive-by shootings, gang member confrontations, one Hector, blue eyes, found shot to death along an off-ramp. One Edward and his daughter, both found stabbed to death in a neighbor's backyard. Others shot to death, strangled, multiple gunshot wounds at a gas station on Marengo Street. At East seventy-sixth Place, in Boyle Heights, along South Halldale Avenue, on Yosemite Drive and South Berendo Street, on North Broadway in Lincoln Heights—"

"STOP RIGHT THERE!" the DA cried out in a panic. "Your honor, may I speak with you a minute?"

"Speak."

"In private?"

"Oh alright." She was perplexed and irritated.

Jack Winston whispered in her ear, "There is something very seriously wrong here. Our office only hours ago was notified of the killings he's just referred to. There is NO WAY he could have known about all of them. He's been behind bars!"

"You're saying he's a psychic?"

"I'm not saying anything. I'm only telling you."

The DA went back to his seat.

"Mr. Rosenbalm, any others? Killings, I mean?"

"Yes, your honor, twenty-eight in all."

"And, you know this for a fact? Did you read it in a newspaper or hear it on the radio?"

"I don't know how I know it, but I do."

"And you know the other streets where it will happen?"

"Yes."

"You know the actual people killed?"

"Not personally. Some have not been killed yet."

"This is quite serious, Mr. Rosenbalm. Are you a psychic, as well as being a Jain?"

"Your honor," Gautama broke in, not certain what was happening, or how things had suddenly shifted. "My client is a monk. Monks have visions. He has eaten little since his confinement during the past week. I would only advise you that we were discussing the issue of his nudity, not his alleged powers of prophecy."

Gautama was shaking inside. Leonard was beginning to frighten him, as well.

The DA and his staffers looked bewildered. The judge tapped her finger on the table, mightily puzzled.

"I think Mr. Gautama is right. Let us leave that subject, at least for the time being. I will ask Mr. Winston to take up that matter in his own time."

"Jesus," Winston muttered to his staffers.

"Where was I?" Judge Newcomb said, flustered.

"You were wondering what possible reason I might have, other than ego, to display my wares in a crowded, downtown setting."

The room was gripped by additional discomfort. "Wares" was not exactly the phrase a sober monk would use. Even Gautama was addled. But, the judge was more so. Those were virtually the very words that had been floating in her brain. Her silence was crystalized by her fear. There was no doubt, now, in her mind that this man was not what he appeared to be. She felt compelled to clear the air.

"Mr. Rosenbalm, I don't know who, or what, you are, but I guess you and I both know that those were essentially the words I was thinking to myself. Unless it was an amazing coincidence."

Leonard did not react.

"Well, I don't want to pursue this aspect of your beliefs and convictions because I don't understand it. So we're going to stay to the issue at hand."

Gautama was trembling even harder now. He put his pen away to relieve the problem.

"I am trying, Ma'am," Leonard said.

"I know you are."

"I wrestle with that pain, not just among humans but among all forms of life. I think I can help. I truly believe that what has happened to me was for a reason. I will not speculate on that reason because it would seem unbecoming. But, I can assure you that my nudity is a blessing and will be looked upon by others not as an offense, or something stemming from the ego, or as a confrontation. People will mostly view it as a form of honesty. Some will find me pathetic, some will spit at me, some will be inclined to join me. Whatever transpires, the result, I am quite sure, will be beneficial to the people of Los Angeles and elsewhere. A man need not possess anything in order to be fulfilled. We are humans, but we are animals. Born naked. And, our nudity is what reminds us of our simplicity, our vulnerability, the fact that we—like all organisms—feel pain, and want comfort. No organism wants to suffer. A worm, a mouse, a dog, a mother. All organisms wish to feel happiness. My nudity, and the words which I have to say, will serve as a reminder to myself, and to all those that I meet. A reminder that peace and harmony on Earth are the only solutions to such pain. I can think of no place in this country in greater need of peace and love than downtown Los Angeles."

Leonard looked into her heart and said, "From the ruins of the old, will come a new Earth for the redeemed."

He'd pressed the right button. In Judge Newcomb's mind, this man was beginning to make perilous sense. She, too, was a firm believer in faith and in practice, which included caring for one's body as if it were the very temple of the Holy Spirit. That meant no alcohol, tobacco, flesh of any kind. She also believed in prophecy, as well as other gifts of the Spirit which people possessed. And, her profession allowed her to practice that aspect of prophecy. In keeping with her beliefs, she was also certain that Christ had to be crucified for all of our sins. Leonard, a Jewish Jain, was no Christ. But, he was nevertheless beginning incisively to alter her mind, to remind her of what she herself most cherished. Such transformation gave her skin an added glow, or aura. Leonard could see it.

"You are some idealist," the judge said.

"All Jains are idealists, your honor," stated Gautama.

Miss Harrisburg conferred with Mr. LeRusso, then whispered something to the DA, while calling up something on her computer.

"What is it, Miss Harrisburg?" the judge asked.

"Your honor, this discussion has meandered away from what we consider to be crucial to determining Mr. Rosenbalm's rights, and violations, under the law. We do not dispute his First Amendment guarantees of personal belief. But there are compelling and indisputable precedents which should guide us in recognizing the valid difference between one's beliefs, and one's actions. You already referred to the polygamy ruling of the last century. In countless other cases involving one church or another, it has been handed down that only the freedom to believe is absolute in this country, whereas conduct must remain subject to regulation for the protection of society. This seems basic, to us. We haven't had a whole lot of time to prepare for this, as you know, but I'm staring on the computer at half-a-dozen precedents which are indisputable. I mean as far back as Manfred versus the People of Fairbanks, and Lawson versus the State of Washington it was stated, and re-stated that those activities enjoying *prima facie* protection under the First Amendment did not include nudity in public."

"Exactly," Winston added.

"And that the right to the free exercise of religion was not absolute. Conduct must remain the province of regulation in order to protect society from perverts, extremists, and other dangerous sorts."

"May I?" Jack Winston broke in, speaking as much to Mr. Rosenbalm as to Gautama and the judge. "This is a basic case of competing values. We have to exert a balancing test in which the state's interest is weighed against the severity of the burden imposed on Mr. Rosenbalm's religion. I can think of no better example of this test than that utilized in the Thomas Leery case many years ago."

"You mean the business of marijuana?" Judge Newcomb said.

"That's right. He was indicted for smuggling marijuana from Mexico and claimed it was part of his Hinduism. He'd set up a shrine in his home. He smoked it regularly. He insisted that the smoking of marijuana constituted an important ritual among certain religious sects throughout India. But, the court did not consider that relevant, nor did it concern itself with Mr. Leery's personal opinions or beliefs. It was the judgement of the U.S. Court of Appeals, fifth circuit, that in the interest of the public welfare, and the protection of society, certain laws can and must be enforced even if they may be contrary to a person's religious beliefs. In other words, the freedom to act is conditional and relative, as my assistant has stated. That's all we're saying here. I think the point is fundamental and should be enough to weigh your honor's decision here."

"Mr. Gautama, do you have a response to that?"

Gautama considered what to do. He stared at his computer screen. He looked to Leonard. He had a plan. Finally, he stated it.

"Your honor, I would raise three crucial points here. First, Carrington versus Rhode Island—this dates to nineteen forty. A state statute forbidding the practice of Jehovah's Witnesses canvassing door to door, was deemed invalid because it constituted a censorship of that religion and threatened its very existence. Nearly all of the thirty cases brought before the U.S. Supreme Court, in which the very existence of some religion was allegedly threatened, have been won by the religious defendents in question. The court system has time and again sided with religious freedom. Not just religious belief, but religious action. My client is one of only fifty-six naked Jain monks in the world. As far as I know, he is the *only* one, at this time, in North America. I should point out, in addition, though it is not being tested here, that my client is part Indian. I have traced his family tree and interviewed key individuals who sit on those historical records within India."

Leonard looked up at Gautama. The two men had not discussed Gautama's research with the archivist in Cranganore. Leonard's dark blue eyes seemed to quiver—a tear formed—then became brighter.

"To deny my client his religious freedom of expression, namely, the right to practice naked asceticism as prescribed in the ancient and revered Jain doctrines would be to wipe out the re-birth of an important tradition before it even got started. If ever there were a reason to uphold the First Amendment, it is now. This is an extraordinary case. I can assure you, people will be watching. And regarding nudity, well, Mr. Winston has already agreed to the point—the crucial point—that there is no law prohibiting nudity in public, period. That law was tested in nineteen sixty-seven, in Wayfare versus L.A. County. The result was that a woman was granted the right to go topless in public. She could have gone stark naked, had she wanted to, merely on a whim, as long as she wasn't soliciting sex. My client is not what'd you'd describe as whimsical, or sexually motivated, as I have repeated. He is a *bona fide* monk. He has much to offer society. He asks only to be allowed to be himself. This is a rare opportunity, your honor. He is the only naked Jain monk in America. Please."

The judge looked at Leonard who stared back with a kind of wild and loving surmise. There was contact which for her, Judge Newcomb, was very disturbing. She caught the fire in his look, or felt the allure. She sensed the forlorn, believing it to be weariness, but could not fail to recognize a conviction and a vigor that was all-encompassing. What nobody knew, because she did not advertise it, was the fact that she and her husband were Seventh Day Adventists who attended Church regularly in Loma Linda, a world headquarters. Part of her own beliefs centered around vegetarianism, though one would never suspect it looking at her, because she was large, her size accented by her robes. Her largeness suggested a big meat-eater, but she was not. She was a dainty eater and, as it turned out, any vegetarian was a friend of hers.

Mr. LeRusso pointed out something quietly to Mr. Winston, who immediately ran with the information.

"Your honor," the DA began, trying to short-circuit any turnabout in the Judge, whose mood and expression had visibly changed towards Leonard's position. "We must remind you that as of a week ago, we can provide evidence from several witnesses who will testify that Mr. Rosenbalm was, to all appearances, a merchant working in the garment district, a few miles from here, and systematically pursuing millions of dollars in profit. A WEEK AGO! your honor. That hardly squares with the dramatic claims Mr. Gautama here is making for his client."

"What about it, Mr. Gautama?"

"It is true, your honor, that Leonard Rosenbalm until recently was engaged in the garment business. I can only tell you that his subconscious had to have been evolving even then. Perhaps, he has been ready to come forth for years. It took the death of his parents, his own near demise, the loss of his business, and a series of dreams and revelations to shake Mr. Rosenbalm into the religious expression that has brought us all together today. As a Jain, one raised in a traditional Jain family in India, I can assure you with all the powers of my legal and religious training, that he is more Jain than most Indians. He is an inspiration. And, what is extraordinary is the fact that Mr. Rosenbalm had never even heard of Jainism a week ago."

"Your honor, to me that invalidates his whole case," the DA resolved, seizing the only apparent crack left in an otherwise unmarred argument. "Are we to believe that Mr. Rosenbalm is only now experiencing his profound conversion? That seems terribly convenient for the purposes of eluding criminal prosecution."

"It can happen," the judge herself exclaimed, to everyone's astonishment. She and her husband and all their Seventh Day Adventist friends had plodded through the *Book of Revelations* for months at their Sunday morning Bible readings. She was an expert on the subject of revelation.

"Your honor," Gautama gratefully added, "in Clayborn versus Davis, nineteen eighty-one, it was stated that so long as one's faith was religiously based at the time it was asserted, the free exercise clause is entitled to complete constitutional protection. And I can assure you that this is not an instance where Mr. Rosenbalm will believe one thing today, and another thing tomorrow."

"I hope you're right about that Mr. Gautama, because frankly, I'm very anxious to know how things turn out. I wish you well, Mr. Rosenbalm."

Leonard stood up and bowed before her, solemn and serene.

"But your honor!" Jack Winston burst out.

"Mr. Gautama, you're a fine lawyer. Mr. Winston, this was unusual. I would not have expected it. Please be sure to convey my judgement to the proper authorities over at the L.A.P.D.. Mr. Rosenbalm is to be left alone. Indeed, if his lawyer should request it, I would like police protection for Mr. Rosenbalm. Do you understand?"

"Yes, your honor," he uttered, deflated totally. Gautama was not sure why the DA had pursued this so vehemently. He clearly had his own motives.

"May I say something?" Miss Harrisburg went on.

"Yes?"

"The U.S. versus O'Henry, nineteen seventy. One religious group cannot be favored over another."

"Forget it," Judge Newcomb said with a feminine finality that nobody in that room would have predicted, save perhaps Leonard. "This case is closed. I did not think it possible but I have come to the conclusion that the U.S. Constitution was invented for people like Leonard Rosenbalm. A lover of freedom. Of the naked truth." And looking to the acquitted, "You're my kind of man," she declared. "God bless you."

CHAPTER EIGHT

The Sermon of the Leaves

When Leonard left City Hall downtown, he had no idea where he would go, what he would do, how, exactly, he would survive. Yet, everything had thus far transpired naturally, with little or no consternation. In a very real sense, he had surrendered to forces around him, inside him, as if a great comedy had elicited his uninhibited laughter, a tragedy his sorrow, a memory of past lives—his own tribute.

He passed through the revolving door, between two well-dressed bureaucrats who had spent their lives trying to get somewhere. Did they even know where? He emerged onto the street, looked both ways, and headed in the direction of nearest darkness, the East. His head was aching, his body fatigued. Gautama was nearby, wanting to protect his client, wanting so much to be a new man himself.

"You needn't worry about me, Gautama. You've already earned your dinner for this day. Go home to your wife," Leonard said with a grin.

Gautama called Asha on his little Fujitsu mobile phone and had what Leonard perceived to be a brief and private argument. Gautama, bearing up with no sign of such altercation, put the phone in the pocket of his tweed jacket and said with manly confidence, "It's all taken care of."

Before them was the universe of skid row, compass readings that might resonate poetically in some other, literary context—avenues like Ceres, San Pedro and San Julian, Maple and Omar, and the first seven streets of the city. They strode past, and were ignored by, a huddle of out-of-work Guatemalans playing their version of Church-farthing and shuffle-cap against a brick wall littered with leaflets which read, "Long Dong Condoms." They continued up a sidewalk that was emptying quickly of pedestrians, as if night signalled a curfew. A patrol car drifted by, slowed down, then came to a stop. The patrolman on the passenger side rolled down his window and asked, "Are you Leonard Rosenbalm?"

"Yes, Sir," replied Leonard.

"Have a good night," the cop said, staring in wonderment at the naked man as his vehicle drove off.

"You need to find a shelter," Gautama urged him, feeling the bite of a cold evening.

"It's a starry night," Leonard reminded him, apparently oblivious to a temperature that had already dropped below fifty degrees.

They came upon an old woman, or she looked old, seated amidst a little peak of cans. Her sanity seemed to hinge upon the shopping cart against which she leaned. She bit down on a security blanket held in place by her left thumb. Part of the thumb itself looked like it had been chewed. Her bowled legs were sprawled before her, jutting out at the knees from a torn skirt, revealing open chancres and enflamed calves. The sidewalk was wet around her. Gautama noticed herpes blisters on her face. One eye was nearly shut and blue. Her breath was raspy.

To Gautama's horror—though he should not have been surprised— Leonard chose to sit down beside her. He at once struck up a conversation, such as it was, borrowed Gautama's coat (Gautama kept the phone) and covered the woman's exposed legs with it.

As Leonard spoke with her, his right hand drifted towards the back of her head and he slowly began to stroke her caked and breaking hair.

"Ruth," he said, before she'd even told him her name, "look at the stars . . . "

The very same scintillating stars, that same delayed light shone brilliantly across the white granite boulder-strewn summit of Mount Vipula, one of five hills surrounding the village of Rajagrha, in the year 556 B.C.. As Leonard softly lulled the homeless woman to sleep, unmindful of the pebbles and broken pieces of glass cutting into his bare buttocks, he felt the presence of that hill, and heard, or imagined, Mahavira's own words.

In the gloaming dusk, a gaggle of calling peacocks emerged over the crest in dignified formation, females in the lead. Behind them and below, out across the mingling plains, the northern Indian tropics rose up in a chorus of Earth, excited by the coming of night. Their delicate talons stepping over the claret-hued loam, like some choreographed pizzicato, the peacocks arrived at length beneath the great asoka tree and sat down, as peacocks do, amid their fanning splendor.

Insects, too, arrived, stag beetles in haste, glow worms more slowly but determined, and rodents of all varieties. Well-behaved children were there with their hopeful mothers, lonely farmers whose crops had failed them, former military men, haunted by the deaths of their friends. Old men had come, patiently awaiting the solace for which they had travelled far. Adolescent boys arrived in a rowdy legion, skeptical and combative. Beautiful striped antelope, skittish and unsure, took positions among the rocks, while a large, old Indian lion, graceful and tenacious, took up a perch opposite the hollow-horned ruminants, silent and unseen. He, too, had wearied of killing.

They came from all over the region. And from as far away as West Bengal, Rameswaram Island and Bhutan, alighted flocks of several thousand plum-headed parakeets chattering gravely in high roosts overhead the assembling congregation below. The Salmalia, Butea and Bassia blossoms were everywhere in profusion, adding to the birds' excitement.

Darkness was somberly illuminated by fireflies coasting over the territory.

Other ascetics had climbed the mountain earlier that day. The Kottiya, who slept on bare ground, the Thalai, who carried everything on their person, the Ummajjaka, known for bathing with a single dip, and the Sammajjaka, who bathed by taking several dips. Came the Sampakkhala, men and women who cleansed their bodies using mud. There were ascetics from the north bank of the Ganges, and different ascetics from the south bank. There were those who lived under trees, those who ate only moss, and those who lived—said they—by drinking only water. Some dwelt in caves, some dressed in bark. They recited Sutras, Vedas, *sastras, stotras* and *slokas* of a hundred ancient texts. Some believed that God was lust. Others, that God was gravity. And still others insisted there was no God. But all had heard of this man they called Mahavira. Not a God, but some other force to be reckoned with. A Great Victor, a *Dharmacakravarti*, leader of the whole world, it was rumored.

Lay pilgrims arrived from the village below, some carried on bamboo palanquins, some walking in sandals fashioned from tiger skin, still others barefoot. They came in cloth as clear as crystal, blue and scarlet robes bordered with threads of gold.

They spoke mutually incomprehensible tongues, Marathi, Bengali, Telugu and Tamil, Kannada and Punjabi. Yet they all shared a common adventure, namely, the soul.

It went this way until sometime after midnight, when the naked man arrived.

With him was Indrabhuti Gautama and his brothers who followed behind, all of them clad in white linen robes and undergarments.

Without bustle, Mahavira took up a place amid the throngs, at the foot of the giant weepless tree and began to speak.

"*Namo Arihantanam, Namo Sidhdhanam, Namo Ayarianam, Namo Uvajzayanam, Namo lo-e savva Sahunam,*" he sang. "I bow to the

Arihanta. I bow to the Siddhas. I bow to the Acharyas. I bow to the Upaddhyayas. I bow to all the Saddhus in this world . . . "

Most of those surrounding him listened without reciting. Few knew the words, or the meaning. Some seemed disappointed. They had hoped for a big show, a miracle. Others were yet expectant, or perplexed, or ready to reject this so-called holy man altogether. Still others yawned themselves into total distraction.

Mahavira acknowledged a world bereft of disciples, only onlookers. But that was quite alright. He'd known from the beginning of his journey that he must proceed alone. There could be no comfort in followers anymore than in strangers.

"I am no miracle worker," he volunteered, reading the minds of many. Countless maimed individuals, missing appendages, in obvious distress, bodies peppered with ailments, stripped of their senses, had made it to this mountain top in hopes of deliverance. All Mahavira had for them were words. Mere words and the example of himself. For many, it was a profound disappointment. He could not instantly bring the blind to see, nor the crippled to walk, nor the dead to rise up from their graves. All he could offer were glib comforts and a smattering of wisdom. But what was the use of these things, if a man's stomach was empty, or his head, for that matter? If he had no shoes, no house, no money; if she were incapable of having children; if he was a slave; if she were unattractive. . . . What use words and rhyme?

There was dissent among some of the people, though not a single animal stirred. In literal fact, the miracle was taking place all around them. Some noticed, some did not. The lion ignored the sheep. A tiger sat quietly beside a deer. An eagle beside a mouse. A child was born whilst Mahavira spoke, and that child's first impulse was to laugh. Some noticed, some did not.

"As the fallow leaf of the tree falls to the ground when its days are gone, even so the life of men will come to an end," Mahavira went on. "As a dewdrop clinging to the top of a blade of Kusa-grass lasts but a short time, even so the life of men. Be quick, as life is so fleet and existence so precarious. Knowing whence we come and whither we go, a man or woman versed in empathy, trained in ahinsa, devoted to the universal law of compassion, rejoices in the reciprocity of all beings. Speculation has no room. Such liberation is not long nor small nor round nor triangular nor quadrangular nor circular. Neither black nor blue nor red nor green nor white. Neither good nor bad, pungent nor astringent nor sweet. Neither rough nor soft. Heavy nor light. Cold nor hot. Harsh nor smooth.

This liberation is without body, without resurrection, without matter, feminine or masculine or neuter. It perceives and knows but the verbs are not entirely correct. The essence of which I speak is formless. It is only recognizable by one thing, the soul."

"And, what is the soul," asked a voice from the rear of the assembled. A voice which Mahavira knew at once to be that of Gosala.

"What is the soul? The soul is the life force," said Mahavira. "*Jiva!*"

"But what is it?" asked the voice.

"The life force is true conscience," replied Mahavira, using words to encircle it, words like *ahinsa, anukampa, jiva-daya, samyama, jiva-cetana,* and *sadharana-vanaspati,* all pointing to a clemency of plants, a tender-heartedness of animals, a sympathy of atoms, the leniency of matter, that saving grace of impulses in the cosmos whose destiny was bound up with love. And to that end, Mahavira elaborated, hour after hour, upon the *yathakhyata-caritra,* or conduct conforming to such perfect purity. He outlined the appropriate vows—non-violence, truth, not stealing, sexual abstinence and non-possession. And, he went on to enumerate some fourteen methods whereby the vows could be consistently kept. Spiritual stages, levels of restraint and renunciation, and a perfectly practical psychoanalysis of pain, violence, ill-deeds and ill-thoughts. The entire meditation, conducted out loud, could only be described as revolutionary.

Leonard managed to hear every word. Or, he thought he did.

By dawn, multiple rainbows emanated from Mount Vipula. Some among the multitudes had fallen asleep, others had walked away, but most remained attentive, even transfixed, particularly eleven men, Gautama and his brothers Agnibhuti and Vayubhuti, an older gentleman named Arya Vyakta, a literary fellow called Sudharman, middle-aged men called Mandika, Mauryaputra, Akampita, Acalabhrata, and Metarya, and a bright, innocent sixteen year old by the name of Prabhasa. Among them, Sudharman alone had the proper accessories for writing down Mahavira's words, a *lehani,* the *masi,* and a *kambiya*—a pen, the ink, and a wooden board.

There were those who'd exchanged tendernesses, or made up, or made knew friends, their good feelings sparked by things Mahavira had said. The parakeets seemed particularly affectionate with each other, almost embarrassingly so, to Mahavira. And there were those whose boils and goiters mysteriously vanished throughout the night. And others whose joints no longer ached, whose hearts were refreshed, and sight improved. The lion wanted to attach itself to Mahavira, just to be near him, but did not know, exactly, how to do it tactfully.

Everything seemed to have gone well.

But by morning there was trouble down in the village of Rajagrha, the capital of Magadha. Mikhali Gosala, Mahavira's former acquaintance, was intensely jealous of the sage's growing audience and presently mocked the so-called Jina's assertion that such things as stones, and salt, wind and worms, leeches and onions, garlic and fire all contained souls.

"He's insane!" Gosala screamed. "He's dangerous! He'd have you believe that monsoons, King Cobras and the plague are all equally alive, sentient, in need of love! He'd protect frogs and virgins with equal verve!" And, before the King of Rajagrha, Srenika, he warned that Mahavira would compel him to disband his army, to melt down all weapons, to free all prisoners, to refrain from eating meat, keeping pets, or harming wheat; to ignore implacable destiny and place men's lives in their own hands. He would insist upon mercy for enemies, and compassion for invalids. In short, said Gosala, he would threaten civilization and cripple the King's empire.

But the King, unbeknownst to Gosala, had already converted to Mahavira's teachings and the more stinging Gosala's contempt, the more pathetic he looked to the royal family. And, when Gosala learned of this, he flew into a purple rage, flinging his fire all around him, killing a dog, burning down a tree, and injuring an old woman. He knew that Mahavira would be descending the mountain later that day and he plotted a warm embrace of an old friend.

When Mahavira reached the village, Gosala snuck upon him and flung his inner heat at two of Mahavira's initiates, killing them instantly. It seemed possible that Mahavira—despite his emphatic message of non-violence—might now be forced to retaliate. Indeed, he shed a noticeable tear for the two victims, and a third and a fourth and a fifth tear when he subsequently learned about the murdered dog, the murdered tree, and the injured old woman.

Now Gosala lifted his arm in a gesture that was determined to kill Mahavira. But nothing happened. The fire never left his arm. Something in Mahavira's command of nature prevented it. The build-up of the fire was its own retribution, Gosala's whole body went up in a blaze. With a wink, Mahavira conveyed a soothing cascade of water from nowhere to put out the flames.

"You will die within six months!" the ailing Gosala cried, more pitiful than penetrating, his body smoking with ire.

"You are the basis for love," Mahavira said of him. "Dual nature is the beginning of consciousness. Consciousness, turned inward, the beginning of insight. Insight the beginning of action. And, action the possibility for love."

Gosala's lover, the potter Halahala, was there. So ashamed was she of her man in the dirt, she spit at him. Everyone laughed. And Gosala felt ashamed of himself.

The mob taunted him. He declared, "I am unafraid of death!"

There were many who demanded the murderer be summarily executed. They grabbed him, tied his body by a long rope to the saddle of a camel and chased that camel through the market place until Gosala was unconscious and bloody. Then, they prepared to bury him alive.

Mahavira stepped into the fray and gently liberated Gosala from the angry public, untying him from the camel. "This is the essence of moksa," Mahavira continued, as if the entire saga were part of his earlier discourse, life imitating art. "The soul is thus liberated from the dust, the *karma*, which clings to it!"

And, Mahavira thanked Gosala for providing so graphic an illustration of this first principle.

Gosala was speechless, a study in anguish. And then, Candana, Mahavira's chief nun, the beauty he had once rescued, came to Gosala and with a medicinal balm rubbed his body to ease the pain. This was too much for him. Gosala broke down and wept with contrition.

"Save me!" he pleaded with Mahavira.

"Wash yourself off, you're a mess," replied Mahavira, who then checked to see that the camel was alright.

But, only Leonard noticed that when Mahavira approached the churning beast, he whispered something in its ear and the camel seemed to understand.

Sometime before dawn, the homeless woman, Ruth, went into convulsions. Gautama, who had himself verged on hypothermia throughout the night, called '911' but by the time the medics had arrived her color had become that of a Karakoram glacier, her trembling had dissipated at the fingertips, and the mesmerizing calm of nirvana had settled over her like a tropical fungus.

Gautama had struggled the entire night. He had to get back to his life. But, he could not bring himself to leave Leonard's melodious side. At moments, entranced in his vision, Leonard had broken out into lyrical cadenzas in Sanskrit, or An-akshari, or Ardha-Magadhi, Prakrit, or Yiddish. And, Gautama had listened, drawn back into time, into himself. During other long intervals the two men had simply sat silently with the woman, saying nothing, Gautama greatly troubled and self-conscious. Everything he thought about was tangibly exposed to the inward-grazing powers of Leonard and this was obviously unnerving.

More troubling for Gautama was Leonard's—how should one put it—his inexorability, the unavoidable truth of his being. If cosmology and history had somehow conspired to create this man, what did that bode for a lawyer who had simply kept him out of jail? Did he also have to play a part in destiny's grand scheme? Had he not already fulfilled his role? Was one human sacrifice not enough? He was in love with his wife, enjoyed a honeyed, even kinky, sex life, relished his gold-colored Honda, was vainly attached to his escalating power in the legal profession, was fond of his time-shared condo on Lake Tahoe, and—while a good Jain, a vegetarian with his own little shrine in his home for doing puja every morning—he dismissed such contradictions as his silk shirt. Leonard had already reminded him that this particular silk shirt was the by-product of approximately four thousand three hundred and twelve silk worms that had been boiled alive. That was some *chutzpah*, Gautama reflected, considering Leonard's own Bentley and Armani getup of just a week before.

By mid-morning, Gautama found himself paralyzed by indecision. He had no one to turn to but Leonard himself, whom he had fought for on intellectual and judicial grounds. His own personal involvement, beyond the professional crusade which he had proudly won, had never really become an issue for him. But now, after a week of the man's company, Gautama was not only very fond of Leonard Rosenbalm, but addicted to the ideal which he represented, and which he himself had grown up with as part of his Indian heritage, his family, his very self-definition.

Would it really matter if he spent a few more weeks with Leonard? Not at all, he figured. He'd take a month or so off from his job, Asha would bring him extra blankets and pillows, his ski jacket and wool sweater, as well as a delicious hot meal twice a day. She'd do that. He'd start taking Vitamin C in massive quantities, maybe Leonard would too, and perhaps he'd get word of Leonard to the Indian dailies in town. The Jain community at large would surely be interested. Asha could bring him his little tape recorder and he'd start keeping a verbal diary of Leonard's discourses and the events which befell them. And, after a few weeks, Gautama would simply resume his normal life, as if nothing had happened. It was a good plan, anyway.

They meandered East. Leonard moved in the direction of the rising Sun.

"Where are we going?" Gautama asked more than once. "What is the plan?" To which Leonard replied, "Watch that you don't step on any ants."

Would he deliver lectures, would he try to convert the masses? Gautama was wondering. How long would he simply walk? It did not at that moment occur to Gautama that Mahavira had walked for forty-two years, and Moses for forty. Leonard's genetic disposition suggested a good number of calluses on the feet.

Suddenly, Leonard uttered an impossible expression Gautama had never heard, *ukkarapasavanasattikkao*, walked over to a fence and took hold of some scrap newspaper. He continued to a pothole in the road surface, squatted down, and relieved his nature as honking cars swerved to avoid hitting the crazy person. Gautama turned away, deeply embarrassed for Leonard, for himself. And yet, he too needed to go. But where?

He went into a Spanish bar to borrow the key to the restrooms but they wouldn't give it to him unless he bought a drink and Gautama had no money on his person. Down the street he found a more congenial Korean steak house. The lavatory was filthy, the stench resembling that of the plates of meat at the shelter. Gautama did his business then rejoined Leonard. It dawned on him that life with Leonard would be no picnic.

Several patrol cars drove by, inching forward in tandem with the two men, then speeding away. Before long, Leonard and Gautama were not two but five, then ten. The crowd consisted of homeless people who sensed something important. They did not seem to question Leonard's nudity, not with Gautama, in his three-piece, albeit wrinkled, suit at his side. They could read the dignity of circumstance like a halo. It invited not scorn, but accompaniment. Leonard was a happening, and when the police were seen to keep their distance, these first stragglers knew that Leonard was not just anybody, but somebody. The dude meant business.

One of the stragglers stepped up to Gautama and said, "You and your friend here might like to know they're givin' out free peanut brickle, apples and cheese sandwiches at the Misery House! Gotta' move if you gonna' make it. They're usually out of 'em by ten o'clock!"

Gautama, though not Leonard, had an appetite and lacking other concrete plans, they made this their first expedition, heading with the band of stragglers to Misery House. Turning a corner, they discovered one hundred and eight people queued up.

"Cokie, cokie?" a black person solicited Gautama. "Good god, and I thought I had it bad!" he went on, seeing the naked man.

Leonard took his place behind the last fellow in line.

"Hey buddy, just leave me alone, get outta' here, I said get 'cause my wife and I we're talking out a problem, you know, and you're not helpin' none!"

Leonard moved back a few paces.

"Notice," he said to Gautama, "how perfected souls develop in all these men, women, hermaphrodites, orthodox, heterodox and householders. Perfection is reached by the greatest, the smallest, the middle sizes, men of five hundred dhanus, or two thousand cubits, it matters not; women of forty-eight inches, homosexuals of between three and eight feet; on high places, on the ocean shore, in caves, upon the sidewalk."

Gautama found this a curious manner of describing what to him was a depressing assemblage of losers, of mostly dark-skinned men down on their luck.

"You, too, are darkly skinned, Gautama," Leonard broke into his thoughts with an adverting glance.

"You really want that apple sauce?" Gautama asked him, utterly on edge, not crazy about waiting in a long line.

"Such apple sauce is a doorway into your own soul, Gautama," Leonard replied. "These are beautiful people," he went on.

But what Gautama saw were trenches of urine, dried excrement, corners adrift in acrid debris. There was a snoring big-bellied pasty-skinned Latino leaning skewed against a grating, a loud machine just on the inside, like an air conditioner, as if coming from his exposed torso. And, so many black men in worn polyurethene parkas, though it had gotten hot. They fiddled with yellow and black charm beads. There was a white woman in hot pants, her greasy mound of sex blatantly exposed, legs akimbo, seated against the corroded brick, surrounded by cokies, former bruisers, solemn Hispanics, an old, still-dignified Chinaman, short but standing tall, with white goatee, speaking about L.A. sewage disposal with his friend. There were four former truckers, all in their seventies, mostly emaciated, in dirty jeans and moth-eaten sweaters, hanging together; a teenage Mexican, schnockered, limping, his lip burst open, eyes glazed; a slick red-haired Whitey, leather coat, velvet boots, real cool, seen better days, calculating his next hit with a tough-guy cohort, a nude tatooed on his left bicept. And, there was a huge grey-headed white woman playing strangely with a yoyo, two worlds swinging back and forth, like a pendulum, or rubber band.

"That's destiny," said Leonard.

They moved up in line, joined now by several athletic blacks, some bare chested, others dressed as if going to church; still others in filthy basketball shoes and sweats, nondescript throwaway clothes. Once youthful and strong, now wearied and burned out, they sported cropped hairstyles, black and grey curls streaked blue like old womens'. The men whistled at a group of women across the street who were doing something naughty in a ramshackle corner, covered in scrap, half-hidden beyond the alley.

Gautama dizzied. The putrescence, the age-old fetor of piss. A man was peeing against the fence, beside a Mayan-type, handsome bones, maybe fifty, asleep with an open romance novel—he probably kept it with him all the time. He heard talk of the authorities sending back illegals. Behind the fence where the man peed, there were hundreds of pigeons fending for themselves.

Yet, amid this desert, Gautama sensed a camaraderie that seemed to embrace loneliness and make it better. A black man in line started talking with Leonard.

"Hi, I'm Tyrone," he said.

He was probably in his early thirties, tall, in red jogging sweats, his skin broken out in a rash. Essentially handsome, very tired.

"I got four kids, but now I'm divorced. Haven't seen my girls since six weeks."

"You were a professional, I think," Leonard said.

"Used to be, I guess," replied Tyrone. "Three years with General Telephone answering some thirteen hundred '411' calls a day; three a minute, pretty good. I was up to ten bucks an hour."

"What happened?" asked Gautama.

"Got hooked on coke. Had to quit my job. Having a hard time getting General Relief. Doesn't matter, now. Everything a man could need is downtown. Don't want my kids seeing me this way, though."

"Hey, Tyrone!" a voice called out.

"Hey! . . . That's my friend Joe," Tyrone said.

"What's your story?" Joe asked of Leonard. "That's pretty far out."

"I'm a Jain monk," Leonard replied.

"Jain?" Joe scratched his head. Leonard knew he was picking lice. "Those are the ones who let bugs crawl all over their bodies in Bombay and wear masks over their mouths so they don't harm no insects. I read about them in some book once." He promptly popped a minute creature between his fingertips, leaving a minute trace of blood.

"Please don't do that!" Leonard begged.

Joe just laughed. "Where's your mask if you're really one of those Jains?"

It was a good question. Leonard didn't know. He'd never thought about a mask. Gautama hoped he didn't think about one. The caricature in his mind of a naked man with a mask, or *mulpatti*, as the Jains called it, was bound to incite gags from the multitudes, like—'Hey, stupid, you got your fig leave in the wrong place!'

Leonard sized up Joe within an instant, reading between the furrows and the generous smile. The hard luck shone. The character and stamina, even the courage, could not be contained for even a second. He was a construction worker who'd been in Vietnam in nineteen sixty-eight. His knees had gone bad, his shoulder, too. Not good for climbing around on roofs or skyscrapers. He came from western Kentucky. His parents were retired steelworkers. He was once divorced, never in love. He wore prescription sunglasses and a baseball cap and was sadly overweight, built like a triangle and wearing the very thing of Leonard's liberation, namely, Dickie trousers. His cowboy boots were covered in feces, his hair multi-colored and dishevelled.

He'd come to Los Angeles by a variety of trains, first from Miami to Houston. He said it was a problem with so much track, you could get confused and hitch a ride in the wrong direction. But, he finally made it to Colton, then headed down to Yuma, then, by accident, back to Colton.

"See what I mean? Thirty hours in the back of a grainery train, a small cramped hole. All I had was one warm Pepsi. And it was a Diet, which I hate. Hoods sometimes hop on board and toss bums off at sixty miles an hour."

Then he cautioned, "Avoid that Santa Fe line. They throw you in the slammer for ninety days if they catch you. Always approach the train yards at night, get the rundown, figure out which train's going where. Avoid the hot ones with merchandise because the guards are checking those all the time."

He came into Yuma in the middle of the night, trekked across some culverts, sat himself down near a drainage ditch, under a pine tree and along came this eight year old blond kid who laid a five dollar bill, with five ones, in his hand saying, "Take it, Mister."

The boy's Mom evidently lived across the way and this was her own form of penance for something she must have done at some point in her life, or a payback for some other stranger's kindness. It broke Joe's heart, whatever the motive. He thanked the child and bought himself a ticket to Las Vegas, where he put up in the Salvation Army shelter, not bad, he said, and listened to a doctor talking about digestion. He took a final bus trip from San Bernardino to Union Station where he slipped on the marble floor and re-injured his bad knee. He could still feel the shrapnel in there from the Tet Offensive. He had three dollars and eight cents to his name. Someone thought he was perfect for the Misery House.

At forty-three, he had plenty of mirth, seemed to be a lovely man, with big broken teeth, a limp and a walkman. He worried about getting his throat slit at night.

"It's a wilderness," he said of Los Angeles, waiting for his cheese sandwich and apple sauce. "You've got to get inside one of the shelters before nightfall otherwise it's curtains. That's what I hear." He spoke like he meant it. Gautama was spooked.

He'd come to Los Angeles on the rumor of the government's Section Eight subsidized housing, a HUD deal. What nobody told him was that there were already at least twenty thousand homeless families in the city on the waiting lists, usually a single mother and her three malnourished kids holding up in downtown dives, desperate, many beaten up and traumatized, some starving to death, or dying of tuberculosis, or AIDS.

Some slept in abandoned cars, or laundromats while waiting for those mythical houses. If you had the wherewithal to stand in line for two days, which few did, it was possible, maybe, to get a government slum hotel voucher and a General Relief check in some modest amount. But then you had to find a bank that would let you in the front door, let alone cash the bugger. If you had kids, you could also get maybe a hundred dollars of food stamps in a week as long as you could get two signatures which showed you were looking for work in the meantime. There was always a catch.

He pulled out a piece of paper from his pocket. "Would you sign this?" Joe asked Tyrone and Leonard.

They both signed.

"A Jain, huh? That's pretty wild."

"What's it like out in the desert at night?" Leonard asked Joe.

"Terrible," he said. "Rattlers everywhere, curled up on the roads, hiding under every bush and cactus. For every star there's a snake. You've got to listen real good."

With slum vouchers, there were a variety of hold-outs in downtown. Joe pointed to the Russ Hotel, over there on San Julian Street or the Panama, part of the Skid Row Corp. on East Fifth Street, both at forty-nine fifty a week. Or the Leo on South San Julian, sober living, one eighty-five a month. You could get into the Lyndon on East Seventh Street for eleven dollars a night. If you felt like spoiling yourself, there was Brownstone's on East Fifth which was upwards of thirteen dollars a night. In all of them, one had to pay about four bucks extra for a shower. Too expensive, he thought.

Problem was, for all four men—Leonard, Gautama, Tyrone and Joe—none of them had vouchers, or any money at all. Of the four, only Gautama had a wallet. But, somehow, he'd misplaced it. Or, it had been pickpocketed. To his own amazement, he wasn't even concerned about calling the various eight hundred numbers to stop payment on his credit cards. It just didn't matter to him right now.

Tyrone filled them all in. The more he spoke, the clearer it became that downtown was a haven of opportunities and services. A veritable country club, thought Leonard.

It was all there for you. Drug abuse rehab, Alcoholics Anonymous, city jobs, boards where you could check for listings at the Employment Development Department on South Broadway. If you were into girls, they came cheap on nearly any corner. If you were into free drugs you could mosey on over to the Mental Health Clinic on East Sixth Street, doctors available up until mid-afternoon and some of them, at least, eager to inject you with good feeling stuff. You could get a public shower at the Lamp Village, five twenty-six South San Pedro, and free art supplies for artists living on skid row at a place called L.A.C.E.. If you were in trouble, out of a room, there was always emergency food and shelter at the Sundown Service after five p.m.. Tyrone had it wired.

They had their pick of the shelters. There were nine of them, in all.

"Not bad meals," said Tyrone. "Though a lotta guys prefer it over at RSM, the Reunion & Salvation Mission 'cause there you get your lunch at eleven forty-five sharp. Same with dinners, at four forty-five p.m.." What he didn't tell them was the Christian sermon part of it. Tyrone had his own agenda.

They all had their apples and peanut brickle and cheese sandwiches (Leonard gave all his food to Joe and Tyrone) and then headed over to the RSM.

For Leonard, he was marking out the territory. Letting the visions of the night before settle. Thousands of years had elapsed. The nature of the mountain top, the jungle, the arid plains, the tea plantations, the local customs, had changed. The parade of living beings had changed. The animals had changed. But, change was samsara, like that revolving door, like the wheels on Leonard's former Bentley. It all came back. Money came back in the form of General Relief for people like Joe and Tyrone. Animals came back as other animals. Customs, rocks, mists, tea leaves— everything returned. And, everything was negotiable.

Hundreds of men and women were standing around outside. Once in, five hundred folk were escorted to the auditorium in single file. You couldn't get your lunch until you'd sat for an hour in the church service. That was the part Tyrone had failed to divulge.

A black bouncer stopped Leonard at the door. "That's a Christian church in there. What the hell you think you're doin'?"

"Christ went naked into the wilderness," Leonard reminded him in the most soothing and persuasive tone.

The black man relented.

"Transform your pain into a miracle!" the boisterous minister calls out, reaching towards the domed ceiling with both hands. "Say hello to the soul sitting beside you. Take his hand, look into his eyes, tell him, 'Friend, I love you.' Go ahead, don't be shy, say it!"

And, the words—at first tentative, then rising to an unlikely crescendo, mangled miserable cries for food in the name of nameless love—with echo throughout the auditorium. Leonard takes Joe's hand and Joe starts to sweat.

"You're hands are burning up!" Joe says. "I do believe you got the fever of the Lord inside you!"

An image of a hippie Christ stares down from above, with words inscribed to the effect, Christ, Ben Yehuda, the Christ bodily taketh unto you, or something like that, and how this day will become the revolution, amen and halleluja.

There's a well-dressed group of musicians on a stage beside the slick, black minister. They have a drum set, a synthesizer, and there's this good-looking gal with a tambourine. And, they all sing, "He is the one, when you're lonely, poor, starving, homeless, he is the one, the only one; no B path, no A path, only the J path, Jesus, our Lord and Redeemer."

This rousing rendition is proceeded by a chunky white guy from New York who prances onto the stage like it's the Jewish Borscht Belt, except that he's a real off-the-hip Christian evangelist, smooth, gesticulating, greasy. "Redemption is a business word, means he buys us back from the devil if only we accept him, Romans Eight, first verse: ' . . . And all past sins shall be removed . . . ' It begins now, here, this day," he cries out exaltedly.

And then, everyone's invited to come on up to the stage for special ministrations, individual prayers, while that cheesy music continues, black tenors whining in soft harmonies like those of Smokey Robinson, to the heavy drumming and the Roland synthesizer. They've got nearly lovely voices. Louder and louder. Seduction. Christ. Amens.

"I'd trust that man with my wallet," says innocent Joe, speaking of the second minister.

The congregation is then marched into the dining room where they're seated one by one, line after line, very orderly. The "weekly menu planner" is on the wall. Breakfast—fruit juice and creamed beef on toast; lunch—pizza, cole slaw, mutton soup; dinner—chili dogs, beans and ham salad. It varies though. Some nights you get ham and lima bean salad for dinner, hot cakes and sausage for breakfast. Lunch is usually the big meal—meat loaf, grilled hamburger, chicken, beef burritos, even oriental vegetables sauteed with pork. Usually it's hot dogs, meat-balls, rice, pork gravy, pork chops or cheeseburgers.

The eating frenzy begins. Mashed potatoes, peas, meat gravy, three slices of curled, slightly cooked bologna, a pink applesauce, some lemonade until it runs out—Hey, where's the white bread?—a voice calls out. "No more bread," an aproned volunteer says. "No seconds, either. Not today. Sorry."

Leonard feels the rush of nausea once again, as he'd experienced in the hospital. The meat portions and gravy are especially rank with the fact of death. Gautama feels a similar pang. Joe notices their reactions.

"If you guys aren't going to eat, I'll help you with that," he says, pulling both plates towards himself.

"A cow died for your sins," Leonard says.

"Yeah, better the cow than this Joe," says Joe.

And, as Joe and Tyrone, along with hundreds of other ravenous and dispossessed vagabonds all devour their modest portions, the queasy horror rises in Leonard until he can keep it down no longer. He turns away, puking all over the floor. Whether a Jain monk, or a prince, homeless or billionaire, puke smells the same. Gautama gags on his own disgorge. Now, one by one, others are similarly afflicted.

"It's the meat!" someone cries out. "It must be rancid!"

The throwing-up has attained epidemic proportions, though not for Joe, who will be damned if anything is going to interrupt this meal.

Single file back out. Napkins in short supply, folks have had to use their shirt sleeves to wipe off their vomit. It's on the floor, on torn leather shoes. In the food.

"Spirit be with you, brother," says Joe, who is happy to see Leonard disappear.

As for Tyrone, he's headed to a less crowded mission. He's heard of some new utopia up the street where they're paying rehab workers six bucks a week, plus room, board, clothes and a new life. They've got drapes, semi-private rooms, they'll give you a haircut, spotless shower. Tyrone wants into that program. He'll commit a year if that's what it takes. Because, otherwise, it's one night per shelter. That's all you get.

"Anybody wanna' come?" he says.

"Daddy?" a voice calls from behind.

Leonard turns. It's Denise. Hal's with her.

"We've been looking for you since yesterday. The judge told me everything." And, she breaks down weeping.

"Hello, sweetheart," Leonard says, comforting her with a soft hand to her hair, not so much as a father, but a distant admirer.

"Lennie, how's it going?" Hal asks awkwardly. He offers him a metal tray of hot spinach lasagna covered in aluminum foil. Leonard knows that that was really something for Hal to have gone and done. Especially considering everything.

"Give it to them," Leonard says gratefully, gesturing to the half-a-dozen stragglers who have stayed with him all the way from Misery House.

"Mom's taking it kinda' hard," says Denise. "She's gone back to work. But, she put all your things in the garage."

"Her heart'll soften after a while," Leonard says simply.

Denise looks at her father, with his growing beard and shaggy hair and blue eyes, unbrushed teeth, uncologned skin. She sees a man who stands at remarkable ease, given his nudity. And, it fills her with pride, or wonder, or trust.—'That's my Dad'—she thinks.—'He's on to something'—.

The group surrounding him is a motley one, baggy pants, a calico skirt, tatoos, ponytails, a Native American, a Latino, an Oriental, some blacks, shuffling strides, a few hands in pockets, others in silent awe, as if before a crucifix. They do not know what Leonard is. Nor does Denise, exactly.

"Let's take a walk," Leonard suggests. "To the Elysium Park. It's a beautiful day." He knew exactly what he had to do, and what would happen.

Gautama separated himself from the small crowd and called the Indian Voice newspaper, as well as a friend at an FM radio station who was, in turn, the friend of a local TV reporter, and explained where the group was headed.

They passed along Olvera Street with its redolent Cocada Horneada (oven baked coconut), past the La Golondrina Cafe and El Paseo Inn with its historic Pelanconi House wine cellar. The street was alive with a Mariachi band before the Casa de Sousa and El Pueblo de Los Angeles. Young fathers and mothers with their children stood enjoying the celebration of All Saints.

When Leonard came down the street, one of them—outraged— pulled a knife and threatened the naked man.

With the scent of candied pumpkins and taffy tarts in her nostrils, emboldened, Denise stepped forward to combat the assailant. "That's my father!" she shouted.

Gautama stepped forward. "I'm his lawyer!"

Hal puffed out his overweight chest and also plunged forth, "And, I'm his business partner, asshole!"

Other Latinos pushed their way into the fray. Other knives were drawn. "Get him away from our women!" they screamed, itching for a fight.

When suddenly a patrol car siren wailed and two officers of the law rushed out of their car.

"Drop the knives, NOW!" they ordered, ducking into firing position.

An amazed grin blossomed on Leonard's face. It was his old friends Davies and Washington. "Drop your weapons, gentlemen," Leonard beseeched. "*Ahinsa Parmo Dharma.*"

The angered hooligans disappeared into the throng. The patrolmen, who had been briefed by the DA's office, kept to Leonard's procession. "From here on in, consider us your guardian angels," Davies said.

Gautama was starving, and he reflected on the fact that Leonard had hardly eaten or taken any drink all week, save for a meager bite of applesauce earlier. He had to think of a way to inform the Jain community. Leonard would die rather than take food for himself. That was becoming clear. Not even Hal's lasagna had appealed to him, and Gautama knew why: any food that Leonard took had to be prepared inadvertently, and by a vegetarian. Leonard, like the Jinas, had delineated sixteen primary rules, or *udgama-doshas* by which food became unfit. The slightest impure particle, manner of preparation, even impure thoughts held by the preparer, would condemn a portion. Leonard's new discipline, however it came to be, was Jain to the core, which meant that in this world of edibles, a monk was bound to introversion. He could not prevail upon any other creature beyond the one-sensed; neither householder nor fellow monk. He would not pluck an apple from a tree, or take a swig of lemonade on his own. Everything had to be offered to him almost by way of accident. He was at the mercy of urban followers.

Otherwise, without even considering it, he should die of starvation. Leonard was on his way to starving to death in the midst of plenty.

Ironically, to Gautama's way of thinking, it was Leonard's very love of life that kept him from taking anything for himself. This had been the path of the Jinas for millennia. Thousands of years ago they were called Nirgranthas, meaning knotless ones, tied to nothing in this world.

They crossed the street to the North and entered the Iglesia Metodista La Plaza. Its beautiful bells were ringing at that instant for the noon Mass. A large assemblage chanted to Nuestra senora La Reina De Los Angeles. A hundred yards away, across the street from a Versateller machine, another group sat praying in the chapel of La Sociedad de la Adoracion Perpetua. The sugar of religion filled the air here.

Leonard prayed out loud, "*Dhammo Mangal Mukkitham, Ahinsa Sanjamo Tavo. Deva Vi Tan Namasanti Jass Dhamme Saya Mano.*"

"What does it mean?" Denise asked.

Leonard could not explain it. But Gautama knew well this famous first gatha from the *Dashvaikalik Sutra*, compiled about a century after the death of Mahavira. It was another of his childhood memories. He tried to translate for Denise.

"Basically, it says that a good and true religion is one that is universally bound to non-violence, to self-control, and to penance. All the gods in the universe will pay homage to him whose mind is engaged in spiritual thought. That's approximately it," he told her.

"It does not sound to me like Jewish," she said.

"It's Indian," he said. "And, it applies to all religions and peoples. Hindu. Moslem. Jain. Jewish. Doesn't matter."

She had not known her father to be a religious person. He had rarely gone to services, except twice a year for the High Holidays, and had not endeavored particularly to raise her in a religious sense either. Her Mom was the one that insisted on family dinners together on Friday nights; who discouraged her from driving her Jaguar on the Sabbath.

The nearly naked Christ figure on the altar, with his tiara of thorns, his dolorous Golgotha, stared downward at Leonard. Leonard stared back at Christ. Everyone in the chapel gazed upon the two of them, who bore an uncanny resemblance to one another. This could not be denied.

The crowd followed Leonard and his stragglers out of the church. No one conveyed any but the most reverential curiosity about the naked man.

The group, now approaching fifty in size, continued past a French dip sandwich bar and stopped at five hundred North Los Angeles Street.

There, on the edge of a small, littered park, was a statue erected in honor of the eighteenth century Father Junipero Serra by the Knights of Columbus in nineteen thirty-two.

Near the statue was a sign that read, "No dogs without leash, No golfing, No beer, No loitering. Closed 10:30 PM to 5 AM."

They walked by the City Market, beyond a square block of rubble and desert over which hung a sign which read, "Who is beyond the law? . . . who is free to choose? . . . who prays loudest . . . " And a second sign "Nuts to you since 1907" beneath which sat a congerie of homeless, of tough dudes hanging out. One of them looked up at Leonard and started cursing him viciously. Gautama, on impulse, stepped between Leonard and the drunk. But, Leonard made his way up to the man, who sat sprawled and eruptive on the sidewalk, and, with the slighest exertion seemed to lift him to his feet, brush off the dust from his clothes, and motivate him with a positive charge. For suddenly, mockery and rage had dissolved into prayer. The man tried to kiss Leonard's feet, which Leonard would have none of. But the situation worsened. The bum having been so inclined, triggered one of those rare and infrequent pandemoniums which throughout history have transformed the mundane swamp into a Lourdes. Now a dozen frantic souls knelt down to kiss his feet. One of the stragglers of the feminine gender started wailing. Another commenced beating her chest and before long the veneration had assumed hysterical dimensions.

Leonard grew faint.

Before him spread the sub-continent of India, and there was Mahavira, having come down from the mountain, setting out on an odyssey that would last a lifetime, every day just like this one. In his inner eye, Leonard witnessed the blurred itinerary, a pageant year after year. Always bare feet. Always travelling with his eyes looking no more than six feet before him so as not to harm an insect on the path. He took little food and little water and lived by a set of rules that ensured one essential fact: his soul would never perish for he would never have killed. An immortal soul! So refreshing, so certain an idea as to clear away all other impediments, to grant the beneficiary so vast a hegemony as to eliminate all other wants, concerns, tribulations and hopes. In an instant to be transported into the heart of nature.

The itinerary of that journey surfaced in his head. So many villages where Mahavira journeyed, spoke, slept, dreamt . . . With exotic-sounding names like Campa, Prsticampa, Vaisali . . . People lived in these towns long ago; lived, loved, hoped, died away. People like Denise, like

Hal and Gautama. Their life expectancy, then, was thirty-eight.
Vanijagrama, Nalanda, Mithila. . . . He was a man, no more, no less. He
stares eye to eye at Leonard, Leonard at Mahavira. Breathe in . . . breathe
out. . . . Let the heart roar like a lion! Freedom from attachment. That's
what he speaks of. Leonard has been listening. Ahinsa. Peace. Love.
That's what he speaks of. Leonard has been watching. And, the procession of peoples in one village after another passes before him . . . At
Bhadrika, in Alabhika, throughout Sravasti and Panitabhumi, town after
town, generation after generation. Children and grandparents. Women
with coconut breasts. Women with only one breast. Animals left out in
the cold. Fathers who have lost a leg, a child, a wife, a parent, a dream.
Young men who have already grown weary of this life. Other monks
who've lost faith. Dreamers who have tried to kill themselves. Kings
who have everything. Poets who have everything. Scientists who know
everything. And the goat, saved from the scimitar, that continues to follow Mahavira wherever he roams.

All the way to the village of Pava-puri.

Harbingers of downtown Los Angeles. Biological haiku, a history
of idealism, compressed into a glance, as one obeisance after another,
each stranger than the last, piled up before Leonard's feet. He could not
curtail this multiplication of embarrassing homage from people who had
nothing else.

Hal Spendetti, walking with Denise this whole time, simply marveled. "I would never have believed it, Denise. Never in a thousand
years."

Suddenly, at Fourth Street, the homeless gave way to tourists con-
verging upon the Plaza, with its spotless sand garden and surrounding
bonsai trees. There was Ike's market, signs for Lancome and Chanel, an
array of mirrored glass and the high-rising New Otani Hotel, its Royal
Suite at seven hundred fifty dollars a night. Leonard had once stayed
there, with its Banquet and Garden Restaurant, its train of Mercedes out
front and impressive brass trim. Now, it was simply a building on the
way to Elysium.

Leonard picked up a few pale white Japanese tourists with their
flashing cameras before a great rock statue near the Japanese Daily Sun
and Mitsui Manufacturers Bank. They begged him to pose for their pic-
tures, which he courteously avoided. So they photographed his derriere
as the core group proceeded beyond Allright Parking, Narumi's L.A.
Sports, and a profusion of storefront windows in which were to be found
such necessities of life as a Zoji Rushi Thermal Teapot, an Iwatani Por-

table Government Stove, Sushi tea cups and a winter clearance sale on Fancy Chirashi lacquer bowls.

An outdoor grocery stall teemed with yama imo—pickled cucumbers—and china peas; young ginger, bok choy, gobo, red and green cabbage, mum leaf, tokyo scallions and d'anjou pears. Gautama, whose stomach churned, but who dared not give in to it, smelled the aromas of Satsu sweet potato snacks, shiro miso soup, Japanese rice, and delicacies at the Ikeda Bakery. Next door, a chef was frying red azuki beans in batter atop a sheet of copper. Leonard warned him that such cooking methods burned up invisible yeast organisms and microbes.

"That's the point, isn't it?" asked the bewildered chef who was proud of his beans and showed off what he claimed to be hundred year old pancakes.

Details swarmed around Leonard like migrating butterflies, as the number of stragglers around him, and the accompanying commotion, increased.

Past the Far East National Bank, along New High Street and the Eagle Cathay Plaza, catching the scent of Kowloon Market, the troubling odor of dead fish and teriyaki beef, the band of a hundred or more stragglers followed Leonard up the mountain, beyond the maze of fast food zucchini tempura and egg rolls, Hikari One hour Photo, Nomoto Master Diamond Cutters, and Bally of Switzerland. Ascending the grassy knoll, the pilgrimage took on new dimensions now, as a news helicopter circled overhead and a reporter from The Indian Voice, a California weekly, showed up and started interviewing some of the Japanese tourists.

"Who is he? Why are you following him?"

Along the hillside emerged a small community of cardboard and plastic shelters. Hundreds of homeless people were scattered throughout the grass, beneath the trees, in plywood lean-tos outfitted with old mattresses. Clotheslines were strung between palm trees.

"You know what this land is worth?" Hal speculated. "Got to be valued at nine hundred a square yard." It was well known that a similar unoccupied mountain in downtown, Crown Hill, sold for twenty-four million in nineteen eighty-eight to a Hong Kong-based development company which planned to build a hotel but had been hit, in the meantime, by the recession.

Hal climbed, out of breath, grumbling to Denise that there had to be an easier way to make a living.

At Elysium, a city park, officials had tried repeatedly to chase the homeless away. Anti-camping and anti-feeding laws were everywhere posted. But, the poor people would return every night. Those on welfare, who got as much as three hundred forty dollars a month, could still not afford the average one room rental downtown, which went for five hundred.

The reporter from the Indian Voice ran up the hillside, out of breath but determined to get a photograph of the naked man coming over the top, with his merry band of followers taking up the rear. Near the summit, the reporter found Gautama, who had called her a few hours earlier.

"What's the story here?" she asked.

"His name is Leonard Rosenbalm. He's a good Jain and he's making an historic journey to the East. Stick around," he said with a tantalizing look.

Leonard sits in a grassy swale beneath a massive tree whose colorful leaves are perpetually floating down, drifting like the group consciousness which now occupies this field of Elyisum. Autumn is crisp about. Leonard feels like he has been here before. Now it comes to him: he and a young girl named Miriam once hugged and desperately kissed by moonlight up here, when they were both students.

A helicopter lands nearby. A television crew, then another, jockey for good camera positions among the hundreds of onlookers who have mostly sat down in the grass surrounding Leonard. Someone with the television people asks Leonard if he wouldn't mind wearing a shirt so that they can put a lavalier microphone in its lapel. Leonard just stares incomprehensibly at the fellow.

A radio person shoves a microphone up near Leonard's feet. There are stray mutts searching for food, their ribcages exposed. And, a large flock of wild green parrots that have lived downtown for decades, arrive in a single flourish. Pigeons and sparrows search the crowd on foot, while several hawks circle above.

Among the homeless in attendance are a number of philosophers in their own right, competing wisemen with their own contemporary schools of thought. Those that will not drink milk. Those that smear their bodies with axle grease. Those who are addicted to sex. Those who become eloquent whilst waxing under the influence of alcohol. Those that live under plastic. Those that live beneath the spell of a fatal disease. Those that live along the northern end of the Los Angeles river, and those that live along its south side. Those that dwell upon hillsides of grass. Those that leech comfortably off more well-to-do relatives. Those who believe in good luck, and those for whom such a luxury is unthinkable. Those who model their existence upon the essence of the shopping cart.

Those who wander amid the traffic in all of its guises. Those who follow pigeons in all of their vagaries. Adepts in casting spells. Those that talk only to themselves. Those who curse all passers-by. Wrigglers who cannot give, on principle, a straight answer to anything but, rather, excel at equivocal replies. Those who are convinced that immortality of the soul can be achieved through pleasure. Those who seek the same through suicide.

Gautama sits nearest to Leonard, a pen and paper in hand. He is taking notes of everything.—'How has it happened?' 'How has it come to be?'—he wonders.

Leonard is not thinking about anything, courageous as it may seem. He is neither happy nor sad. To Gautama's eyes, there sits a mother-of-pearl, the lone horn of a rhinoceros, a great bronze bell ringing out over ice floes in the Arctic. The eye of a cleansing hurricane in the tropics.

The crowd quiets down at once.

"O mother, O father, I have enjoyed remarkable and blessed pleasures whose consequences for an impermanent body entail—it must now be admitted—continuous anxiety. Like the transient, beauteous whitecaps of a forgotten morning in a forgotten lifetime, of a faraway ocean, long ago, so this body one must cast off, sooner or later. To have enjoyed it even for a moment is enough to understand that one moment is equal to all moments. Thus, leaving behind my fields, my house and gold, my daughter and wife, my Bentley and both of you, dear departed parents, I am abundantly at peace," Leonard began.

"Bentley?" the Indian Voice journalist pondered.

"Who is it that longs for liberation, disregards worldly objects, confesses sins, seeks moral and intellectual purity of the soul, obviates transgressions, holds his body in particular positions, denies the self, sings praises to nature, keeps the right time, practices penance, begs forgiveness from all creatures, studies and recites sacred texts, ponders, discourses, acquires sacred knowledge, concentrates on stability of mind, controls himself and achieves freedom from sins, practices austerities, cuts off *karma*, is mentally independent, uses unfrequented lodging and beds, turns away the world, does not suffer the misery of renunciation, renounces food, conquers passions, renounces activity, body and company, does service for the community, is patient, is freed of greed, practices simplicity, humility, and sincerity of mind, is watchful of one's speech and one's body, maintains faith in the soul, destroys wrong belief, subdues fear, conquers anger, pride, deceit, greed, love, hate and wrong belief? Who is it?" Leonard asks.

"It is the human conscience in each of us that has risen above the temptation to commit injury. That has acted at every juncture to prevent harm, to be mindful of one's thoughts and deeds. The plant and animal in my own evolution has suffered. That suffering will not go away, so long as other living organisms are being deliberately harmed.

"An infinite number of times have I been roasted over a blazing fire in an oven, screaming aloud. Being suspended upside down over a boiler, shrieking, with no relation to help me. I was cut to pieces with various saws, fastened with fetters, crushed like sugarcane in presses, thrown down, torn to shreds, lacerated, screaming and writhing. Hacked into edibles with swords and daggers, with darts and javelins. Forcibly yoked to a cart of red-hot iron full of fuel, driven on with a goad and with thongs, knocked down like an antelope. Butchered like a buffalo, suffered hopelessly from mallets and knives, forks and maces. Slit, cut, mangled, skinned alive with keen-edged razors and shears. Caught and bound and fastened in snares and traps. Felled, sawn into planks, malleated, torn, made to drink hissing molten copper, minced, burned, forced into hell against my will, in every kind of past existence. O father, o mother, it is even thus as you have plainly told. But who takes care of beasts and birds in the woods?

"It is he, or she, that stops the whirlpool of pain. One should not permit, or consent to, the killing of living beings. Only then will he perhaps be delivered from all misery. A careful man who does not injure living beings is called circumspect.

"It is thus incumbent upon the feeling conscience to do something, to act deliberately on behalf of all other creatures. That is true conscience. That is the message of the soul."

There were many who seemed, to Leonard, to be getting restless, either from lack of comprehension, or boredom, or from the sheer confrontational nature of his message.

"How can a homeless person like me stop so much suffering in the world?" asked a woman who sat directly before Leonard holding her infant daughter. "Maybe, if I had a roof over my head, and a decent pair of shoes and a new dress. Maybe, if I could feed Lili here properly, or get myself together."

"The homeless are closest to their soul," Leonard declared. "Uninhibited by possessions. Unclouded by the sea of material goods, close to the Earth, you walk in the path of all gods. Fasting in the form of a cube, of any arrangement whatsoever, content below such a tree, in solitude or with one's daughter, aware of the subtleties of nature, whether xylem or phloem, hyacinth or teardrop, fog or red chalk, grasshopper or dolphin,

human ancestors or one's own parents, having thus felt the truth of such
things, only the homeless are truly free."

"That's bull!" a voice cried out. "Ain't no freedom in poverty,
hunger, disease, pain. You're just plain crazy!"

"He whose soul is purified by meditating on these matters is like an
albatross at sea," replied Leonard. "The wind is testimony to its freedom.
Reaching the far shore, however unlikely, the albatross gets beyond such
misery."

"Who can understand such things?" the same voice barked into its
matted beard. A man, greatly agitated. Leonard discerned that he was
an intelligent but mentally unstable person. Another sad case of an individual who was in dire need of medical attention, and most of all, love.
"Meditation won't feed my belly! This woman—most of us, for that
matter—need our next meal, not poetry!"

"And, when your next meal is consumed, then what?" asked
Leonard.

"Then we'll start all over again, worrying about the next meal, and
the next."

"And the next, ad infinitum. No, my friend. That is not the way to
achieve your freedom. Beg for your food. There's dignity in that. Work
for your food. There's satisfaction in that. But, do not live for your food,"
said Leonard. "That is abject slavery."

"What then?" the man pleaded.

"Live for your soul," Leonard went on.

"What does it mean?" the man asked.

"He who does not undertake harmful actions, whose heart is pure,
does not acquire bad *karma*. His vision, his life, remains clear. Understanding the origins of *karma*, of negative energy, negative thoughts, ill-
deeds, darkness and suffering, he avoids such things. Avoiding it, he becomes adept at helping others. Helping others, he is, at once, a Great
Hero. Great Heroes are not born again and do not die. They are immortal."

"But everyone dies," the homeless woman braved. "Some go to
hell, some to heaven."

"God is within you," Leonard said. "Heaven is within you. Heaven
is within every creature. It's up to you to realize that and to take proper
steps each day so that others can also realize it."

There was silence for a time. The bearded man had calmed down.
The woman was lost in thought.

"That's my Dad!" Denise whispered proudly to Hal.

Said Leonard, "See that pigeon! Roam about like a wild animal, I say to you. Such is the life of the pious, whether monk, householder, or homeless person. These are hard times. All the plants and animals are crying out. The sky is melting. The forests are being stripped. The seas and air polluted. The viruses—for so many eons comfortably balanced in their previous hosts—unleashed, as a result of our own ecological vandalisms. The whole Earth assaulted. Human beings are out of control. So, I say unto you, imitate this pigeon; feel this life of animals, this passion of changing-colored leaves, which would clear one's mind, calm one's heart, and make one free from delusion and misery. If you will permit me—" and he reached towards his daughter, Denise, whom he realized looked remarkably like Candana in the afternoon light, as it was filtered through the canopy of falling leaves above, and said,—"Go, my daughter, as you please."

And Denise, not knowing what had come over her, trembling, her voice rising to an occasion she could never have anticipated, looked to Hal, thinking—'He's asking me to walk like a pigeon?'—And Hal just shrugged. And then, she looked to Gautama in panic. And, the terror traveled from her head to her throat and suddenly she uttered words that were incomprehensible to her,

"Kahan Chare? Kahan Chitte? Kahan Ase? Kahan Saye? Kahan Bhujanto Bhasanto, Pavv Kamman na Bandhai."

Which Gautama wrote down and translated as, "How should one walk, stand, sit, sleep, eat and speak so that the sinful *karma* bondage may not accrue to the soul?

—'Where did such words come from?'—Denise cogitated in a frenzy.

And, her father answered in the same language, which Gautama recorded and translated as, "With vigilance should one walk, stand, sit, sleep, eat and talk, thus sinful *karma* Bondage shall not accrue to the soul."

For hours, Leonard went on about the perception of life, the love of life, and the crowd seemed to increase in size. There were other questions and answers and some people took off all their clothes to be as free as Leonard, at least, in theory. The policemen present did nothing to prevent such exposures.

Leonard spoke at length on the nature of non-violence, and of nudity, which he likened to the condition of all plants and animals, to the essence of feeling. "The Earth is naked," he said. "It is the least a man can be."

And then, someone asked him what his plans were, and Leonard said, "To walk across America speaking of ahinsa, of non-violence. To intercede on behalf of all the plants and animals. To help liberate all those who are oppressed by cruel deeds. To spread the truth of nudity. And, finally, to stop the functions of the mind, then the functions of speech, then those of the body, and at last, to cease breathing altogether. This is the final freedom from causation, or *karma*, achieved during pure meditation, which the twenty-four Jinas have proclaimed. At that moment of exquisite freedom, the soul takes the form of a ray of sunlight, and, without touching anything or taking up the slightest space, quickly ascends into its natural form so as to obtain perfection. This perfection is the Earth itself, whose totality eludes easy definition. But, in a man or woman who would transcend the constraints of easy definitions, it is the achievement of non-violence.

"At death, this non-violent, liberated soul goes to a place at the top of the universe—equivalent to every paradise, every dream-come-true, every form of solace and harmony the world over—where the soul sits at rest, overlooking whatever it wants to see, a vacuum the color of white gold and measuring millions of miles in all directions, for all time, tapering off to the width of a fly's wing. Or, a Himalayan expanse. Or the wine country in the south of France. A modest hamlet in the gardens of eternal India. Or the smiling face of a grandchild. Whatever the view, or the name of the religion, however that heaven be described, the soul's true comfort comes to pass at the point of true conscience, there in the place known as liberation, or moksa."

Many of the homeless, and some of the tourists were seen to wipe tears from their eyes.

The radio transmission was live and being picked up by approximately five hundred twenty-seven thousand listeners who were more accustomed to hearing call-ins from L.A.'s lonely hearts.

And, later that night, a minute of Leonard's sermon was broadcast over two local news networks.

Miriam Rosenbalm was at home planning a menu for a job when she happened to catch one of the clips, in which a news reporter, speaking from the Elysium Park a few hours earlier, tried in her own words to sum up Leonard Rosenbalm's speech, or sermon, as she called it.

Miriam's heart pounded as she watched images of a huge crowd dispersing all around her husband, who was seen wandering among the multitudes, as the pretty, female reporter in the foreground, spoke to camera, and to the news anchors back in the television studio.

"And later, Mr. Rosenbalm, whose lawyer has called him a true Jain—that's an adherent to some Indian religion—stated quite bluntly, 'Free the animals.' In spite of considerable eastern mysticism and obtuse poetry, not the normal stuff of skid row, he was rather direct on this business about animals and he actually advocated a new amendment to the United States Constitution on behalf of all of them. He called for national legislation that would mandate a vegetarian diet for all Americans. And he posed the question, 'Why not put an end to all forms of abuse, this moment? An end to the abuse of those dearest to us—our children, our spouses, our parents, our friends, our associates. Why not liberate all pets. Abolish all zoos. Put an end to circuses in which animals are exploited. Ban all biomedical research on animals which does not result in a greater good, condemn the fur and cosmetic industries—any industry— that kills and tortures animals . . . ' And, his list went on to include certain plants. 'People will not stop harming one another until they can act decently towards plants and animals,' he repeated. 'To strive every minute of every day towards the ideal of minimizing violence in an imperfect world.' That was the message Mr. Rosenbalm tried to convey here today. But what seems to have really electrified this large crowd of mostly homeless people," the reporter continued excitedly, "is the fact of Leonard Rosenbalm's legalized nudity. According to the DA's office, with whom I spoke earlier, there is no law against being naked in southern California, if—as in Mr. Rosenbalm's case—the motivation is strictly spiritual. That ruling could have quite an impact in a state like California, where the sun always shines."

The video cut away to an image of Leonard leading a huge crowd of over a thousand souls, some of them unclothed, down the mountain side in an eastern direction, as darkness settled over the twinkling skyline of Los Angeles and the reporter chased after Leonard hoping to secure a private interview.

In Leonard's mind, there was no celebrity. No particular gladness, nor fear. He was only doing what came naturally. Denise was with him, as was Gautama. And, so was Hal Spendetti, two policemen, even Joe, the Vietnam vet, who'd heard back at the Mission that something amazing was happening on the mountain and figured—since he knew all about the Jains anyway—it might be worth checking out.

The descent from Elysium was occasioned by a great calm, a joy in living. Many must have sensed that something historical had occurred here this day. Until the eclectic procession was swallowed up in the city's sprawling night.

CHAPTER NINE

Epilogue

Hundreds slept out that night with Leonard along the railroad tracks. By the morning, word having spread far, a contingent of southern California Jain housewives had arrived with hot vegetarian meals. They set up tables and served everyone lentil cake curry, sukhi bean aur narial, curried chick peas in a rice casserole, yoghurt and layered bread known as paratha.

The fest was aswarm with the odor of spices, of cardamom and cinnamon, coriander and amchoor. Gautama savored each black mustard seed, crunching them between his teeth in near religious ecstacy. Leonard, on the other hand, ate with one hand, standing upright, grateful to the ladies but showing no particular enthusiasm. In his mind, humility, self-control, renunciation and non-attachment—*aprigraha*—applied to everything, a car, a home, even the taste of one's food. His entire meal was consumed in less than five minutes and he privately evidenced sorrow at the fate of those peas and lentils. Such sorrow, he said, was unavoidable while one still lived in this human form.

Denise asked him why it was alright to eat beans but not meat. Were not beans also living creatures?

Leonard launched into a somewhat byzantine, but apparently quintessential explanation of the difference between meat and beans.

"There are one-, two-, three-, four-, five-, and six-sensed beings," he stated. "The sixth sense is the human brain. The fifth sense is the brain of a less neurotic, but equally astute animal, such as the gorilla or the giraffe. Four-sensed beings are endowed with less complicated brains. Evolution has granted them a more simplified circuitry, if you will. They also lack the ability to hear Beethoven. The fly and the sea slug, for example."

"But, even Beethoven could not hear Beethoven," Denise reminded Leonard.

Leonard smiled. "All the more reason for compassion at the dinner table," he said. And, he went on by identifying those "three-sensed beings which lack not only Beethoven in their lives, but the ability to see the finer details of a Sistine Chapel. Lice would fit into that category," he said. "As for the two-sensed beings, such as bacteria, they lack not only

Beethoven and Michaelangelo, but the ability to smell, whether the armpits, or the fresh horse manure, or even a loaf of freshly cooked bread which they righteously inhabit. They too, should be revered, and left alone. Then, there are the one-sensed beings who are without Beethoven, Michaelangelo, horse manure, or even taste buds. Such creatures would include palm trees and bell peppers, rice and nasturtium flowers, yoghurt and beans. Now beans are endowed with the sense of touch, of respiration, life duration and body power. Fundamentally, it is wrong to consume them. Yet, if even one-sensed beings such as beans and flowers are exempted from the law of consuming nature, then a Jain would starve to death," Leonard explained. "And that would be a form of violence. Therefore, respectfully, apologetically, go ahead, daughter, and eat the beans. However, do not pick flowers unless you intend to eat them."

"But, because beans lack nearly all possession of the senses, doesn't that put them closest to monkhood?" Denise asked.

"Yes," Leonard said approvingly. "That is the tragedy of the bean." And, he winked at her to lighten the load of an otherwise ponderous universe.

It was a minimalist philosophy, and Denise understood it. The logic was unassailable: a human being had the power—indeed, the responsibility—to cherish all life forms, to exhibit balance, wisdom and compassion at all times. Since it was quite clear that a human organism could thrive on a diet of nasturtium and beans, rice and yoghurt, or any of the other food types so abundantly available in the modern world, there was absolutely no excuse, none, for consuming the more neurologically advanced, animals; creatures that were, according to Leonard, as capable and sensitive as humans. Animals like cows, pigs, chickens and fish. Denise planned to have a talk with her mother.

She asked her Dad about other things weighing on her mind—like abortion, chemical pollution, euthanasia, capital punishment, mercy killing, war, and self-defense. What prompted this philosophical outpouring would have been an utter mystery to her, two weeks before. To each query, Leonard consistently replied that each individual counted, but that confronted with impossible choices, the greater good had to be considered. And, that meant consciously, insistently striving to disarm situations, to negotiate with compassion and strength, to back off gracefully, to do whatever was necessary to minimize violence. He'd heard from Gautama (who read the newspaper headlines whenever they happened to pause near street-corner vending machines) that over a thousand Hindus and Moslems had been killed in India that week, and he also knew that over six thousand Indian toddlers were dying every *day* from disease and chronic malnutrition. He *saw* those children! And his heart was breaking, but he knew of no other way to address such pain than through individual tenacity and courage. One had to keep going. One had to *insist* on non-violence.

Denise did not understand how her father had changed so radically before her eyes. Naked, philosophical, eloquent, he was more a father than ever before, even if his priorities had shifted from making a living for his family, to making a living for all creatures. In her innocent heart, she was not bothered by Leonard's evident descent into odd evangelism. He did not so much preach as speak his mind. And, if he had become desperately serious, he also retained a little bit of his former humor.

Of course, she, too, had changed, within a matter of a week. Ever since learning that Leonard had actually given his Armani suit to a homeless person and invited him into his office to spend the night on the couch. It was a beautiful gesture, she thought. One that she, too, would like to extend.

"In an imperfect world, one must minimize violence," Leonard decreed, as if in prayer. "Sometimes, you have to be a psychoanalyst, a strategist; you have to compromise, to listen, to be tolerant. The poet needs to be crafty, the he-man a ballet dancer."

And, he could tell that this young woman who was once his daughter was but minutes away from stripping off her own clothes and becoming naked. And, it troubled him deeply but he did not know exactly how to discourage her, or why.

And, he turned away, looking East towards Boyle Heights, to the old Jewish ghetto of Los Angeles, where his parents had first lived when they came to this city, straight up Brooklyn Avenue all the way to Soto Street, as if tracing in his mind's eye an itinerary; and he enunciated dreamily, "Samayag-Darshan-Gyan-Charitrani Moksh marg. Right vision, Right Knowledge and Right Conduct together constitute the highway to liberation."

And, as the words formed, and were spoken, Leonard searched for an answer and found himself staring eye to eye with Mahavira.

He was there, as he had been all along. Looking much older, but no less radiant. Becoming with each added moment the graceful marmoreal presence of his posterity. A man, no less, who with each deep wound had rebounded more vigorously still.

It was raining in the village of Pava-puri. And, if one were to characterize the *feeling* of the surroundings, there was slightly more unhappiness than happiness here, and slightly more happiness than unhappiness there. Human life was short and prone, at times, to great misery. But not so short, and not so miserable, that there was not sufficient time or want amongst the human residents to pursue freedom. Happiness and unhappiness, these two old bedpartners, exchanged vows, whispered sweet cajoleries, and reinvented the universe with each passing hour, with every new recollection, nuance, negation and desire.

In the middle of Pava-puri was a great crenellated rampart punctuated by enormous gates, a deep mote of sporting carp and high surrounding towers. The walls were of stone brought down by countless bullock carts from the hills above Kathmandu and decorated with a pantheon of bulls and crocodiles, yak and lotus creepers. Elevated carvings in the form of benevolent beings looked down upon the village. Domes and flags, garlands and jewels added lustre to the palace of King Hastipala. There was even a machine—a male and female couple—that welcomed guests from above the primary entrance by bowing to the visitors, then turning to kiss one another on their metallic cheeks.

Once inside, the invited guest was met by a maze of cornelian columns, granite balustrades, circular staircases in teak and gold leaf, luscious courtyards adrift in orchids leading in a dozen directions. The ceilings were painted in silver leaf and doorways were fitted with fine jewels. Incense burned throughout each richly appointed room.

Beyond the attendance hall, the fasting hall, the pinnacled hall, and bathing rooms, the gymnasium, the royal quarters, and judge's chambers, was the scribe's hall in the office of the survey ministers.

And, there sat three old men, day after day, while trickles of monsoon rain leaked through the grand edifice of teak-wood beams, down silk-cushioned walls, and onto the cold marble floor.

The rain pelted the exterior of the palace and the sound of shelter and comfort was imbibed by all.

Children chased one another, or played marbles in the halls. A young man quietly kissed for the first time a young girl under the stairs. A servant carried heated water in a wooden bucket to a distant room. Two important district tax collectors discussed customs duties beside a turquoise-studded fountain.

At the far end of the great scribe's hall, or rajjuyasabha, the rajjuya, or survey minister, sat before a shelf of documents consoling himself with the latest figures. Only yesterday, he had himself trekked into a disputed field, calculated just over three janapada by passing a length of rope tied to a stick from one end of the property to the other, making his determination and collecting the appropriate taxes from the owner. All in a driving rain.

Thus, life went on.

Woodchoppers and farmers, hunters and spinners, weavers and fishermen, builders and potters, blacksmiths and bronziers, mothers and children, old men and old women, toddlers and pet animals, survived each day in the downpouring monsoon, huddled under awnings, beneath trees, within caves, under leopard-skin covers, in rusticated hamlets and official places.

No schools were in session because of the unrelieved storms. That and the fact a mysterious egg was found in the road, which no magician or seer could quite explain. Not even the King, nor his astrologers, could make head or tail of it.

And so, the egg was placed upon a warm satin cushion in the palace, near a moist place, and two musicians were told to chant all day in one shift, and all night in another, in order to coax forth whatever creature languished inside the alabaster shell.

In most respects, this particular rainy season was no different from a thousand others before it. As in past centuries, frogs caroused in the mud day and night, while ducks cavorted and quacked in unrelenting bliss wherever there were ponds.

In the words of a later Antonine emperor of note, "Behold and see how many strained every nerve only to fall in a little and be resolved into the elements of life."

And, in the words of a later celebrated poet, "The thing that hath been, it is that which shall be; and that which is done is that which shall be done; and there is no new thing under the sun."

But, in fact, there *was* one important difference this year. A few months before, at the beginning of the monsoons, Mahavira had arrived from the village of Chamani, walking naked, as he had since the age of thirty, mindful of every step, eyes undiluted and bright. Had he read the minds of ages to come? Did he know what he had accomplished?

For nine weeks now he and his chief disciple, Indrabhuti Gautama and his scribe, Sudharman, had remained on the floor of the far corner of the hall, relieving their nature in an ash heap behind the palace, eating virtually no food (and never after dark), drinking an occasional cup of boiled water, but otherwise deeply engaged in the exposition and transliteration of one text after another, one hundred and ten chapters detailing the effects of good and bad action, thirty-six chapters concerning the great inexplicables and unasked questions of life, and a final personal meditation on the secrets of the universe, called pradhana.

Mahavira knew he had little time left to accomplish so much.

Nobody in the palace bothered them. No one stirred before him. Not even a cricket dared to distract him. Yet, out in the rain-soaked darkness, across the vast distances of Bharat, as it was known in those times, hundreds of thousands of Jains were coming by foot from all directions, guided by so much impulse, wanting to be present at the great nirvanabhumi.

Sudharman wrote quickly upon one leaf after another, dipping his pen in the inkpot.

"Oh long-lived one! Thus have I heard the following discourse from the Venerable Mahavira . . . "

And Leonard looked to Denise and recommended that she should leave her clothing on. "There can be no proprietary sensibility with regard to other animals. But, with you, oh daughter, with you I hesitate in this regard."

"Dad, I understand what you're doing. I love you. I'm with you. If Mom understood, she'd also be down here with you."

Was it possible to understand, and to be confused, at the same time? To have desires leading in one direction, and conflicting volitions in another? To know what would happen, and yet to not know? To read another's mind, as in a trance, and yet not trust the reading? Leonard agitated over his daughter's insistent affiliation with her father, and his own grudging protectiveness of this girl. These were undeniable emotions which broke all the rules of true renunciation. He was merely a man, after all. No saint. What he had envisioned for days, now, was another life, some other man born as Vardhamana, eventually known as Mahavira. But, it was not Leonard and he surely knew it. The times were different. The customs. The wants.

True, people were people, obstacles and hardships essentially unchanged, from century to century. But, Leonard's vision of Mahavira allowed for no lingering passions or loves. He saw a man seated on the king's floor of the scribe's hall with no confusion in his heart. That man had achieved utter peace. He knew wherefrom his mission, whereas Leonard had only a vague yearning of such a mission, of that desire for ultimate pilgrimage which by itself conflicted with the goal of being entirely free of such desires. But, he had not yet achieved that goal; he was not there yet, and this distinction made a world of difference.

Anybody, he thought, could be naked. That was the most normal thing on Earth. But, to become, somehow, naked on the inside . . . an enterprise of gigantic proportions. Denise confronted him with his own nudity by her readiness to drop her pants, to unzip her blouse, to unsnap that white nylon brassiere, to slip out of her panties and expose that precious hidden body—velvetine and smooth—to the rash of hungry eyes surrounding her. A sexual twinge jerked his reasoning powers. The burning sun, with its ultraviolet penetration, suddenly frightened him. The hundreds of male onlookers with their loose and unpredictable genitals closed in all around and the world, at once, became a harsh and unfeeling place. That little girl he'd watched emerge as naked as a quartzite crystal, blue-eyed and honey-lipped from Miriam's womb on an otherwise sleepy morning some nineteen years ago now came back to test, or haunt him.

Gurgles mingling with aged gasps. As the squirming naked baby before him re-moulded, enlarged, its bones creaking, its skin expanding, the entire carapace breaking out into the fully-grown body of an old woman, at the very end of her life.

—"Ida?"—Leonard mumbled, staring into himself.

Dead little more than a week, her flesh embalmed without any evidence of decay, Leonard's mother, Ida Rosenbalm, stepped up beside him, also naked, her body gleaming the color of a dull white, the sea-white of a grey winter morning layered in November mist, her breasts hovering over a sunken belly, and flowing with sullen milk.

—"My son!"—she said. And began to sing, "your cradle is of sandalwood, your cushion of silk. Grandmother will come and will sing you to sleep, jojo. Will protect you throughout your days as sure as the Cobra its young. My milk has quieted you, has sweetened your lips, and within the hand of God, I shall deliver your soul, jojo."

—'What did it mean?'—his head perplexed, his hand reaching out to see if this apparition were physical.

Denise took his hand, feeling the weight of her father's discomfort, and said, "No problem. I understand."

Leonard was shuddering. Even he did not understand.

It was certainly no macho *male* thing—or he didn't believe so, no *feminist* thing, nothing to do with double standards or faintness of heart. She was his daughter, after all, despite whatever claims to the contrary his madcap excursion into his head, into his heart, might have insisted.

He feared for her. He feared that others might be offended. And, if this fear contradicted his insistence on religious freedom of expression, then so be it. He could not help himself. Ten days ago, he'd never heard of Jainism. He was no Mahavira, after all. Only Leonard Rosenbalm. Born in Brooklyn, married in Boyle Heights, Los Angeles, his best man a helicopter pilot in Vietnam who'd had a leg blown off in combat; financially broken, mentally unsecured, spiritually alone. Driven by memories, galvanized by words, composed of genes and blood, purposes and hindsight, events and characters, reasons and unreasons, which were not even his own, necessarily, but of all men; compelled towards the great yawning East by impulses that were greater than any one individual; as vague and over-used as the cliche, 'higher callings'.

He was relieved that she had agreed not to take off her clothes.

"Time to go," Leonard said abruptly.

And the procession continued, picking up reporters and pedestrians along the way. Numerous Jains now began to attach themselves to Leonard's ensemble of the homeless, while most of the tourists had dissipated the night before with the onset of the cold.

Near the State Street Recreational center, they encountered a pack of In Touch With The Lord Club supporters who stood cheering Leonard on and passing out their business cards inscribed with God's address and a "700" number.

Gay rights activists showed their support, and their flesh, as Leonard and his flock turned East off Brittania onto Broadway. It was a scene out of the 1960s.

This was the old neighborhood for Leonard and he pointed out places of interest to both Gautama and Denise. To everyone Leonard confronted, he bowed and said the words, "*Ahinsa Paramo Dharmah.*" When asked what it meant, he would spend a minute and explain how a soul which never killed would never die. Immortality, he stated repeatedly, came to those who had learned to listen, to believe, and to be tolerant. Or he'd shift the emphasis upon gentleness, or empathy, or upon learning the language of the albatross.

He passed Lubovitcher Hassids who moved quickly on the other side of the street in their four fringed *tzitzits*. Their jacket buttons were on the left and button holes on the right. Their heads were covered with fur *shtreimels* and some, the Sephardic Jews, were clad in yellow striped robes. For them, this was a Friday morning of the year 5753 and many of these Jews were on their way to the synagogue. One of them, seeing the naked man and imagining a demon before him, rubbed his shoe hard on the sidewalk, as if trying to blot out dog poop, and muttered a curse against Amalek, Haman's descendant.

"Leonard?" an old woman's voice rang out.

"Leonard Rosenbalm?"

Leonard turned to see Mrs. Fleishman, in her blood-stained white apron, coming out of her family's Kosher meat market.

"My God, Mrs. Fleishman!" he proclaimed. "How are you?"

"You haven't changed one bit!" she smiled, pinching Leonard's ear. "Oi gods, I was so sorry to hear about your parents, bless their dear souls, but I was sick, or I would have come to the funeral. You know my Melvin passed away last year, too. God bless him."

"We sent a note. I was so sorry to hear it. I'd like you to meet my daughter, Denise," Leonard said, a bit awkwardly.

Mrs. Fleishman, who stood just under five feet, took Denise's head in her two hands and kissed her. "Wonderful, darling!" she cried in tribute. "I used to play with Leonard when he was shorter than I am currently." It seemed that she intended to mean that she was still in the process of growing—shorter.

Her eyes having settled on Leonard's mid-section, Mrs. Fleishman suddenly opined, "Leonard, what's that?"

"What's what?" Mrs. Fleishman.

"Leonard, darling, where are your clothes?"

"Gone, Mrs. Fleishman, gone for good!"

She paused, trying to get through to his meaning. Then, recognizing it with a long-suffering sigh, she said, "Oh, I know. It's this neighborhood now. You can't leave anything! Not even for a moment. They'll kill you for a jar of sweet pickles if they have a mind to. Imagine! You know, I keep a semi-automatic?"

She led Leonard inside the small market.

"You used to come around spinning your dreidle as a child, remember? Always asking for halavah. And, you always got it, too, because Melvin had such a soft spot for you, Lennie."

Eviscerated chickens hung from clotheslines above the butcher stand along the wall. Slabs of beef and dozens of sausages hung there as well.

He remembered these signs of his upbringing clearly. Jewish dietary laws were never intended to be understood by the mind. The *Torah* is filled with seemingly intractable contradictions. For example, he recalled that one is allowed to eat only those marine animals with fins and scales. None others. Why was that? No real explanation. And one could only eat the meat of an animal that chews its cud and has split hooves. That means cows and deer, but not pigs. His Aunt Nelly used to say that the swine rub their bellies in the dirt, like snakes, and therefore are unclean. But, if you've ever spent time with a cow, as Leonard had once at a 4-H Club farm in upper New York State, then you know that cows lie around all day on their bellies, too.

The *Torah* itself—the most holy book to the Jews—is traditionally made from pieces of dead Kosher skin sewn together, skin that more than likely had been repeatedly rubbed in an animal's own excrement.

He had grown up with this, never before giving it a thought. But now, in a hemorrhaging of clarity, with rosy-cheeked Mrs. Fleishman proudly displaying her ghastly array of suspended animal corpses, Leonard saw through to the gross deficiencies of Kosher logic. He remembered from synagogue a well-worn saying from somewhere in Deuteronomy, "You shall not consume blood, because blood is the life force." That was a clear dictum. It should have been understood by all who read the Old Testament. But, many Jews, like Mrs. Fleishman—and like his own parents—did not read the Old Testament, or, if they did, had not considered that this was simply another way of saying, "Thou Shalt Not Kill."

Instead, they assumed it meant that blood should be drained from the dead animal before it is eaten. And, that is all. It meant purity, or something akin to purity. As if killing could ever be pure. Meat was soaked in water, then salted, or roasted over an open fire. Every last drop of blood was cleansed and exorcised from the flesh. In other words, every minute particle of the animal's intrinsic life force was washed down the drain. And that was Kosher. The Jewish Shohet *U-bodek*—the meat slaughterer and checker—used a knife which had not a single nick on it, a practice continued today. And this was meant to ensure a quick, and compassionate slicing of the animal's wind- and food pipes. But it was all a terrible and tragic misinterpretation of YAWH's will, written into mortal law.

There were other, more subtle contradictions to Kosher which simply reflected those of the vast Christian culture all around it. Leonard remembered how his father had once told him that Jews were prohibited from eating animals considered to be themselves merciful, like the stork. Even as a boy, Leonard knew that there was never going to be much of a rush on storks at the market, Kosher or no Kosher. But, of course, that wasn't the point. Why were storks considered merciful and not cows and chickens? If mercy truly entered into it, why kill any animal at all, ever? None of his Jewish or Christian friends could ever explain that.

Leonard felt a profound nausea which he could not shirk, which had dogged his childhood and now returned in the guise of the old neighborhood. The whole market was saturated with the aura of colossal pain, the scent and blood-red of animal entrails. Gautama, who had gone inside the market with Leonard, recognized that certain expression on his friend's face—that 'Look-out!' kind of gesture which signalled a messy upheaval, as Leonard closed his eyes, ground his teeth, and tried to fight back the sensation overcoming him. But, there was something else happening to him, as well. A truly Indian equanimity that seemed to envision the whole world at once, in all of its minutia . . .

Sudharman wrote rapidly. He detected Mahavira's voice growing weaker, from proclamation and decree, to counsel and discourse, to quiet conversation. For hours, the Jina had clarified and countered prevailing heresies, like those of his old arch nemesis, Mikkhali Gosala. He had set forth the rules of behavior for a monk, embarking on a rather detailed explanation of the *dharma-tirtha*, or holy path. He explained such concepts as *jiva-daya*, namely, compassion, empathy and charity; of care in walking, all manner of forgiveness, universal friendliness and love (*mettim bhavehi*), affirmation, the sharing with guests, the whole arena of critical self-examination and constant meditation, a vast realm of personal restraints, and an increasing aversion to all things, leading ultimately to renunciation. And, he stressed that evil, sin, wrong-doing of all sorts, was rectified the moment a person, or any other animal, vowed to change his or her ways, to do better in the future. Guilt was not passed down from father to son, or from a former to a later life. People could change. They were not victims, not even of their own past mistakes.

These many assertions of a daily quest, taken together, said Mahavira, were the basis for liberation in this life.

"He who looks on creatures, big and small, of the earth, as his own self, comprehends this immense universe," he murmured. "All souls are interdependent. One who neglects or disregards the existence of earth, air, fire, water, animals and vegetation, disregards his own existence which is entwined with them," he summarized.

Outside the palace, standing day and night in the rain, the huge crowd had congregated. Some would later insist that there were as many as fifty thousand monks and nuns standing there, three hundred and seventy-seven lay followers, three hundred scholars who had memorized everything Mahavira ever said, thirteen hundred followers who had toiled with him up every hill and mountain, seven hundred excellent disciples who had achieved the highest knowledge, five hundred exceedingly wise persons, seven hundred followers capable of occult transformation, and so on. All Jains.

On the fourteenth morning of the month, an unexpected friend came to visit him.

"Sakra!" Mahavira called out in the faintest voice.

"*Jai jinendra!*" his old school friend said, grinning vigorously.

"You haven't changed," said Mahavira.

"Nor you," Sakra admitted.

They just sat, side by side, for most of the day, Mahavira in a yogic posture, Sakra more relaxed. Both felt deep and lasting friendship for one another. Words were not necessary between them.

The moon was in conjunction with the svati constellation. It had stopped raining. A mist rose up from throughout the village and the frogs and crickets had become silent. The year was called Candra, the month known as Pritivardhana. The day they called Suvratagni.

It happened then, in the midst of lustres and great silences, in the middle of the fifteenth night.

Mahavira ceased to breathe.

And a sudden tumult arose in the world.

Hours later, Indrabhuti, a homeless mendicant of the Jnata clan, Mahavira's chief disciple for over a decade, attained his own boundless enlightenment.

In trying to grasp, or reckon with, what had transpired in their very own village, the elders exclaimed, "The lamp of inner light is extinguished. Let us now burn lamps of ordinary clay."

At that moment in the palace, atop the satin cushion, the mysterious egg cracked open and a creature emerged. It was not exactly what might have been expected.

"See that!" Leonard exclaimed, grabbing hold of a headless chicken. "You see!" It was a worm. "A little WORM!" extending blindly from the neck cavity, wriggling in open air, confused. "A worm that will haunt us for the remainder of our days, Mrs. Fleishman!"

"Lennie, what are you talking about!"

"These animals require a proper burial," he went on. "How much for everything?"

She did not know what to make of this request but conceded with a vague calculation.

"Denise, dear, write Mrs. Fleishman an IOU."

Denise did so and Leonard then instructed two dozen of his followers—they were no longer merely stragglers—to gently carry the myriad corpses to the nearest park with him, which they did.

And, in the dirt, they found a spot that seemed appropriate, though not entirely legal, and buried every creature with homage and respect.

The policemen who'd been protecting Leonard's cavalcade even helped dig the hole.

"That worm does it," said patrolman Davies, who'd already given up sushi for the same reason. "I'm cutting out all meat from my diet."

One week later, Leonard and his more than one hundred followers continued along a railroad track across the deserts of Nevada.

At night, from a mountain pass where they bivouacked, they could see the jeweline lights of Las Vegas.

The lights skipped across Leonard's mind as he fought off the freezing gusts of wind that scorched his bare chest and benumbed his fingers. Others in his company sat huddled around a single fire, wrapped in blankets, holding each other, singing.

Out of the singing emerged a high-pitched threnody—or was it some celebration?—of far-away chants, the orchestral music of chimes and the myriad ringing of triangles. Leonard heard it all. And, he saw thousands of candles throwing their reflections across the Earth-dark waters of the sacred Ganges, all in homage to the transcendence of Mahavira. It was the first Divali, the Festival of Lights, and it warmed Leonard's insides even to witness it from afar.

But his problems were multiplying. Miriam had decided to accompany the group. With Denise and Leonard away, she was feeling very much alone and sorry for herself. She missed Lennie and it seemed to her that the only way she was going to ever get her family back was to join them.

Asha had also joined the procession, though she was not thrilled about it. She'd left India precisely to avoid all that religion, all those exhausting pilgrimages her parents dragged her on as a child. But, she went where her husband went.

It was the day before Thanksgiving. They were encamped just outside the city fringes of Las Vegas when it started to snow lightly and the freezing wind picked up. In short, conditions were rotten. Denise had a bad cold. The procession had woolen blankets, some tents and sleeping bags for comfort. Some had followed the procession by vehicle all the way from Los Angeles and now those same automobiles evacuated several who had lost their motivation to keep going in such weather. Others deserted the cause for hotels in town, long hot showers, and for those huge cheap breakfasts at the various casinos.

But a goodly number stayed on, including Joe, some of the original stragglers from outside Misery House, and the barking fellow with matted hair from Elysium who had been turned around completely in his own whirl of pain. In addition, numerous Jains, local environmentalists, a group of Seventh Day Adventists who had some how heard about Leonard, a contingent of a newly formed "*Jews For Jains*" organization out of Berkeley, even a number of tourists had ardently joined the procession, among them, a delightful young Japanese couple, newlyweds, touring this country for the first time. They planned to go all the way across America with Leonard Rosenbalm. To everyone they said the same thing, "Sakai! Sekai! Sekai! Jinruiga Heiwade Arimasuyouni!" May peace prevail on Earth!

There was, in addition, a curious, middle-aged Indian man in jeans and polyester parka who hadn't said a word since joining the group.

Where the cavalcade sat, amid desolate peaks and dreary eye-stretching distances, resembled the dark side of the moon. Gautama was feeling the cold. He was tired and even a little frightened, mostly for Leonard. Seeing his wife Asha after a week away from home had reminded him of many things. Nevertheless, he was not about to leave Leonard's side. Especially now. For it was reported that a large gathering of state troopers awaited the procession at the entrance to the city proper. They stood armed in their shiny black leather knee-boots and hunting jackets, with restless German sherpherds and long-range rifles and a roadblock of two dozen police vehicles and armored vans. They evidently felt they needed all that in order to take Leonard in, according to a set of charges, laws and alleged community standards that didn't even exist in California, or India for that matter, however ironic. Gautama was not licensed to practice law in this State, but he knew one or two other Jain lawyers who were.

Leonard sat in the wind and snow pondering the situation. His body had acclimated to the cold. He was not worried in the least about those policemen. His two nights in jail, thus far, had proven exhilarating to him for reasons he alone would be able to express. Now, it was simply his hope to avoid anymore premature burials. He wanted all animals to live, to be free, and so it was his goal to try and save as many turkeys as possible from slaughter.

The group had taken up pledges. It was an awkward moment. Most were homeless, and many of those who were not, in the strictest sense, were not necessarily carrying large sums, or credit cards. Some were not prepared to have to spend their money to save turkeys, despite their show of support for Leonard. The result was that the group managed to produce only eleven thousand dollars in actual cash or credit card pledges. Much of it came from the Jains. In addition, the young Japanese newlyweds committed nearly all of their traveler's checks which their respective families had given them as a wedding gift. They had already seen enough to trust that Jains throughout America would feed and shelter the procession wherever it wandered.

But, at seventy-two cents a pound, the money was nowhere near enough to save what was estimated to be fifty thousand turkeys awaiting slaughter and housed in deplorable conditions a mile away. Some felt that the whole enterprise was going to create more problems than the group was prepared to cope with. Where would the liberated turkeys go? Wouldn't they just starve to death with the onslaught of winter, and was that any more merciful than a quick execution? How would the group single out those to be saved from those to be left, considering their finite cash supply?

Leonard did not enter into these debates, but, in his own heart he knew very well that the saving of even a single life was worth everything. The simple words of Mahavira kept coming back to him, " . . . a wise man should not act sinfully towards animals, nor cause others to act so, nor allow others to act so."

And, he remembered how, in Jewish tradition, God was said to have spared the world for just one good soul. "Do unto others as you would have them do unto you."

And while the many followers sat stymied, debating all the pros and cons, the strategies and counter-strategies of their *ahinsa* and animal liberation goals, something like a miracle took place.

It was no lightning bolt, no rainbow in the hail, no giant leap. Just one small step for a man named Leonard Rosenbalm, who stood up determined, undeterred, breathing easy, and walked naked across the lunar-like landscape in the direction of the turkey farm. He needed no space suit to protect him.

And, as he continued across the harsh desert floor, against a strong icy wind, the silent Indian gentleman who Gautama thought he'd recognized, also stood up and followed behind Leonard.

It then hit Gautama who the man was: a Jain widower from New York, childless, whose various businesses had placed him among the very highest of the Fortune "500" set. Gautama had seen his picture on the cover of several business magazines.

All that money was certainly not necessary, Gautama thought. But on this day, at least, it couldn't hurt, either.

Vinay Jain   June 5, 1995